TWICE REMOVED

by Zee Lacson

ISBN 978-1-966628-99-6 (Paperback Edition)

Some characters and events in this book are fictitious. Any similarities to real persons, living or dead, is coincidental and not intended by the author.

Editing by Kathy Waghorn
Front Cover Art by Zee Lacson
Book Design and Layout by John Lacson

Visit www.zeelacson.com

for anyone struggling to belong.

MANANANGGAL

Tagalog: mana'nang'gal, lit. 'remover'

The Manananggal is a Philippine Mythical Creature that splits itself in half from the waist.

The upper torso grows large bat-like wings and detaches to seek victims.

AUTHOR'S NOTE

This is a vulnerable story.

As a first generation immigrant myself, I experience my own set of challenges. My children, American by birth, face different obstacles. Our family is one of many with roots in two different countries. It can be complicated. Sometimes, people force us to choose and we feel divided. We wonder where we belong, if we even belong anywhere.

The characters in this story experience much of this. They're victims of prejudice, ignorance, bigotry, and circumstances that may be difficult to read about. They, too, learn to adapt but the lessons often leave scars.

I did not include a glossary or list of terms even though the story is rich with what may seem like new words or foreign languages. I think, if you allow yourself, you'll follow along well enough. Just as so many families learn to do with an open heart.

Because what you discover when you're torn between languages and cultures is that borders can change but we are all children of one world. And I hope this story will help broaden yours just a little bit.

Be brave. Be vulnerable. Be kind.

And always, always, choose the light.

My girlfriend is a monster.

And I don't mean a monster like she's one of the mean girls in class. The popular girls in my high school use the term fairly casually. Like when Suzy Perkins tells her sometimes-best-friend-sometimes-biggest-rival Jessica Harris that her skirt looks like a tablecloth, then all of Jessica's friends put their perfectly manicured hands to their perfectly glossed lips and exclaim, "Oh em gee, she is such a monster."

It's a term that can also be used for the opposite sex. Like when Brad Johnson breaks up with Suzy right before the prom. All the girls get together in herds and whisper loudly amongst themselves, "What kind of monster breaks up with his girlfriend before prom?"

So there's that kind of monster.

My girlfriend isn't like that.

She's more like the monsters parents in the old country would tell their kids about to scare them into submission. "Don't go there or the monster will get you." The boogeyman-type monster of nightmares and horror stories. That kind of monster.

My girlfriend is a manananggal.

You haven't heard of that before? Me neither. Not until after she became my girlfriend, which was a challenging journey to begin with. Then in less than one summer, I learned everything there is to know about this mythical self-segmenting flying terror.

And it's not pretty.

I mean, my girlfriend is pretty. I'd say beautiful and I wouldn't even be talking about something as shallow as her looks. No, she's just amazing. She's sensitive, considerate, and sees the best in everyone. Even me. She's really an incredible human being.

It's her not-so-human half that isn't great. It's the half no one else sees. Or knows about.

So if I thought my life was complicated enough being a second-generation Filipino immigrant trying to discover who I am in New Orleans right before the beginning of the millennium, being in a relationship with a cursed vampiric mutant certainly has its own set of challenges.

One of which is trying to stay alive while she's actively trying to kill me.

CHAPTER 1
JAY

Bacon.

Sizzling bacon grease popping in a cast-iron skillet and sending that tantalizing fragrance of frying pig fat into the air. Maybe with a stack of pancakes dripping with thick maple syrup waiting on the table. The perfect smell of sweet to balance the savory. That's the scent the majority of Americans my age might wake up to.

Not rice.

I don't have to open my eyes to know that's what's waiting for me. Fried garlic rice with egg and sweet meat. It's expected, and I can smell it.

"Jay! Bangun na, anak! Mag-almusal ka na! Wake up! Eat your breakfast!" my mother yells, presumably from the kitchen, translating her Filipino into English like I didn't understand her the first time. My bedroom is the loft of our house, accessible only by a ladder attached to the kitchen wall. I'm the only one in the family who can climb it, so even if there is no actual door, I have all the privacy. Her voice carries through the open hatch easily, but I already know she won't be able to hear my groan of defiance as I make it. She yells again.

"I'm awake!" I growl back in a yell. She harrumphs in response. She's probably muttering to my father what a disrespectful child I am.

I roll off the mattress with a reluctance that reflects my stance on the injustice of my existence in this world. I do a couple of shaky push-ups to help wake me up. I pretend that I would do more had I the time, but the reality of the situation is that I'm not a push-up kind of guy. I did a whole summer of lifting weights back in freshman year, but all it did was make me hungrier. I'm never going to be the buff football quarterback my fourteen-year-old self envisioned me to be. At seventeen, I've accepted that I'm naturally skinny, and with some effort, have just enough muscle to not look weak.

There's a thin film of sweat on my back. Had it been up to me, I would have headed to breakfast sans a T-shirt, but the last time I tried that, I got a lecture from my mother on how inconsiderate it was to everyone else at the table. It isn't worth the argument.

Putting on an old shirt, I also slip on my well-worn flip-flops—indoor slippers that have never been outside the house. They are worn in all the right places, which means that in just a few months, a hole will inevitably appear and I'll have to start all over again. I'm already sad on behalf of my future self.

"Ayan na siya. There he is."

It's like listening to a *how-to-learn-English* tape. I used to think she did that for my benefit, but I learned it was her way of practicing the language. Mom was born in a small province of the Philippines. Some backward town that probably didn't even have running water. She always talks about it with the rose-colored glasses of nostalgia, but honestly, how great could it have possibly been if she had been so eager to leave?

My maternal grandmother is sitting at the table, her thin gray hair pulled up in a bun. I've rarely seen it in any other way. She smiles at me when I enter. I possess the esteem of being her favorite. She has other grandchildren, but I'm the eldest and the one she's taken care of since the day I was born. My parents were always at work at one time or another, but my grandmother, my lola, took me everywhere with her. She is more of a mother than a grandmother.

She offers me her hand. I take it and bow low enough so I can touch the top of her hand to my forehead, like I've been taught to do in the traditional show of respect. "Mano po, Lola," I mumble. She pats my cheek with her other hand but doesn't say anything. She doesn't say much these days. When I was younger, she spoke straight Filipino or broken English. She's the reason I understand the language even if I can't speak it fluently. Not because of Mom's livestream translations.

I straighten up and turn to my mother. She doesn't require the same greeting. She wants to be more American. I don't know how American she thinks she looks in a formless housedress with large floral print. She has different outfits with similar unflattering patterns, worn exclusively at home, the Pinoy duster. Probably because no one should be caught dead wearing something so ugly in public.

I give her a kiss on the cheek. Not because I really want to, but because if I don't, that will mean another lecture. I'd rather avoid such conversations this early in the morning. Her hair is still rolled up in tight bright pink rollers all over her head, and she smells of hairspray and Ponds Cold Cream. It's a daily ritual she endures for that poodle look that was popular in the eighties. Almost twenty years later, she still can't move on.

I sit at one end of the table, across from my father. Mom sits to his right, across from Lola. The food is already laid out, but no one takes anything. My father makes the sign of the cross with his right hand, a Catholic tradition before the beginning of every prayer. We all bow our heads and murmur the words of a blessing I learned to recite when I was three. We do this before every meal, and I no longer pay attention to the words. My mind is a few strides into the future, thinking about finishing breakfast and getting out the door.

Mom reaches for the rice bowl to serve my father. He sits at the head of the table, his reading glasses perched precariously on his flat nose as if he enjoys challenging gravity. I wait until he's served before I reach out for my turn. It's going to be a long day, so I pile on a few spoonfuls of the fragrant white grains. I stare at the heap on my plate. There are chunks of roasted garlic in them, beautifully golden and slightly seared. Lightly salted. Lola's handiwork, no doubt.

"When was the last time we had pancakes for breakfast?" I wonder aloud.

The wrinkles on Lola's brow multiply. She does most of the cooking, and she doesn't make pancakes. Mom cocks her head to the side as if she's been introduced to an unusual sound. I don't think Dad even heard me.

"Ano daw?" Mom asks. She looks at me, then Lola, then Dad, then back at me. "What did you say?" No one answers her. "Pancakes? Did you say pancakes? You want pancakes?" She looks at Lola for confirmation. Lola frowns. It's much more of a production than it should be and I remember why I avoid speaking my mind.

"No," I demure. "Nothing. Never mind." I reach for the plate of sweet meat. It's an almost unnatural shade of bright red. Tocino is a sweetened cured meat. It's still pork but nothing like bacon. It's chewy, not crisp. Sweetened by brown sugar, not salty. I slide it on top of my bed of rice.

Mom frowns a little but lets it go. "May trabaho ka ba ngayon? Do you have work today?" It's as if she's afraid of silence. She should already know the answer. My work schedule is on the refrigerator. I bite back a sarcastic response.

"Opo," I say, nodding. It's better to just play along.

"Gabriel is good to you." She says this often. It's her way of reminding me to be a good employee. Don't make a fuss. Don't cause problems.

Fortunately, I agree. Gabriel, or Big G as we know him around the neighborhood, is good to me. I've been working for him at his restaurant all summer, and while exhausting, it's been great. I'm paid well, and I get to eat for free.

And, sometimes, I get to see Maya.

Lola passes me a plate. There are two greasy fried eggs left. Slightly browned around the edges but runny in the middle. I take them both, layering them over the meat like some kind of mutant breakfast parfait. The trifecta is complete. Tocilog, a Filipino breakfast staple.

"Salamat po." I thank her. She smiles at me and puts the empty dish on one side of the table. She's not having any of the food she cooked for the family. Instead, she has a shallow dish in front of her with soupy rice topped with dried fish. She'd rather have that. I don't see the appeal.

"I need to leave soon," I say, semi-distracted by the small dish of vinegar near my plate. Bits of onion, tomato, and pepper float to the top. I dip my spoon in. It's not maple syrup. I take a big spoonful into my mouth. There's a bite of sour and heat with sweet. I don't wait until I swallow before I add, "I'm supposed to open today."

"Chew with your mouth closed," Mom reminds me. She's parenting on autopilot. I almost roll my eyes, but I know better. Dad doesn't look up from his plate. I doubt he's even part of the conversation. He likes to space out over meals. Maybe because Mom talks enough for both of them. "Breakfast is the most important part of the day." She's her own Public Service Announcement.

Lola squeezes my upper arm, then points at the pitcher of water on my other side. I nod, take it, and pour into her glass. She lifts her hand, palm up, to tell me to stop. Her hand is wrinkled and soft. She's not as strong as she once was, but her hand doesn't shake. She's still as steady as she is sharp.

"Your dad has clinic today." Mom continues her announcements. When Dad has clinics he usually isn't home until after the rest of us have had dinner. Part of the deal when you're a doctor, I guess. I look at her and wonder if coming home late is actually a perk of the job. "What time will you be home?" she asks.

I shrug noncommittally. I know what time I'll likely be home, but I don't want them to expect me to be home. "I dunno. Later."

This infuriates her. I know it does. She glances at Dad, but he's scraping up the last spoonful of rice off his plate and isn't at all interested in our exchange. So she just rolls her eyes and sighs. I am victorious.

In a manner that's too intentional to be accidental, Lola drops her spoon. When I bend over to pick it up for her, she raises an eyebrow ever so slightly. This is her way of rebuking me without calling me out. I frown. My sense of triumph is short-lived, and my stomach drops a little with guilt. I don't like this feeling. When I hand the spoon back to her, she smiles and thanks me aloud, knowing full well her message was received.

"Uy! May bisita darating!" Mom says, distracted by Lola's tactic. "We will have a visitor!" She beams at Dad, and he smiles at her like they're sharing a secret. She says this every time anyone at the table accidentally drops flatware. According to her, a fork signifies a male guest, and a spoon means female company. I have never known this to be true.

"I'll probably be done by four," I say reluctantly, knowing that it's what Lola wants me to do.

Mom looks happy that I volunteered more information. Lola looks placated. I feel like I compromised something I shouldn't have. I'm not so pleased with myself. I lose either way.

"Basta umuwi ka bago dumilim," she responds. "Come home before dark."

CHAPTER 2
ALL WORK AND NO PLAY

New Orleans is famous for, among other things, its streetcars. The brightly colored metal tubes stop conveniently around the more popular destinations in the city. The route I take to work on my bike is parallel to one of the railways but I'd much rather be on my own two wheels than in an enclosed space with strangers. Experience has taught me that taking public transportation would put me at the mercy of lost tourists asking the driver the same maddening questions at every stop.

"Which way is Bourbon Street?"

"Does this go to the Garden District?"

"Is there a Cafe Du Monde nearby?"

Over and over again. If the streetcar wasn't already on a rail, I'd be tempted to grab the controls and drive it into a wall.

You would think this would aggravate the driver but Southern hospitality kicks in every time. The driver will stop the ride, even so far as to step out of the streetcar, just to point a helpless stranger in the right direction, complete with a smile and a tip of the hat. And I get to sit next to a six-year-old who smells of too much sunblock with parents who are too hungover to control their kid.

We're a tourist destination, I get that. You don't get to be called The *Big Easy* if you're uptight. People come here expecting to slow down and have fun. We're the epicenter of *Mardi Gras* and the birthplace of Jazz. And ever since *Interview with the Vampire* came out in theaters five years ago, we've seen more vampire-obsessed visitors than ever before, wanting to check out the *Crescent City* in person. It's no wonder we are considered America's most interesting city.

Except that means we're also never without perpetually lost sightseers. Everywhere. They travel in groups, wearing large hats and clothes louder than the music on Frenchman Street. They snap photos with contraptions they clearly don't know how to use, or with disposable cameras you find in every corner convenience store. And they talk to locals like we aren't all speaking the same language.

I avoid them whenever possible. I'm more exposed to the sun when I take my bike but it's a small price to pay for speed and peace.

When I get to the HotHouse, I lock my bike to the black ornate metal fence between buildings. The fence is meant to keep the overgrown bushes from spilling out into the wide, cracked sidewalk, but I use it to make sure my bike doesn't tip over or get stolen. Not that it's a particularly fancy bike, I just don't want to be another statistic. Being an Asian American minority is statistic enough.

A Black teenager with tightly cropped curly hair and a wide nose is leaning against the yellowing wall of the HotHouse. He's in a shirt that's two sizes too big and baggy shorts that hang right over scabby knees. There's a skateboard under one arm. I've known him since we were in fifth grade together. And now we're about to be seniors in high school.

We don't go to the same school anymore. While we're still both in the same graduating class of '00, dubbed the class of the new millennium, my parents moved me out of public school before entering ninth grade. Marcus stayed my best friend anyway.

"How come you're here already?"

Marcus grins at me. My question is largely rhetorical. Marcus lives a few blocks away, close enough to the HotHouse. And he's always hungry.

"I'm hungry." He's unapologetic.

I'm not surprised. "So, eat at home."

"I did."

I roll my eyes but I'm grinning when I unlock the back door of the HotHouse. Marcus follows me.

It's dark when the door closes behind us, but I know where the light switch is and feel for the toggle. I find it on the first try, and the long fluorescent bulbs mounted on the ceiling of the cramped kitchen flicker on. One continues to flicker long after the others have steadied. I grab the handle of an old broom that's leaning against the wall specifically for this purpose. I hold it near the frayed bristles and jab the other end at the offending bulb. It just reaches and taps the metal edge without hitting the glass. The flickering stops. I return the broom to its resting space. It will be used many more times during the day.

Marcus is already walking into the dining area, or what counts as a dining area. There are a little more than half a dozen chairs resting upside down on three round tables. Only one table with two chairs will stay inside. The rest will be moved out front after I open the main doors.

The HotHouse is less of a restaurant and more of a take-out counter. We don't serve customers at the tables. They sit there with their take-out containers and clean up after themselves.

We supply napkins, plastic utensils, and the requisite courtesy condiments. I clean up at the end of the day before I drag everything back inside.

Marcus leans his skateboard against the wall and starts turning chairs right side up one by one. He doesn't work here, but he knows the routine, and if he's in the right mood, he might help me out. I trust him and focus on the kitchen instead.

Two aprons hang on the hook beside the fryer. I grab mine and get to work. My job is to make sure everything is ready for Big G when he comes in. We do a lot of the prep together after closing the day before. In the morning, it's all about mixing the sauces fresh for the day and setting up the dining area.

The HotHouse is essentially a one-man show. Gabriel Williams started it all from his kitchen before putting all the money he had set aside for college into this small property on the very edge of Uptown. It wasn't a recommended course of action but years later, he claims he has no regrets.

On the prep table is a jumble of plastic and glass containers. Nothing is labeled properly. Blue painters tape wraps each container, and numbers are written on them with permanent ink. That's how I know how much of each ingredient to put in the bowl. For the most part, they're basic: mayo, sweet onions, lemon juice, capers, hot sauce—but then the relish and seasonings are not so easy to identify. The magical mystery sauce.

Big G might trust me to open up shop but he doesn't trust anyone with that sauce.

Even mixing it is a process. I was trained to whip up the wet ingredients and then fold in the dry until fully incorporated. I don't see what difference it makes if I just blend everything together at the same time, but Big G insists. As if the spell of successful sauce won't work if you don't follow the instructions perfectly.

Marcus is back in the kitchen with me. "Wanna catch a movie after work?" he asks like it won't cost me at least two hours' pay to do that. I give him a side eye so he knows what I think about that suggestion. "Oh, come on," he whines. "Live a little, you tightwad. What's the point of even having a summer job if you won't spend the money you're earning?"

"I'm not spending it on a stupid movie." I top off the fryer with more oil before I set it to preheat. I turn my attention back to the bowl. "And I'm not lending you any money so that *you* can go watch a stupid movie."

We've had this conversation before. Marcus likes to spend money. Even when he doesn't have it. And he's never paid me back.

"Buzzkill." He pushes take-out cartons to one side and pulls himself up on the counter behind me. I ignore him. He kicks me with one swinging foot. I'm holding a spatula with one hand and a mixing bowl with the other. My options are limited. I attempt to elbow him without turning around. He evades my clumsy attack and counters by pushing my elbow away and kicking me with his other foot. But it means he slides sideways on the counter and a row of take-out cartons spill to the floor.

"Look what you did." I jerk my chin toward the mess to deflect attention away from my failure to get him back. "Clean that up before Big G gets here, or *he'll* kick your ass."

"He'll have to because you clearly can't," he taunts but gets off the counter to pick up the fallen boxes.

"Bite me," I retort.

He laughs, collects the wayward containers, and puts them back in order with lightning speed. He's a great worker when he's motivated. The problem is that he's not consistent. Today he's on top of things, but tomorrow he might decide to spend the entire day working on his tricks at the skatepark. You never know with Marcus.

After he sorts everything into place, his attention is back to me. I'm pointedly ignoring him because that's the only way to get back at him for besting me. He nudges me and rocks me a little off balance. I scowl at him. "Come on, Buttercup," he teases, "what are we doing after you're done earning money you'll never spend?"

"Probably getting into trouble," a baritone voice interrupts. Marcus quickly steps away from me, and I almost drop the mixing bowl in surprise. Big G is standing by the door with a look of tired amusement.

"GoodmorningBigG," Marcus says so quickly that his words run together. Suddenly, he's not acting so tough. Technically, Marcus shouldn't be here with me but Big G has long given up trying to keep him away. He's accepted that Marcus and I come as a package deal.

"Hello, Marcus," Big G responds. He nods at me. "Jay."

"We didn't hear you come in," I say without thinking. As if it were a valid excuse for our behavior.

"Obviously," he snorts. "Do I really have to remind you to keep the horseplay to a minimum in the kitchen?"

I give Marcus the accusatory side eye he well deserves but he's looking down and shuffling his feet. "No," we chorus sullenly like a couple of misbehaving children.

He sighs, waving his hand in the air as if to dismiss the entire situation. "As long as no one's in the hospital, I guess."

Marcus takes advantage of the dismissal and escapes into the dining area, leaving me alone with Big G and my feelings of guilt. I can tell by the droop in his shoulders that he hasn't really forgiven us yet.

"I'm sorry," I say, chewing the bottom of my lip. It's easier to apologize when Marcus isn't in the room.

"I get it," he responds, looking at me more earnestly. "I've messed around in the kitchen myself." He lifts his left arm to show me the scars of an ugly burn running from wrist to elbow. "And I've paid the price for it."

I wince. The image of a fresh burn on a teenage Big G drives his point home. I squirm a little, uncomfortable at being the focus of his attention.

He must see that I'm genuinely remorseful because he drops his hand. "Look," he adds, "I'm not trying to be a downer. I just don't want you to get hurt. You remind me a lot of a younger me." He laughs, shaking his head. "Boy, does that make me feel old."

Now, he sounds like he's really forgiven me. "Well," I agree, relieved I'm back in his good graces, "that *was*, like, twenty years ago."

"Watch it, you little whippersnapper," he threatens with a fake scowl. "I'm not that old. It can't be more than sixteen years."

I shrug and grin instead of giving him the satisfaction of agreement.

"Speaking of sixteen, that's about how many days you have left for that dish proposal to be ready," he reminds me, putting me back in my place. "Days," he repeats, "not years."

Last week, Marcus and I made a comment about the HotHouse limited menu. We had meant to suggest Big G add variety to the selection but instead, he turned it around on me, challenging me to come up with something new.

"Variety would be great," he had agreed. "Let's do it. Show me what you've got."

I didn't have anything to show. He gave me until the end of the month to come up with a recipe, price out ingredients, and have it ready to serve. The deadline for me to save face and come up with something good is fast approaching.

"I know, I know. I'm almost there," I lie.

"Oh, I can't wait." He flashes me a row of bright white teeth.

I narrow my eyes. "Why does that sound so threatening?"

His smile is even bigger following my question. He looks rather pleased with himself as he pulls his apron over his head and wraps the string around his waist. It sports the words *#1 Fry Guy* and the logo of the HotHouse on the front.

"I don't know what you mean, Jay. I'm just being the super encouraging boss that I am." He winks.

CHAPTER 3
MAYA

"**D**on't look now," Marcus mumbles under his breath. He's facing the wall and giving the peeling paint more attention than it deserves. "But guess who just walked in."

I'm wiping down the counter but look up at the door. Maya Hebert, the girl from school I've had a crush on for the past three years, is looking right at me.

Marcus groans. "I *said* not to look."

I look back down. I don't know what to do. I'm examining my hands but I've stopped wiping. I've stopped moving. I may have stopped breathing. I'm like a trapped animal with no way out. Marcus groans again.

"Too late," he reprimands. In the same breath, he turns around and acts like he sees Maya for the first time. "Hey, Maya!" He's trying to distract her and give me time to recover. He really is my best friend.

It works. Maya turns away from me and smiles politely at him. "Hi, Marcus."

That's all she says but that's all it takes for my knees to weaken. I'm leaning heavily on the counter, holding myself up completely with just my arms. Good thing I've been doing all those push-ups.

18

As she walks toward us, I remember to breathe before I pass out. There's a delicate flowery smell in the air. It's overpowered by the aroma of deep-fried fish and strong spices from the kitchen, but I can tell it's there. I know it's because of Maya.

Her hair, impossibly straight, reaches almost halfway down her back. Black like agate, not charcoal. She has one side tucked behind her ear but the other curtains down, hiding her face from me. I stare at her hair as if I can see through the shiny black. It's like I'm looking at the industry standard for all shampoo commercials. Too perfect to be real.

"Here for the usual?" Marcus continues the conversation while I'm lost in my own head.

"You don't work here," she reminds him. She pulls the double strap of a backpack, too small to be practical, over one shoulder.

"*He* does." Marcus thumbs at me and leans back against the wall. When Maya turns her attention to me, he grins and steps away to give us the appearance of privacy. I'm grateful but also terrified.

"Um—" I forget what I'm supposed to say. I repeat the same spiel several times every day to dozens of customers, but whenever Maya is in front of me, I can barely remember my own name.

"Thank you for your welcome." I stumble over words. This happens every time; you'd think I'd have figured out a way to deal with my nerves. "I mean, thank you for coming and welcome to the HotHouse, where the only fish you'll find fresher than ours is in the water. What can I get for you?"

She smiles at me and a dimple appears on her cheek. It's unfair for someone to look this cute. "Hi, Jay. The usual."

I blink at her, and she blinks back.

Marcus is standing behind her and making large circular motions with his arms. He's telling me to move things along and keep talking. What a great idea. I wish my brain would work.

I pick up the order pad and fumble with the pen. It falls behind the counter, giving me an excuse to hide and collect myself for a second. I take a deep breath. It prevents me from hyperventilating. When I straighten up, I start over. *Fake it until you make it.* That's what I'm doing. Faking confidence.

"Two orders of a three-piece fish fry dinner with potato wedges. Only one container of sauce." I recite from memory. Not because I'm particularly obsessed with her, but because that's what she orders every time she comes in. And she comes in regularly. But also because I *am* actually obsessed with her.

She nods. "You got it."

"Coming right up." I escape to the kitchen to put her order together and I hear Marcus chatting her up. It comes easy for him. It always does. It helps that he has no vested interest in her but he's also just naturally good with people. He has confidence and charm. I have neither.

It's easy enough to put her order together. I make sure she has the best pieces, perfectly golden and even. I know one is for her father and the other is hers. I don't know which one, so I make sure both are the best examples of our product.

I'm happy that when I get back to the front, there's no one else waiting in line. Maya always arrives after the lunch rush but sometimes we get stragglers.

"Here you go. Fresh and fried!" I try not to make that sound lame and it comes out sounding fake. Marcus is behind her again. I can see that he's trying not to laugh.

Fortunately, Maya does not look offended. Instead, she smiles at me in a way that I decide to consider encouraging. "Thank you," she responds. It's basic courtesy but she makes it sound better than it is. She's always so dignified and classy. She's royalty in a purple tank top and black denim cutoffs.

Behind her, Marcus is mouthing out words with extreme exaggeration. He's coaching me, telling me to compliment her. Good advice.

"Maya—" I say too suddenly as she starts to turn.

She's waiting for me to say something else. I've got nothing. She tilts her head to the side, and her eyebrows come together ever so slightly.

I'm frantically thinking of something to say. What do I compliment her on? Her outfit? What do I know about fashion? Her purse? It's completely inefficient. I can't say anything good about that. Her makeup? Or lack of it? What does one say?

"Um, your hair—" I finally decide.

She's holding her take-out order with one hand but the other automatically goes to her hair. She looks concerned. "My hair?" she asks. "Oh my gosh, is there something in it?" She quickly escalates from mild confusion to controlled alarm. Her eyes get wider. She spins around and her hair fans out. "Get it off!"

Marcus steps back to give her room, making it seem like there *is* something in her hair that he's trying to avoid. He looks equally worried.

"No, no," I assure her, throwing my hands out to the side as if the gesture would level off everyone's emotions. "There's nothing there. You're fine."

She turns back to me, still looking anxious. "What about my hair then?" She isn't letting go of the strand in her grip, protecting it from imaginary bugs.

"It looks fake."

Behind her, Marcus is audibly defeated. He closes his eyes and winces at my attempt. His shoulders slump, and I know he's given up on me. He had such high hopes.

"Fake?" Maya looks hurt. Still confused but also hurt. She looks down at the lock of hair she's holding and everything about her is suddenly smaller.

I'm such a loser.

I backpedal so fast I'm mentally in a different country. "I mean," I say quickly in hopes of interrupting her next thought, "it looks like you should be in one of those commercials, you know? Where they show how good your hair can look if you use the right product? Except that behind the scenes, it's not real. Things on TV aren't always real. They use special effects and tricks. Like with the commercial, I know they use all sorts of hairspray and staple hair to cardboard to make it look right. Your hair looks like that. Fake but it's not."

There's a heavy pause.

"My hair looks like it's stapled to cardboard?"

Marcus takes two steps back. He doesn't appear to want to be associated with me and my burning ship. I don't blame him.

"It looks better," I finish lamely.

Maya looks at me, then down to her hair, then back up at me. "Thank you," she says but there's a lift at the end of the sentence that makes it sound like a question. She's not certain if what I said was a compliment. I can't actually say if it can be considered a compliment but I know I meant it to be one.

At this point, all hope is lost and there's no way to save it. I give up. "It sounded better in my head."

She stops short and considers this, a blank expression on her face. Marcus is also frozen. I don't move. There is a collective holding of breath among us. The scene is one out of *Jurassic Park*. Marcus and I are skittish smaller dinosaurs waiting for the T-Rex to make a move so that we can react appropriately.

Her lips twitch.

I brace myself for retribution.

CHAPTER 4

DIPPING SAUCE

Maya's laughter isn't just delightful but also a reprieve. I'm redeemed. I can breathe again. I make eye contact with Marcus. He's also laughing, a little too loudly, actually. But I don't care. I have a second chance.

"That is the worst compliment in the history of compliments," Maya declares, shaking her head. I allow her smile to encourage me.

"So what you're saying is that I'm immortalized and unforgettable," I say with unfathomable confidence. In my peripheral vision, I see Marcus's eyebrows arch up, and he nods. I'm on the right track.

Maya smiles wider. She has perfect teeth, the favorable result of braces when she was younger. I can tell because I wore braces for a couple of years too. The idea that we have this in common makes me happy.

"Oh, for sure, Joshua Abayani. You are far from forgettable."

My name has never sounded so good before. The fact she even *knows* my full name is already more than I could hope for. I'm not a total loser, after all.

She lifts the bag of food slightly and says, "Thank you. I'm sure I'll be back soon. My dad loves your fish fry." She turns to go.

I don't want her to leave. Not after I was able to make her laugh. Not after I was able to come out of that dumpster fire without burning. This is the most conversation we've ever had together and I don't want it to end.

"Are you sure you only need one thing of sauce?" She always asks for just one, so I know it's a useless question but it's all I could think to ask.

It works. She faces me again and shrugs. "I know everyone loves it." Her tone is apologetic. "But I'm not really big on mayonnaise."

I don't like mayonnaise either. Another thing we have in common. I grin. "Oh, yeah? Me neither." The dimple on her cheek is back. Even with a slight smile, she can summon its presence. So unfair. "Want to try something different?"

She tilts her head to the side. "Sure," she says. "What have you got?"

"Stay here, don't leave yet." I wait until she nods before I run back to the kitchen. I know I don't have exactly what I want on hand but could make do if necessary. This is definitely necessary.

I take an empty sauce container and fill it halfway with white vinegar. I add a pinch of the unidentifiable mix of spices. The powder floats on the surface. I throw in a few bits of chopped onion. It doesn't look very appealing. I scowl but I can't think of what else to add. With not much else to work with, I seal it with the lid and shake it until the liquid is tinged red. It would have to do.

I wasn't gone long. Neither Marcus nor Maya have moved from where I left them. They both turn to me when I enter the room. I hold my hand up and show them the container.

"What is it?" Maya asks. She sounds optimistically curious, not wary. This is a good sign but for a split second, I'm second-guessing myself. What if she hates it? How will that make me look?

I put the container down on the counter between us. "I made it up. Try it!"

She isn't one to back down from a challenge. I can tell by the way she grins at me. She puts down both her mini backpack and plastic bag with her order on the counter. She starts to open the bag.

"You're going to make her dig through her own order? Bogus!" Marcus rebukes me. "At least get her a fresh strip or something!"

I falter. I'm not authorized to give out free samples but I don't want to lose face in front of Maya. I'm allowed a free lunch. I can just give her mine. I turn back toward the kitchen to get her a fresh meal but she stops me.

"Don't worry about it," she assures us both. She opens up her box and breaks off a piece of fish. "I'm excited to try this." Without hesitating, she dips it expertly in the vinegar and pops it in her mouth.

Marcus is bending over to sniff at the container. He recoils right away from the sharp vinegar smell. I pray Maya doesn't react with the same distaste. I watch her intently, taking in all her micro-expressions and trying to interpret them.

Mercifully, her eyes widen and she smiles. "That's what I'm talking about!" She has one hand demurely over her mouth when she speaks. Then she nods and points at the sauce with her other hand. "So much better than mayo!"

I love the taste of salted fish fry dipped in spicy vinegar. She's just like me and I'm the one to introduce her to it. This is the best I've felt in a long time.

"I knew you'd like it," I say, even though it's so far from the truth. "But I can make it even better."

She takes another piece and dips again, clearly delighted in this new discovery. "I don't know, Jay. This is pretty fresh."

I exchange a quick glance with Marcus. He gives me a thumbs-up. We both recognize this incredible moment for what it is. My chance.

"I promise I can make it better," I insist. "This isn't the real thing. I've got the good stuff at home." Then, before I can overthink it too much, I go for it. "If you want, I can make a batch for you."

"Tell you what," she counters, "if you can bring some over to my house later, I'm buying another three pieces right now." She picks up a second strip. "I think I might finish this right here."

This keeps getting better and better. I can't believe everyday table sawsawan is going to get me time alone with Maya.

"You've got a deal!" I fail miserably at trying not to look too eager. "But, hey," I add, trying to recover, "that one is on the house. I'll grab you a fresh meal." It's the perfect way to end the conversation: cool, suave, and totally confident.

Too bad Big G has other ideas.

CHAPTER 5

ANCESTRAL PRIDE

Are you giving away free food, Jay?"

Big G's booming voice catches me by surprise. That's twice in one day. My faux composure crumbles instantly. I go from winning this confidence game to all-time loser in one sentence. The sudden drop makes my stomach hurt. I'm apologizing before I even turn around.

Big G is smiling. He holds up a hand to stop my words before they leave my lips. I think he's trying to help me, but I'm also hesitant to hope.

"Good to see you, Gabriel," Maya says politely. "Jay wasn't doing anything wrong. I'm paying for my meal." She's down to her last fish strip, unless she plans to eat her father's too.

"Lagniappe," he says, dismissing her protests with one word. It is a unique New Orleans sentiment, meaning I have his permission to give her something "a little extra." I'm exonerated. "You're one of my favorite people. Jay knows this." He puts one hefty arm on my shoulder, and I feel both the heaviness of responsibility along with the relief of leniency. He's not only giving me an excuse, he's making me look good at the same time.

Maya smiles. "Thank you, Gabriel." She's perfectly polite.

"Call me Kuya Gee! We Filipinos need to stick together, right?"
Big G shakes me a little to indicate that I'm part of the group. The
weight of his arm feels heavier and I can't make eye contact with
Maya. Why does he have to say that?

"You're Filipino?" she asks him; she looks like she isn't sure if
he's just teasing her. "Honestly? I didn't know that."

Many people don't know it. People rarely see past his skin color,
just about as dark as Marcus. And with his confident attitude and
strong accent, everyone just assumes he's a Louisiana Creole.

Maya, on the other hand, confuses everyone she meets.
Between the shape of her eyes and darker features, people
can't tell for sure. She doesn't look completely Filipino and is too
naturally tanned to *not* be Filipino. For whatever reason, the idea
of a mixed heritage doesn't come to mind as easily as it should
in a place as diverse as this.

"On my mother's side," he announces proudly. "Just like you."
He points at her and winks again. "Except really, really far back."

He waves her toward the closest chair and drags me along
with him around the counter. My feet are heavy. I don't want to
go. Marcus joins us at the table, looking mildly amused.

"Big G," I interrupt, "shouldn't we be getting back to work?"

He must hear me but gives no indication of it. It's intentional.
Any hope I have of redirecting this conversation is already lost.
I've heard this so many times before, I'm already mouthing out
the words of Big G's first sentence a split second before he says
them aloud. I know what's coming.

"I'm a direct descendant of one of the families at St. Malo,"
he says, puffing up his chest. "The very first permanent Filipino
settlement here in this country!"

"St. Malo?" Maya echoes. She's left her meal on the counter. A
sign that she's invested.

Big G looks even more delighted to be egged on. He lets go of me so that he can have full use of his hands. He waves them around when he speaks as if he's literally building the world he's talking about. "St. Malo was the largest fishing village on the southern shore of Lake Borgne in the eighteen hundreds."

"The eighteen hundreds?" Marcus scoffs, sounding like a student trying to point out a mistake the teacher made in front of class. Except Big G didn't make a mistake.

"You bet! The eighteen hundreds," Big G reiterates. If his six-foot frame isn't already imposing enough, he stands even taller sharing this fact. "Filipinos have been around longer than you think! They built their cypress homes right on the bayou. They had wharfs where they could dock their boats. It was a community of over a hundred Filipino fishermen!" He pauses, as he does whenever he tells this story, to stare off into the distance as if he were watching the scene unfold the way he described it.

"Wow," Maya says, and she sounds like she means it. "That's just wild. I can't believe I've never heard this before." Why is this so fascinating to her?

"It's too bad that being out in the bayou also made them vulnerable. Storms destroyed the settlement every decade or so." He bows his head, and it's likely we're all thinking about how things were when Hurricane Andrew hit Louisiana seven years ago. I was ten years old when that happened, and I'm told it was nowhere near as devastating here as it was in Florida, but I don't know anyone in Florida. I don't know their stories. I just know what happened here.

I remember the rain coming straight down, then slanted, then horizontal. We shuttered our windows but the whole house still shook. Glass still broke. Power went out. It was frightening. I can't imagine what a tropical storm would be like in a cypress home built on the water.

"More families left to surrounding parishes." Big G continues, spreading the fingers of his outstretched arms like he's scattering the families into the wind. "Then, finally, a hurricane completely destroyed the settlement." His shoulders heave and then slump. "It's all underwater now."

As sad as Big G looks, Maya looks even sadder. Her eyes brim with tears for the Filipino families that lost their lives and their homes to the elements. She has such a big heart, and I find that all I want to do is comfort her.

"If St. Malo was the first Filipino settlement, how come there aren't more Filipinos around here?" Marcus asks. Valid question. Filipinos barely make up half a percent of the population in the whole state. There are more of us in California.

Big G shrugs. "Many migrated north. Others, like my forebears, integrated into the rest of the community." He points to Marcus. "You never know. If you check, you might find that you're of Filipino descent too. It's been over a hundred years. Maybe there are more of us than we realize."

"I wish I were Filipino," Marcus declares, leaning back on his seat. I roll my eyes. He grins. "Seems like Filipinos get special treatment around here."

Big G doesn't deny it. Instead, he laughs, a deep sound from his belly like a Southern Santa, if there ever was one. "Being Filipino isn't a badge to be displayed or hidden away in shame. Until you recognize your heritage as part of who you are, you may never be able to recognize yourself. And how can you accept yourself if you don't know yourself?"

Both Maya and Marcus nod. I don't react. He isn't talking directly to me but his words resonate, and I don't like how it makes me feel.

"I didn't know I was Filipino." Big G taps his chest for emphasis. "But I wanted to know myself, so I started a personal dive into my bloodline. That's how I met my Carmelita. She helped me trace my lineage all the way back to St. Malo." The hand that was tapping his chest rested over his heart, a little over dramatically. "I fell in love with her the same time I was discovering my heritage. It was like finding my past and my future all at the same time."

He shrugs and lands his arm back on my shoulder. "So, sure," he admits. "Maybe I have a soft spot for Filipinos."

This job has been a huge learning curve for me and I often wonder what stops Big G from firing me. Saved by my heritage. How strange. I'm more familiar with it being a disadvantage.

"And speaking of soft spots," he continues, looking past us to the door, "here comes my biggest weakness now."

A very pregnant Carmelita Williams is making her way toward us. She has one hand over her rounded tummy and carries a purse with the other. Her hair is pulled away from her face and gathered together with a large scrunchie. That's what the girls in my class call it, anyway. It's basically just a regular rubber band wrapped in colorful material and made to look … big. She used to have much shorter hair but hasn't had it cut since she's gotten pregnant. Apparently, long hair ensures an easier delivery. According to superstition anyway.

Big G steps outside and helps her in. His wife is graceful and doesn't seem to need his help but takes it anyway. She smiles at him, accepts a kiss, and then greets the rest of us.

"Oh, are we just not working today?" she teases.

I smile. Carmelita is just as nice as her husband but significantly less intimidating. She's as tiny as he is large. And unlike him, there's no doubt that she's one hundred percent Filipino. From her stature, dark features, and easy tan down to the unmistakable accent. Even non-Filipinos can tell, judging her immediately as an outsider and assuming that because of her accent, she's not well educated. But she's so likable that within minutes, they'll forget they even stereotyped her for her skin color. I've decided that it's because everything about her is maternal. She has a calming aura that instantly puts everyone around her at ease.

Except for Maya.

Maya is shifting in her seat like she sat in something squishy and uncomfortable. Her expression switches from vulnerable to guarded. She looks away and lets her hair fall over her face again. There's a flux in the general atmosphere. I look around but no one else seems to have noticed this sudden change in her.

"Good afternoon, Mrs. Williams," Marcus and I say almost in unison. Maya mumbles a greeting, further confirming my suspicions. Maya always displays an impressive level of class, like she was trained in some boarding school. Her greeting now sounds much less impressive.

"Boys! I keep telling you, Mrs. Williams is my mother-in-law. You can call me Carmelita." She says this but we know Big G likes it when we're more respectful toward her.

Maya gets up. The sudden movement and the scraping sound of the chair on the floor gets everyone's attention. "I have to go." Head bowed, she takes the two steps to the counter to collect her stuff and hastens to leave. She's out the door before anyone can properly say goodbye. I exchange a confused look with Marcus before I chase after her.

"Maya!"

She stops but doesn't turn around. I catch up to her easily and walk around and face her. She's looking down, her hair falling on either side of her face. "I'm sorry," she says in a tiny voice. "I have to get home. I stayed too long."

"Yeah, I get it." But I don't. "But, um, I said I was coming over later and I will. I just, well, I don't know where you live."

She looks up, meets my eyes, and smiles. "Oh, of course! Here, hold this." She hands me her bag of food. I take it, and she rummages through her little backpack. She pulls out a small colorful notebook and a glitter purple pen. She struggles at first, looks around for a surface to write on and her search lands back on me. She makes a circular motion with her hand. I know what she wants. I turn around and bend over slightly.

I stare at the broken sidewalk under our feet, just a few steps away from the entrance of the HotHouse, and wrestle with unfamiliar emotions. She puts the notebook on my back, and leans her arms on me to write. I hold my breath. I tell myself the reason I'm doing this is so it will be easier for her, but the truth is it's because I fear any movement will reveal more than I'm ready to share.

This is the longest physical contact I've had with her and my whole body is in a heightened state. Every stroke of her pen sends a ripple across my skin, even though she's not pushing very hard. I can feel the tightness of her muscles as she writes.

It's over before it begins.

"There," she says, and I can breathe again. I turn around. She rips off a page and hands it to me. Her handwriting is perfectly level and all in loops. So much better than mine. But she didn't just write her address, she also drew a rudimentary map with main streets to show me how to get to her house from work. My final destination is indicated with a star. "Got it?"

It's fairly simple. From this, I can figure out how to get there from home or work. I give her a thumbs-up. "Got it."

She points to a series of numbers at the bottom of the page. "But if you get lost or something, this is my number."

Her name, Mayaari Celeste Hebert, is next to the digits. The ink is purple with a hint of an artificial fruity scent but I'm not about to put it up closer to my nose to confirm. Maybe later.

I hand her back her food and realize that I never gave her that extra meal. "I'll bring you a hot batch too."

A dimple is my reward for that promise. "I'll see you later," she echoes. "Thank you." Maya is back to being herself, as gracious as before. She tilts her head as a final farewell and continues on her way, head held high this time.

CHAPTER 6

FAMILY HISTORY

'm still confused but also delighted when I walk back into the restaurant.

"What was *that* about?" Marcus blurts out. "That was weird. I know she's cute and all but …" He doesn't finish his sentence. Instead, he makes little circles by his temple with his finger.

"Jay likes the strange ones," Big G teases. I can tell there's heat on my face but can't deny his accusation. His wife bumps him with her hip.

"Stop it, Riel!" she admonishes, calling Big G by another of his many nicknames. "You're embarrassing the boy." She shakes her head and waves a finger at all of us. "And shame on you! You should all be kinder. That poor child has been through more in her young life than anyone should."

Big G, properly chastised, nods solemnly. I look at Marcus, and he shrugs. Neither of us knows what they're talking about.

"What do you mean?" Marcus is always braver than I am.

"Oh, you were both too young to know this, I suppose," she responds. She takes the chair Maya recently vacated and sits down. There appears to be a longer story behind the answer.

"Ah, so this is one of those days we're just not working, eh?" Big G teases. She slaps him on the arm. He laughs, bends over, and kisses her forehead. She accepts the kiss but scowls at him playfully. Seeing how the two of them are together makes me smile. They have a great relationship. Someday, I'd like to be in one just like theirs.

"Anyway," she continues, her Filipino accent a little deeper with mock annoyance. "Maya was very young when she lost her mother." She looks up at her husband. "What was it? Back in Nineteen eighty-nine? Nineteen ninety?"

"Around that time," he agrees, counting on his fingers. "She must have been only eight when it happened. I didn't even have the HotHouse open yet."

"Yes, so young." She shakes her head. "Her father is a police officer, you know?"

Both Marcus and I nod at the same time. Marcus has a theory about why Maya isn't dating anyone. Her father won't allow it. And who would want to challenge a cop?

"He's the one who got the call," Big G interjects. "He was the one who found her."

The way he says that makes my skin crawl. Maybe it isn't so much what he's saying but more of what he *isn't* saying. There's something between the lines. Something too awful to say.

"She was in a major car accident," Carmelita continues. "It was so bad that they say her body was cut clean in half." She puts a hand to her mouth, trying to hide the words. As if she isn't the one saying them.

"*What?*" Marcus pushes his chair back a little, distancing himself physically from the image conjured by her words. "In *half?!*"

She nods solemnly and makes the sign of the cross, more of a compulsory action rather than the beginning of prayer. "It was terrible." Big G lays a hand on her shoulder in silent comfort. He stands close enough to the chair so she can lean her head on his arm. "He was the one who had to call it in. Then, even before the paramedics could arrive, the whole car burst into flames."

The scene becomes even more horrific with every added detail. I'm imagining the carnage and my breakfast threatens to come up. I'm removed from my body, like I'm in the past, floating above the site, witnessing it as it happens while also standing in the middle of the HotHouse entry. "Was Maya there?" I hear myself ask.

"Thankfully, no. Only Officer Hebert." In a conspiratorial tone she adds, "There was talk in the parish after that. Some people were suspicious of him. They say that he was behind everything and got away with murder."

If Marcus could lose color, it would've drained from his face. And I'm equally aghast. *Murder?*

She shakes her head, reading our thoughts so clearly on display. "He's such a nice man. It's difficult enough to be a single father raising a young child in tragedy but to deal with such ugly rumors on top of that?" She sighs. "Such a pity."

"Yikes," Marcus says indelicately. "That's enough to mess anyone up."

"You never know what battles people are fighting," she reminds him. "So always be kind." She reaches her hand out for her husband to take. And with his help, she hoists herself up. She tiptoes and kisses him on the cheek as a thank you. He bends low to accommodate her. Immediately after the kiss, she slaps him lightly on the arm. "No more dilly-dallying! You can all get back to work!"

"You heard the lady. I think we're about done here anyway." He starts to untie his apron. "I'm going to take Carmelita home. Go ahead and close up shop." He jerks his head toward the kitchen and purses his lips in a way that makes me believe he has Filipino blood in him for sure. "I think there are some extras back there. You can take some home." There's a glint in his eyes, and he grins. "Or you can take some to Maya."

I'm mortified.

"Riel!" Carmelita chides.

He holds up his hands in surrender but does not look remotely apologetic. He winks at me before following his wife back to the kitchen.

I'm alone with Marcus. He leans back on his chair and puts one foot on the table. "Who knew, huh?"

His casualness bothers me. I push his foot off the table, and he almost topples. "Feet off," I say as an excuse for being physical. "I just wiped that down." That's not true but he doesn't argue with me.

There's a heaviness in my chest I can't explain. Now that I'm thinking about it, Maya is always so reserved at school. She's well liked and welcome in any group but doesn't spend exclusive time with any one person. She's almost always alone, even in a crowd. What a painfully lonely way to live.

I look at Marcus, who's swinging chairs over tables in preparation to close. Even though he doesn't have to. He can be super annoying but he's my best friend and I know I can count on him. Does Maya even have that?

In my mind's eye, I see an eight-year-old Maya learning about her mother's death, and my heart breaks for her. I look out the door as if I can see her walking home. As if I can see through walls and distance and emotions.

And all I see is that she's alone.

CHAPTER 7

THE MAGIC IS IN THE SAWSAWAN

The only thing that stops me from speeding down the street on my bike is knowing that I have two important fish fry orders in a plastic bag that need to stay upright. I don't have to worry about sauce but I'm still concerned that jostling will crush the perfectly golden crust on top. While that doesn't change the flavor, it does make it look much less appealing.

Mentally, I'm already home. I'm planning what I'm going to use to transport the sawsawan I'm taking to Maya. Proper sawsawan needs stronger vinegar. One that's packed with spices already in the bottle. Enough to turn the white vinegar a brownish color. I like to add finely chopped fresh garlic, red onions, and siling labuyo to the vinegar after it's poured. Lola says it's made with calamansi, a kind of lime that's native to the Philippines. Nothing else tastes like it. I've tried ordinary lime and it doesn't work. Lemon is a better substitute but still lacks the right kind of sour. A dash of soy sauce will complete things.

Maya is going to love it.

I think about her reaction to the dipping sauce I cobbled together earlier. I did that. I put that smile on her face. And I'm going to do it again. My chest swells with a kind of pride I've never experienced before.

The back door is unlocked, as always. Lola is in the kitchen washing dishes by hand. We have a dishwasher but for whatever reason, she prefers washing things by hand and putting them in the dishwasher when they're clean. Our dishwasher is essentially a cupboard of clean dishes.

She smiles when she sees me and holds her hand out to me. I place the bag of food on the counter and take her hand. It's still damp but gratefully, no suds. "Mano po, Lola," I say in greeting.

Mom walks into the room. She doesn't greet me. Instead, she purses her lips toward the bag on the counter and says, "Ano yan? Hapunan mo ba yan? What's that? Your dinner?"

I'm instantly defensive. She likes to assume things and her assumptions are often wrong. "No," I respond, a little more aggressively than I intend to. She raises her eyebrows, and I make the effort to control my tone. "I'm taking it to a friend. I just have to get something together first before I go."

"Aalis ka nanaman? You're leaving again?" She doesn't look irritated but the way she asks sounds like she is.

"I'm just dropping it off. I'll be back in time for dinner," I promise, hoping that's enough to get her off my back.

"Anong kailangan mo dito? What do you need here?"

I can't tell if she's trying to be helpful, just nosey, or looking for a reason to scold me about something. I don't think I'm doing anything wrong but Mom likes to find mistakes in everything I do. I've learned that it's best to provide as little information as possible. "Nothing. I can handle it. Just don't touch anything."

She throws her hands in the air dramatically. "Excuse me, Mr. Know-It-All." She rolls her eyes, landing a sideways look to Lola. "I won't touch your precious things," she adds with a smirk before leaving the room again. It's like the sole purpose of her even coming into the kitchen in the first place was just to ruin my day.

I hate that she has the last word, but I can't think of anything to say that won't turn into a full-blown argument. I don't have time for that right now. So I just grit my teeth and turn my attention to the cupboards where we keep all our spices.

It's easier to focus on peeling and chopping than it is on processing the volatile emotions my mother has a talent for bringing to the surface. I power through the tears brought about by the onion skin. It means I have to make a conscious effort not to touch my face when I chop up the single siling labuyo needed for this. I made that mistake once, and I'll never forget the burning sensation in my eyes from the potent pepper. Lesson learned.

There are no strict measurements when making sawsawan. At least none that I've ever been taught. Everything is "to taste" or, basically, however much you want to add. I add enough chopped onions and garlic so the jar is choked with them.

It doesn't take long and I'm done within ten minutes. By the time I add the jar to the bag, I'm smiling again.

"I've got to change," I announce for no reason. I don't want to smell like the HotHouse. Lola looks up from her task of putting away things I used for prep but doesn't stop. I hesitate and half-heartedly make a move to help her. She shoos me away. I don't know if she actually enjoys the busy work but I know *I* don't enjoy it, so I don't argue. It seems like a mutually beneficial situation.

I wash up in the bathroom sink and study my reflection in the mirror. I've been trying to control the acne on my forehead all summer but every time the worst of it heals, new pimples pop up. I brush my hair forward with my hands in an attempt to cover it up. It does but it's too reminiscent of the bowl cuts my parents had me sporting as a child. I shake it off.

Looking for inspiration, I rummage through the cabinet by the wall to find that jar of gel I bought last Christmas. I've used it a couple of times but I can't seem to get the hang of it. Would it be a good idea to try it now? I glance back up at my reflection.

Wouldn't hurt.

If it's really bad, I can wash it off. I rub a little on my palms and run it as evenly as possible through my hair. I try to hide the zits again and with the help of the gel, swipe my hair a little to the side so it doesn't fall straight down into its preferred bowl shape. I spike it up a little to break up the monotony. The result is an improvement.

I brush my teeth. Not because I'm anticipating any close contact but because I don't want to be embarrassed by bad breath. And it gives me confidence.

Cracking open the door of the bathroom, I see Lola is still in the kitchen. I don't see Mom anywhere. I prefer it that way and open the door completely. I hate it when every little action I make is questioned. I'm sure Mom will notice the slight deviation in my hairstyle and give me a hard time, so I'd rather avoid her altogether.

No one interrupts me as I climb the ladder to my room. Once I'm here, I'm safe. This is *my* space. No one ever comes up here.

I push the dirty laundry I've left on the floor to the side with my foot. I shed the clothes I'm wearing and add them to the pile. Once on the floor, it's like it's left my realm of existence and have no bearing on anything of consequence at the moment. I do my own laundry. I'm just not doing it now, so why would it matter?

It's still hot out but I want to look good. I unfold a plain collared shirt my parents bought for me for my last birthday. There's a little horse embroidered where a breast pocket should be. I don't always agree with their fashion choices but this shirt feels cooler than most of the other ones and the collar is a step above the T-shirts I usually wear.

I check myself out in the cheap full-length mirror I have leaning against the wall. I try popping the collar like Marcus sometimes does. What look am I going for here? Bad boy? Boy next door? Boyfriend material?

Anything but just *Jay*.

One last look at my reflection in hopes I miraculously look better in real life than I think I look in the mirror. I smooth the collar back down. That may be something I have to work up to.

Lola is peeking into the food bag when I get to the kitchen. It's annoying when Mom is nosey but adorable when Lola is curious. I look around to make sure Mom isn't within earshot and I whisper conspiratorially to Lola, "It's for a girl."

Her eyes light up and she gives me an approving expression. She asks me in Filipino who I plan to give it to. I answer her in English. That's how our conversations always go.

"Just the prettiest girl in class," I say. "Maybe even the world." I enjoy feeding the mystery. She looks delighted and asks for specifics.

"I should go." I use this as an excuse to leave and avoid her questions. I look toward the hallway and yell, "I'm leaving!" I don't wait to hear back from Mom. My job is to let her know when I leave the house but it's not my responsibility to make sure that she hears me.

Lola looks out the window. Her expression has changed. She looks concerned. There's still plenty of light out but she stops me to warn me about staying out at night.

"Yes, Lola," I tell her, wondering if Mom's paranoia originated from Lola. "I promise I'll be home before dark." I wave goodbye and close the door behind me. I see her watching me from the window.

She doesn't look reassured.

CHAPTER 8

INTRODUCTIONS

I follow Maya's directions as best as I can but my progress is slow to make sure I don't spill anything. The closer I get to where Maya lives, the easier it is. There are more tourists to avoid but the sidewalks are level and there aren't as many cracks in the road.

Maya lives in the Garden District. It's an older and more famous parish. I pass many tourist groups taking pictures of houses. If this happened anywhere else, the neighborhood watch would call the police to report suspicious behavior. But in the Garden District, it's just a Monday.

The houses are beautiful, and every one of them is unique in its own way. Like most of the houses in Louisiana, shutters are a standard survival tool against the frequent storms, not a stylistic choice. Here in the Garden District, they find a way to make the utilitarian into something fashionable. Some shutters are long, starting from the floor and only stopping where the roof begins. Others slide to the side instead of swinging. And some are even installed behind the glass.

The larger houses are left over from a time when rich families had slaves or staff. As grand as those are, they always give me the creeps. Enough that I pedal faster when I go by them. I like the quaint little houses, just as fun and colorful as the people of New Orleans. Maya's is one of them.

I slow to a stop in front of a small home with blue-gray painted walls, white trim, and dark double shutters that span the entire door and then some. It looks too decorative to be functional but as I get closer, I see it's styled intentionally to look that way. There are layers to the design so that the shutters can be used when necessary without compromising beauty.

More than size, that's how I can tell I'm in a different kind of neighborhood. The cast-iron gates are extra ornate. There are added curves on ends that serve no purpose other than it can be done. It costs more and the people that live here spend on details like that. Even the porch is wrapped in iron, not standard wood banisters, and even more ornate than the gate. A subtle display of wealth. The front gate is unlocked, and I navigate my bike just inside. This isn't the kind of neighborhood where bikes get stolen, but I'm not going to make it easy for anyone in case they are tempted.

The brick steps that lead to the front door are in different shades of complementary red. The porch ceiling is painted a cool shade of green-tinted blue. It's tradition to ward haints, or evil spirits, away from the home, meant to mimic the appearance of the sky and trick them into passing through. Or it can look like water, which ghosts are believed to be unable to cross. Either way, it's protection for the family. I wonder how much of that is something Maya's family believes in or if it's just tradition. Maybe it's just a pretty color.

Concrete planters sit on either side of a dark wood door inlaid with black iron and stained glass. Healthy leaves of ivy spill stylishly over the planters and end right before they hit the brick. Even Nature herself conforms to the aesthetics of the

Garden District. Or maybe a hired gardener makes sure it does. In contrast, as if to prove the occupants are grounded people, a common old-fashioned gas lamp hangs from the eave. I can barely see it because it's still bright out but the pilot light is on.

The house is as welcoming as it is intimidating.

I park my bike parallel to the gate and away from the steps. But before I go up the stairs, I take the food out from the bag so that I can present it properly like the present it's meant to be, and not like a bag of groceries.

Maya opens the door before I finish climbing the steps.

"I knew I saw you out there," she says. She sounds much more relaxed now than she did when she left the HotHouse. "Why didn't you knock?"

"I come bearing presents." It's not an answer to her question but I had that quip in my head prepared before I even left my house. I default to my rehearsed pitch because it prevents me from saying something dumb. I lift the containers a little to distract her further.

She opens the door wider as an invitation to come in. I might have said more but my concentration is on my steps because I'm very aware that all it would take is one misstep to turn this dream opportunity into the trauma moment I'll be talking to my therapist about for years to come.

"Here, let me get that from you," she says, taking the items from my hands as I walk over the threshold. I relinquish the dinner with welcome relief. At least if anything were to happen to it now, it isn't going to be because of me. "Oh," she adds before I can take another step. "Could you take your shoes off right here? We don't do outside shoes inside the house." She gives me an apologetic look. "Is that weird?"

I think it's endearing that she's worried about it. It's exactly the kind of thing I worry about all the time and one of the reasons

I never have anyone over to my house. The house rule makes sense to me. It minimizes outside dirt and helps keep the floors clean, but all it took was one weird look from Marcus in fifth grade for me to realize this isn't as common a practice as I thought.

"Not at all," I assure her. "We do the same thing at our house."

"It must be a Filipino thing." She indicates a small bench by the door. "You can sit there if you need to. Just slide your shoes to the side so my dad doesn't trip on them when he gets home."

I do as she suggests. "Your dad's not home? You're here alone?" More importantly, we're here alone *together*? Knowing that excites me. This feels like a date.

Or maybe I'm just relieved her father isn't home to judge me.

She's walking away from me before my shoes are off. "Yeah." She raises her voice the further away she gets. "He should be back in a bit."

I look toward the entry, expecting him to arrive just as she says that, but the solid door remains shut. I remove my white Nike Airs, tuck in the laces, unlike I would have done in my own home, and carefully push them out of the way. I follow her voice to the next room.

This is my chance to see another side of Maya. I don't imagine a whole lot of people get to see the inside of her house. How much of her can be found here?

A large chandelier hanging from the ceiling is the first thing I see. It's made of several layers of flat, thin, circular iridescent shells that hang from invisible strings, independent from each other. Each circle slowly spinning on its own axis. It looks alive.

I recognize the material as capiz, a type of seashell popularly used in the Philippines. Lola has a jewelry box made out of the oyster byproduct. I've never seen it used extravagantly this way.

The walls are painted white but the furniture is all made of the same heavy wood, elaborately carved and stained dark. An imposing cabinet with a glass front is tucked in the corner. It's filled with items that don't look like they have anything in common with each other. Framed pictures of different sizes cover every surface. There's little evidence of actual living happening in this living room. Instead, everything feels preserved, like a museum. This might not be a direct representation of Maya, because it's more a reflection of her parents, but it does tell me a little about the environment she grew up in.

Maya is yelling to me from another room. "It's cool if we wait for Dad before eating the food you brought, right? I'd feel bad if I started without him."

I walk toward her voice and find her in the kitchen. In contrast to the dark living room, the kitchen is sunny and painted a happy shade of yellow. When she turns to look at me, she lightens the room even more.

"If you want to keep it wrapped in the foil and maybe pop it in the oven until your dad gets home, that might help keep it crispy," I suggest. I didn't know I would be invited for dinner. I'm largely unprepared.

"Great idea." She uses a toaster oven on the counter instead of the big gas range. "I don't know why I've never thought of that. We always just eat it slightly soggy."

I must've made a face because she laughs.

"I'm not the culinary pro," she says.

"Clearly."

She grabs a towel that is lying on the counter and swats me with it. I take the hit. It isn't hard. "You take that back!" she demands.

"Hey, *you* said it! I was just agreeing with you!"

She wrinkles her nose and it's just the cutest thing. "Whatever," she says, bobbing her head. She throws the towel at me. I catch it and grin at her. She shakes her head.

I don't hear the door open but a commanding voice yells from the other room. "Maya? I'm home."

It's clearly her father and suddenly I feel like I've been caught doing something illegal. Would he consider being in a room alone with his daughter a capital offense of some kind? Am I about to be yelled at?

Maya must not be feeling any of this because she's smiling when she responds. "We're in the kitchen, Dad!"

I like the sound of "we" in that sentence. Maya and me. A unit. She says it so casually and it makes it seem real, not just a hopeful idea in my mind. The tangent thought helps calm my nerves.

Unlike Big G, Lieutenant Hebert is a man of average height and build. He has a full head of sandy-colored hair, swept to the side. He is wearing the light blue New Orleans Police Department uniform, complete with a clip-on tie. He isn't an imposing man but I am very much intimidated. He raises both eyebrows as he regards me.

"Who's this?" he asks. His tone is casual but it doesn't quite mask his suspicion.

Maya steps toward her father. He leans down a little to her but does not take his eyes away from me. He allows her to kiss him on the cheek before straightening back up.

"Jay," Maya says, "this is my dad."

Hoping my palms aren't as sweaty as I think they are, I extend my hand out to him. He takes it with a tight grip that I attempt to match.

"Dad, this is Jay."

"Good to meet you, sir," I say, trying my best to remember any etiquette I've ever been taught in my life. And just when I think that I've been holding on to his hand too long, he releases me.

He regards me with sharp blue eyes darkened by age and experience. "How do you know each other? School?"

I can't tell if he's asking me because he's looking at me or if he's asking Maya and doesn't trust me enough to take his eyes off me. Maya answers him before I can.

"Jay's in school with me but we're friends because he works at the HotHouse." She picks up the glass jar that is still in the bag I used to transport their food. "Look what he brought."

Mercifully, that makes Mr. Hebert look away from me. "What is it?"

"It's dipping sauce." She shakes it slightly to make the little pieces inside swirl around, a snow globe of flavor. "It tastes incredible. Wait until you try it."

"Dipping sauce," he repeats, seemingly unconvinced.

"It's sawsawan," I offer, clearing my throat a little because I suddenly sound hoarse. "It's a Filipino dipping sauce." I mean to sound like I know what I'm talking about but I end the last sentence like I'm asking a question. I clear my throat again. "It's vinegar based. We use it a lot in my family." He looks suspicious enough for me to want to convince him I'm not trying to charm his daughter with a voodoo love spell.

He takes the jar from her, opens it, and breathes in. Maybe cops undergo secret training to identify questionable ingredients. Or maybe he has experience in Filipino spices because he seems assured by what he smells.

"OK," he concedes. He lifts the jar up like he's toasting with it. "Shall we try it?"

The invitation seems genuinely optimistic but a sense of dread settles in my stomach and I don't know why.

53

CHAPTER 9

FILIPINO FOODIES

The dining area is on the other side of the kitchen. On the wall is a comically large set of wooden utensils, made of the same dark wood as all the furniture. They're clearly for decorative purposes but it feels like it belongs more at a large cafeteria than in someone's home. I sneak a sidelong look at Maya, who is quietly laying out placemats made of thin strips of wood woven together with colorful thread. I decide my unflattering opinions shouldn't be voiced.

The dining table is big enough to fit eight people but there are only four chairs. There's a bowl made of carved wood in the center of the table. In it are blocks of the same kind of wood masterfully carved in the shape of fruit, unpainted and varnished. Outside of a banana and a pear, I can't identify the rest of them but it looks like a better conversational piece than the oversized spoon and fork.

I pick up one of the unidentifiable wood fruits. It looks like a grenade. "What is this?" I ask.

"What does it look like?" she volleys back instead of answering, a mischievous glint in her eyes.

Her look encourages me to be silly. "A grenade?" I mime like I'm throwing it, then duck behind the table. "Fire in the hole!"

She laughs. I like making her laugh.

"Dork," she says, taking the roundish checkered wooden piece from my hand. She holds it in front of my face. "Obviously, this is an atis."

"A what now?"

She puts the carved hand grenade back in the bowl with the rest of the wooden produce. "How do you not know what that is?" she asks but looks delighted to be the one who gets to tell me about it.

"That's not my fault." I shrug.

"It's a Filipino fruit." She adjusts all the inedible fruits in the bowl. "These are all examples of Filipino fruit."

"I've never had an atis," I admit. "Where can I get it?"

"The Philippines?" She laughs when my response to that is a sardonic look. "I mean, I don't think they sell it around here," she amends.

"Then how the heck am I supposed to have tried it then?"

"You've never been to the Philippines?"

I shake my head. "Nope."

Her expression changes to one of pity. There's a little sadness in her eyes. "Aww, that's too bad. The Philippines is beautiful."

I nod but I don't agree. I'm not missing anything. This is my home. New Orleans, not Manila. The United States of America, not the Philippines. I have no desire to leave here. "How often do you go?" I ask because it looks like she wants to talk about it.

She still looks sad even though she smiles. She sits down on one of the dining chairs, and I follow suit. "Not often. The last time I went was before my mom died." That explains the sadness.

She traces her finger on the grooves of the placemat in front of her as she talks.

"I was seven," she continues, looking down at her finger. "My mom took me to the Visayan province she grew up in to meet cousins of cousins and all sorts of other extended family."

"There are three regions, right? Luzon, Visayas, and Mindanao." She seems to know so much about the Philippines. I only know one city, Manila, the capital. I want her to think I know more. "So how come you didn't go to Manila? That's in Luzon. You didn't go to Luzon?"

She shakes her head. "I've been there once, and it's nothing like the province. If you want to see the beauty of the Philippines, you visit the provinces and beaches. It's breathtaking." She tilts her head to the side, as if the action triggers the memories in her head. "My mom's province is small. I swear I'm related to every single person there."

"That's probably true," I agree. "Small towns tend to be that way. Even here."

She nods absentmindedly. "She gave me a dollar. I mean, the equivalent of what a dollar was in pesos anyway. And when I went to spend it at the corner sari-sari store, I had enough to buy *all* the kids in town some candy and a bag of cola."

I know what a sari-sari store is from Lola's stories. It's a neighborhood convenience store usually connected to someone's house. They sell everything from sugar to detergent in individual sachets. Sometimes they even sell street food. But her description of the drink confuses me.

"A *bag* of cola?" I ask.

"That's how they gave it to us," she insists. "They pour the cold drinks from the bottle into a clear plastic bag and serve it to you with a straw."

"A plastic bag. Like a grocery bag?"

"No!" She laughs again. "Way smaller." She makes motions with her hands to indicate the size. It's a clumsy attempt and not very accurate. "And super thin. Like the kind you put a goldfish in when you win one at a carnival."

That does not sound appealing, and I make a face. "Goldfish-flavored cola. Yum."

"Stop it!" But my expression makes her laugh, so I do it again. "It's not the *same* bag. It's not like they recycle goldfish bags and use them! It's *like* the bags they use at carnivals. That's all!"

"So candy and sugary drinks for the kids," I say. "Good choices. I mean, even without the goldfish."

"I was *seven*," she repeats. "But it *was* a good choice because I think that made me the most popular kid in town!"

"Buying into their affection, I see," I tease her.

"It was such a great summer. I got to swim in the ocean, eat the freshest seafood, run around with the rest of the kids ..." Her voice trails off as she's lost in memories.

I let her linger in them. I can see they make her happy, and I don't want to interrupt. I watch her stare off to the side, seeing scenes in her head that I'll never know, and it occurs to me that I recognize the look.

Sometimes, in the cafeteria at school, she'll be in the company of friends, but she'll have this same expression on her face. I realize that every time she did, it meant she wasn't actually there with her friends but lost in her memories half a world away at a time when she still had both her parents. A time when she was happiest.

I'm probably the only one in this world that knows this. I'm humbled to be entrusted, whether or not it was intended, with this knowledge. I'm already silently promising to protect it.

She pulls herself back from her reverie, maybe suddenly aware of how long she was mentally absent. "The Philippines is beautiful," she repeats in summary.

"You haven't gone since?" I ask gently.

She shakes her head. "No." She's sad again. "The flight takes forever—like two days. Dad doesn't have a whole lot of vacation days, so …" She shrugs. "By the time we got there, we'd have to turn right back around."

"You can't go by yourself?" I'm trying to problem-solve this for her. Give her options that she may not have considered.

"Dad won't let me." She should sound angry. If I were her, I'd be angry. But she doesn't sound upset at all. Just resigned. "It's OK," she assures me. Probably because I look unconvinced. "I get it. He's already lost my mom. He's not going to risk losing me."

I hadn't considered that. I nod, understanding now.

She gets up and I follow her back to the kitchen but stop before I leave the room. A small round table sits by the entryway. Two framed photos of different sizes are displayed on it.

One is of a toddler—Maya—with a bowl cut and her father in uniform. She's sitting on his shoulders, her arms wide open like wings, unafraid of falling. A younger version of her father is looking up at his precious daughter. It's a photo full of laughter.

The other frame, made of capiz shells like the chandelier I saw earlier, holds a photo of a slightly older Maya. Her hair is longer, down to her shoulders. She's eating a beignet, her lips coated with powdered sugar. Next to her is a woman with even longer hair. She looks remarkably like Maya but with darker skin, a broader nose, and thicker hair. She has the same eyes and dark features. Unlike the child, her lips are free from powdered sugar but her smile is wide. She must be Maya's mother.

"She was wonderful." Mr. Hebert is standing behind me. He's caught me studying the photos but doesn't seem bothered. His eyes are on the image of his late wife, not me. "The purest soul I've ever met."

I study him in this unexpected light. He's a young father, younger than my own parents. But the lines by his eyes are deep. I don't know what that means other than the cause is beyond my own limited experience.

"She made the best pandesal," Maya adds when she reenters the room carrying plates. "She would make them fresh for me every morning at the end of her nursing shift. They were heavenly."

I welcome the interruption. The atmosphere had become heavier without me noticing. I take the plates from her. She allows me to and goes back into the kitchen to grab more things while I set the table.

"You know what pandesal is, right, Jay?" she asks loudly from the other room, intentionally putting me on the spot.

"Yes," I say, proud that I can answer with confidence. "I know how to make pandesal."

That catches Mr. Hebert's attention. He turns to me with a half-smile on his face. "Oh, you do, do you?" I can't tell if he's challenging me or impressed by my claim. Either way, I'm suddenly less confident.

"My lola taught me," I reply, faltering a little. Pandesal is like a Filipino dinner roll. But I've only eaten it for breakfast. Maybe as a snack, but never with actual dinner. "We eat it with a slice of cheese."

Maya is delighted when she returns. "Have you ever dipped it in hot chocolate? Or had it with ice cream?"

I make a face. "Ice cream? What? No."

Both Maya and her father laugh. I'm not so thrilled with this because I'm not actually trying to make them laugh, which means that they're laughing at me.

"When I was in the Philippines, the sorbetero would come by with three different flavors of ice cream." She goes on to describe the colorful cart of the Filipino street ice cream man. There were no ice cream trucks when she visited. Only the mamang sorbetero with his colorful two-wheeled cart that he would push down the street. "You could have your ice cream in a cone, a cup, or in pandesal!"

I can't imagine putting ice cream inside the slightly sweet, slightly salty bread roll. The combination doesn't seem agreeable. "In *bread*?" I repeat, unable to get past this. "That's not how you're supposed to make an ice cream sandwich."

They laugh again, but this time it doesn't bother me.

"I didn't think so either," Maya says. "But I figured I should try it and, honestly, it wasn't too bad!"

"But not necessarily good, right?" I prod.

"I like the cones better," she admits, and I'm vindicated. She flashes me a winning smile then disappears into the kitchen. I take a step to follow her but Mr. Hebert stops me.

"Sit down," he instructs, not aggressively but also in a tone that is used to getting what he wants. I sit on the chair he motions to.

Maya walks back in with the rest of the food on a tray. She's divided the sawsawan I brought into three sauce bowls. It looks like the toaster oven has done its job satisfactorily. The fish looks crispy.

"Do you need help?" I offer. I want to stand and help her but I also don't want to disobey her father who had given me clear orders to sit.

She puts down the tray and waves a hand. "Don't worry," she assures me. "I've got this. Everything is pretty much here already. Just need to grab the wedges." Then she disappears again.

"Her mother used to be the one to do all that," Mr. Hebert tells me. "Now Maya does it."

There are many things that could mean but Mr. Hebert doesn't elaborate. We sit in silence. It's so uncomfortable, and I'm looking anywhere but him. On the wall behind him, there's a large elaborate wood carving of thirteen men sitting on one side of a table. I'm familiar with the image.

It's *The Last Supper*, a scene from the Bible. Jesus is in the middle, and his disciples spread out on either side. We have a painting of that exact scene hanging in our dining room. I've seen many versions of the scene but never in carved wood. Why thirteen men would all sit on just one side of a table doesn't make sense to me but I'm not an artist.

I clear my throat. "I've never seen *The Last Supper* carved in wood," I say because it seems like a neutral enough topic.

Mr. Hebert twists in his chair to look at the hanging. I can relax a little when he's not looking directly at me. His attention is unnerving. I don't think I'm doing anything wrong but just being in the same room alone together is enough to make me feel guilty for everything I've ever done in my life. I can't imagine living with that kind of presence but then again, I'm not his precious little girl. I'm just the guy who likes his precious little girl. It's probably a very different experience for Maya.

"It's much heavier than it needs to be," Mr. Hebert complains about the piece. "My wife insisted we take it with us all the way from the Philippines. It wouldn't fit easily into any of our luggage. We had to bring it home in a large box with a whole lot of other things. That thing was such a pain." When he looks back at me, there's a smile on his face that tells me he didn't mind as much as he claims. "I've traveled to many places in my life but it's only when we visit the Philippines do I have to travel with boxes."

"It's called a balikbayan box, Dad," Maya says, bringing in the rest of the meal. "It's not just *any* box."

I know what a balikbayan box is. My own parents have filled boxes of them to be sent to distant relatives in the Philippines. As far as I can tell, it really is just a regular corrugated box. The only thing that would make it special is the **BALIKBAYAN BOX** printed on the sides of it. And maybe it comes in specific sizes.

Her father doesn't argue. He reaches out to take the items from Maya, and when everything is laid on the table, he takes a closer look at the sawsawan. "I've seen this before," he observes.

"This tastes better," Maya assures him in a way that makes me swell with pride.

"It's not exactly the same thing you had earlier," I warn her.

"No, this is going to be even better. I can tell." She smiles at me, and it's like we're the only two people in the room.

Mr. Hebert fills his plate. Then with a fork, he takes a piece of his crispy fish to dip in the sawsawan. He chews it thoughtfully. I hold my breath. It isn't until he swallows and his expression changes to one of grudging acceptance that I exhale.

"Not bad," he says. "I've had salt and vinegar with fish fry before."

"Not the same thing," Maya insists. "This has a Filipino flavor to it."

He nods and dips the remainder of his piece into the HotHouse signature sauce. "That it does. I'm glad you found something you like."

Maya rolls her eyes. "Don't mind him," she says to me. "I really like it. And if I have to keep eating fish fry because Dad wants to, I'm always going to have it with this." She dips her piece in the dish next to her and pops it in her mouth. "So good."

I'm thrilled. I'm having dinner with Maya. She loves the sauce I made so much she's defending me against her own father. Her father isn't kicking me out. Everything is going so well. Even better than I could have imagined. I could leave right now and ride this high for the next month. Marcus would be proud. I'm on top of the world.

CHAPTER 10

QUACK

This is what I want to show you." Maya bites her bottom lip, as if she'd say too much if she didn't. Her tone is conspiratory, and I'm caught up in the mystery of it.

We've just loaded the dishwasher and her father is in another room. Maya is leaning against a door with glass windows. A door that looks similar to my own back door but significantly more ornate. "Go grab your shoes," she instructs.

I don't pass her father when I retrieve my sneakers from the front entry and carry them back to where Maya is waiting. She's already slipped on a pair of strappy sandals. She waits for me to jam my feet into my shoes before opening the door.

Warm air greets us when we step outside. The sun is getting ready to set. I can tell because even though it's still bright enough, it doesn't burn the same way it does when it's at full blast. The sun sets much later in the summer, and I estimate that I have less than an hour before it gets dark. I promised to be home by nightfall but I have no intention of leaving Maya now.

The backyard is large, twice the size of the house. There's little flowers but plenty of grass. An uneven stone path greets us at the door and splits, leading to two different sheds.

One shed has no windows. I assume that houses things like gardening equipment and stuff you don't want inside your house. We have one of those too. The other shed is more interesting because it's less of a shed and more of a chicken coop. But with ducks. Fat white ducks with bright orange bills and equally orange feet.

"Are those *ducks*?" I ask the obvious.

A low-slatted fence surrounds the structure. As we approach, a small artificial pond installed behind the shed-turned-coop comes into view. I count almost half a dozen ducks, one in the pond and the others waddling about. I can't see if there are more inside the coop. There's straw everywhere.

The fence is low enough to step over with some effort but there's a built-in swing door made of planks of wood nailed together. Ducks noisily funnel toward the entrance. They are louder as we approach and my nose wrinkles involuntarily at an unfamiliar smell of dirty pond water, musky and damp.

When Maya unlatches it, the door swings open, and the ducks swarm out like water pouring out of a faucet. One duck is unusual. Two is quirky. Three is excessive. She has more. She has an alarming number of ducks.

I take an involuntary step back but Maya bends over to greet the ducks by her feet. "These are my ducks!"

"All of them?" I ask in a much smaller voice than I intend. She doesn't hear me over the sound of quacking and feather ruffling. I make an effort not to flinch as four of her ducks surround me. I anticipate pecking, and I prepare to control my reactions. I don't think Maya will take it kindly if I kick one of her ducks across the yard.

I'm trying not to make eye contact with any of the birds. They may be able to sense my fear. My biology teacher once said something about birds being descendants of dinosaurs. I'm not ready to test that theory. Instead, I keep my eyes on Maya and shuffle my way to her. There's a duck trying to peck at Maya's hair, but she isn't bothered. Others are vying for her attention. She looks delighted instead of annoyed.

"Why do you have so many ducks?" I ask, louder this time.

She straightens up with a duck in her arms. She holds the duck out to me. "This is Papan. She lays me the most eggs." She tilts her head and starts talking to the duck in a voice reserved for babies or things that can only hear high-pitched notes. "Who is the queen of egg laying?" Papan shakes her head and rears a little. She might flap her wings but Maya has a good grip on her. "That's right," Maya continues in the same high-pitched tone. "You are!"

To my surprise, Papan tilts her head to meet Maya's and they bump foreheads in what seems to be a shared moment of affection. Then Maya lets her go. Papan flaps her large wings and waddles after the rest of the flock.

"Have you ever had balut?" Maya asks. I make the same face I made when she talked about pandesal ice cream. Around us, the ducks wander about, no longer interested in the humans. They peck at things I can't see. Some flap their wings but don't fly. One waddles back to the pool.

"Once." I shrug. "Fertilized duck egg, right?" Balut is considered a Filipino delicacy, but I don't see the appeal. It looks like a regular hard-boiled egg from the outside but nothing like it on the inside. I think of it more like a dare than a dish. When Lola first introduced me to this, I felt tricked. There's a kind of soup in the egg when the very top of it is cracked and carefully peeled. It's savory and delicious. But once the egg is peeled all the way, an actual chick is revealed.

There's something about seeing the veins and a partially formed chick that makes me lose my appetite.

Maya nods. "My mom raised ducks before I was even born. She started with just two of them, and by the time I came around, she had more. They don't all lay eggs anymore." She spreads her arms to gesture at all the birds as if I could possibly miss them. "I grew up always having ducks in our backyard."

She starts to walk around the fence, so I follow. I don't have a lot of experience with girls, much less visiting them at their homes, but everything that's happened since I parked my bike outside this house is a surprise. Maya herself is a surprise. And the more time I spend with her, the more fascinating she is.

"Dad tries to tell me about her," Maya says in a quiet voice. She's not looking at me, and it takes me a moment to realize that she's talking about her mother. "But most of the stuff, I already know. There's just so much I don't know."

What do you say to that? I don't say anything.

"It's strange, you know?" she continues. "She was born in a province in the Philippines, and my dad only really knows about who she was here. That's only a small part of the story." She sighs heavily. "She's from a whole other country. A whole different culture with a whole different history. And I want to know it. I want to learn everything about it."

Is that why she's talking to me now? Because I happen to be Filipino?

Suddenly, I'm not having a good time. There's a distaste that twists my mouth and makes my stomach queasy. It occurs to me that she's not at all interested in me like I have been hoping. She doesn't care about me. I'm just a source for her research project, someone who may be able to tell her more about the Philippines.

I'm more than just a brown-skinned Filipino. It seems that's all everyone sees. It defines everything I do. I have a job because Big G likes Filipinos. Maya is talking to me because I'm Filipino. That sounds great, but I'm also the kid who sits alone at lunch.

I'm the kid that gets made fun of. It's my skin color, my height, my nose, my food. I'm an outsider because my family is different. I'm different. No matter what I do, I'm just Filipino, never American.

"Who cares?" I say in a tone I have never used with her before, one I'd never have imagined I would use with her.

That catches her attention. She looks back at me and recoils a little. Whether it's my tone or the expression on my face, I don't know.

"I mean"–she falters, then turns the question around to include me–"don't you want to know more about your heritage?" Like I was the one who brought it up.

"Not really," I say, trying to keep the hostility out of my voice. "I'm American."

"Yes," she interrupts. "But you're also Filipino."

"Am I, though?" I'm spitting out my words. "I was born here, just like you. Just like Marcus. I grew up here. I don't speak the language. I've never even *been* to the Philippines. Exactly what about me is Filipino? My skin? My hair? My fresh-off-the-boat parents?" My voice is getting louder with every sentence. I see Maya shrink from me, but I don't stop. "What is my heritage? My heritage is *here*. Who cares who my ancestors are? I don't know them. What have they ever done for me?"

I give her a moment to respond. She opens her mouth to speak, but nothing comes out. There's no argument because I'm one hundred percent right.

"I'm *American*." I'm not yelling but I know there's intensity in my words. Even the ducks give me space. "If I wanted to be Filipino, I'd *be* in the Philippines."

I'm done. The whole evening is in ruins. I feel guilty almost as soon as I stop speaking because the look on Maya's face is the opposite of how I want to make her feel. Her eyes are shining with unshed tears. She's making an effort to keep them there. There's a tremble in her lips and her breathing is shallow. She's not angry. She's hurt. I hurt her.

"I need to go," I mumble. "Tell your dad thanks for having me for dinner."

That's how I say goodbye. I don't go through the house but through another gate that leads to the front where I left my bike. And right before I close the gate behind me, I catch another look at her.

She's sitting on the grass, facing away from me. Her ducks gather around her in a protective circle. Her head is down, and I see her shoulders shake.

I made her cry.

CHAPTER 11

BREAKING CURFEW

Mom is standing at the door. Of course she's waiting, ready to catch every little mistake. I know what's coming before she even opens her mouth. The sun has set. I officially broke curfew.

"Sabi mo uuwi kang maaga," she accuses me. "You said you'd be home before dark." She gestures out the window to support her argument. "It's dark."

I don't greet her. I walk right past her into the house, and she follows close behind. "It *just* got dark," I say. "The sun literally set one minute ago."

"Then you're one minute past your curfew," she responds in heavy accented English. She acts like I've committed some kind of cardinal sin and she's the one who gets to take me to hell. "You need to be responsible. It's very irresponsible for you to break your curfew."

"I'm not that late." I'm trying to keep my voice level but I hear myself getting louder.

"You're still late. Where were you?" she asks, matching my volume. When I don't answer, she continues her tirade. "You're inconsiderate. Did you know that Lola made you dinner? Now it's cold!"

"I'm not hungry," I mumble. I feel bad that Lola went through the trouble but I wasn't going to give Mom that victory.

"What?"

"I said," I repeat through gritted teeth and in a much louder voice. "I'm. Not. Hungry."

"Your lola made you a good dinner and now you're not even going to eat it?" She makes a sound in the back of her throat, a huff unique to Filipino mothers. "Where did you go? We didn't even know where you were! You said you'd be home before dark but now it's dark! It's so irresponsible!"

"Oh my God." I throw my hands up in the air as I turn to face her. This is pointless. She's just going around in circles, trying to find the button to make me lose my mind. I may as well give her what she really wants: an argument. "What is the big deal? I'm home now, aren't I? It's not like I was out doing drugs or something!"

"Don't raise your voice at me, you disrespectful child!" she stutters in anger, her hands on her hips, acting like she's taken aback by my attitude. Like she's not the one that triggered it. "Akala mo sikat ka?" She doesn't translate that last sentence and I actually don't know what it means. But I also wasn't about to admit that.

"I'm *not* a child!" I kick my shoes off, not bothering to put them away properly and grab the ladder up to my room. I cannot deal with this right now.

Mom is still yelling at me when I get into my room. She can't follow because she's afraid of falling off the ladder. But she knows I can hear her, and not for the first time, I wish I had a door I could slam. I want that satisfaction.

Instead, I throw myself face-first into the bed and scream into my pillow. I throw punches into my mattress because it's safer than punching the wall. I do this until I can no longer hear Mom yelling.

She must've retreated to the living room or bedroom to complain about me to Dad or Lola. It's better than yelling up at an open hole, I suppose.

I roll over on my bed and stare at my ceiling. I know at some point, I'm going to have to go back downstairs and take a shower. I wonder how I'm going to be able to avoid further confrontation.

I stay in that position for a while before I reach for the phone next to my bed. The phone is attached to the wall with an extra long cord I bought with my own money. I even bought the phone with my own money. Worth it.

There's a phone jack on one end of the wall that I could tap into but it's not located conveniently near me. The phone and cord are a great investment. I pick up the handset and punch in Marcus's number.

It rings a few times before his sister picks up. She sounds annoyed when I ask for Marcus, and I hear her yell out his name. There's sounds of a scuffle and a bit of sibling back and forth before he picks up.

"Yo!" That's his typical greeting over the phone. I hear him moving the phone around, presumably to try and get some privacy in his house. "Spill."

"I mean, it *started* good," I admit. Part of me doesn't want to talk about it but a bigger part needs to analyze the situation. "Even met her dad."

"Yo," Marcus repeats but with a tone of respect. "And you lived to tell about it. Kudos."

"He's not that bad," I lie, quickly following it up with a better point of pride. "And Maya even talked me up to him."

"She did not! You lie!"

I rise to the challenge. I tell him word for word what Maya said in defense of me. I talk about dinner and every incident that made Maya laugh. In my narrative, I'm killing it and can do no wrong. I'm the perfect dinner guest. By the time I get to the end of dinner, Marcus is hooting at my conquests.

"My man!" he exclaims. There's pride in his voice, like a teacher with his student on graduation day. It makes it more difficult to admit what happened next.

"Yeah, but then I messed up." I sigh and stare up at the ceiling again, seeing the scene play out in my head. I cringe at my behavior.

"Oh no," he groans. "What did you do?" The ease with which he accepts that the failure was entirely on me should be insulting. Except that it's realistic, and I can't get mad at him for it.

He laughs at my commentary about her ducks, so I linger on that for a bit, trying to delay the inevitable. If I don't talk about it, maybe it never really happened. But ultimately, we get to that point in the story. Marcus groans when I tell him how I lost my temper.

"It's not my fault," I say, but I know that it is. "She just sees me as *the Filipino kid* and nothing more."

"So what? Why are you trippin' over this?" he asks. I bristle but don't respond. "No, duh, you're the Filipino kid. That's your *in*. She wants to know all about your ancestors? You *tell* her all about your ancestors. Make stuff up if you don't know. Just *give her what she wants*."

I'm quiet. I don't agree with him. We stay on the line in silence. I can hear him breathing. He sighs.

"Listen"—his voice is much calmer now—"she wasn't dissing you. Can't you see that?" I shake my head. He doesn't see me but somehow, he knows my response. "She misses her mom."

There's a sinking feeling in my chest that travels down my stomach. I'm so busy feeling sorry for myself that I didn't see that. The more Marcus talks, the more I realize what he's saying is absolutely true.

"I wonder all the time," he says. "And I've got no one to ask." Marcus knows firsthand what he's talking about. The only boy in a family with three children, he felt close to his father. His parents divorced when he was thirteen. It was messy. His father moved out and he hasn't heard from him since. He doesn't even know where he lives. Maya's struggle hits close to home for him.

"You're right," I admit, ashamed that I missed what was so clear to Marcus. I'm a terrible friend. "I suck."

"She's just holding on to everything that reminds her of her mom. You're lucky enough to be what she's looking for. And you wasted it, you dipstick."

I swear. "What am I supposed to do?"

"Duh. Apologize."

I groan. "How? There's no way I can face her now!"

"You're already an idiot," he says matter of fact. "Don't be a coward too."

"Gee, thanks, *Mr. Miyagi*." I'm sarcastic, referencing the name of a fictional karate master.

"You're welcome, *Daniel-san*," he responds gamely. "I gotta go. The she-devil wants the phone." His sister in the background protests the nickname. His response to her is muffled, so he must've covered the receiver with his hand. "I'll see you tomorrow," he promises before hanging up the phone.

I return the handset to the cradle when I hear the dial tone on the other end. Marcus is right. I need to find a way to apologize to Maya. I need to make things right.

But how?

CHAPTER 12

MIDNIGHT INSPIRATIONS

I wait until it's almost midnight before I sneak back downstairs. Everyone should be asleep and that should give me privacy.

The lights are all off in the kitchen. I'm not worried. We've lived here almost four years now. I know my way around the house. I navigate the stools I know are there and turn the corner for the bathroom. Safely inside, I shut the door before switching on the lights.

Showering is more than just getting clean. Mom says I'm wasting water because my mind wanders when I'm in the stall. I could stand under the spray for a full minute getting soaked before I even start with soap. Maybe I use up more water than I should but I solve problems this way. Not all problems, but a few. Too bad there's no shower-solving magic this time.

By the time I'm done toweling off, I've considered and rejected twenty different ways I could make things right with Maya. I know I can't just come up to her and blurt out an apology. I don't know if I'll be able to muster up the courage to say the right words. Eloquence is not one of my strengths. And words just aren't enough.

I'm operating on a routine. I brush my teeth without really thinking about what I'm doing. And when I look at myself in the mirror, I don't see me; I see Maya. I remember how dejected she looked when I left her. I not only made her feel that way but also left her feeling that way. I wash my mouth out and just stand there looking at my pathetic reflection. The guilt chews me up inside. I have no answers.

I leave the bathroom in nothing but my boxers and the towel around my neck. It's too hot to wear anything else, and I'm fairly confident that no one is lurking outside to see me. Still, I open the door slowly and make sure the coast is clear before actually venturing out. My eyes acclimate to the darkness. Everything is in its place. Except on the usually clear counter, I notice something sitting on the surface. I take another look around, and satisfied that the rest of the household is still asleep, I investigate.

There's a plate on the center of the counter, covered loosely in cling wrap. The plate holds four pieces of Lola's ensaymada, a sweet pastry similar to a cinnamon roll but with sugar, butter, and cheese instead of cinnamon. In spite of my bad mood, I smile.

Lola has an innate ability to know when I'm having a bad day. Her ensaymada has a way of making a bad day better. And these look even more perfect than usual. I'm not hungry but I'm still tempted to have one, just for its therapeutic ability. If I hadn't brushed my teeth already, I might have gone for it.

Inspiration hits me and I'm suddenly smiling. I know exactly what to do. Not ensaymada but pandesal. Just like her mom would make her.

I want to kiss Lola. She always has the answers.

I rush up to my room as quietly as possible and almost trip on the shoes I didn't put away earlier. I throw the towel to the corner, adding to the pile of laundry I'll deal with another day.

I'm not one to get up early. On days that I don't have to, I could sleep in until noon. But not tomorrow. Tomorrow, I'm going to get up before Lola does. Tomorrow, I'm going to make the best batch of pandesal I've ever made in my life. Tomorrow, I'll deliver it personally to Maya. Tomorrow, I'll apologize.

Tomorrow, I'll make Maya smile again.

My alarm wakes me up when I feel like I just fell asleep. But instead of hitting the snooze button, I'm up. It's still dark outside. It'll be another hour and a half before the sun rises completely but it seems the sky is already lightening.

It's hot, even with the fan facing right at me. I'll have to apologize to Mom for my behavior last night. My parents are not the type to accept responsibility for any kind of wrongdoing, so it's always clearly my fault and my fault alone. I'm going to have to take the brunt of things; I may as well wear a clean shirt and not add to the list of how I disappoint her with my existence.

When I get down to the kitchen, I'm happy that Lola isn't there yet. Lola is usually the first one in the family to get up and putter about. When I was younger, it seemed she was always awake, and I didn't think she even slept. Beating her to the kitchen feels like I've won a contest.

The pressure I felt on my chest last night eases when I pull down all the ingredients I need to make pandesal properly: flour, sugar, salt, milk, egg, butter, yeast, and some breadcrumbs. There's something about the faint nutty smell of raw flour that raises my spirits. It represents a clean starting point with seemingly unlimited options. I can make cakes, breads, or all sorts of desserts with flour. But I can also make gravy, breading, or savory pie crusts. I have the power to make it anything I want. Today, I'm going to make magic happen.

I hear Lola walking into the kitchen behind me, and I turn to her excitedly.

But it's Mom, not Lola, standing there.

My expression freezes and falls. She sees it too. She's in a bathrobe, her hair still in rollers, not yet dressed in her duster. Her expression is flat, neither happy nor unhappy.

"Oh." I break the tense silence between us. "Hi, Mom."

One side of her lips twitch but she doesn't say anything. She's looking at all the things I put on the counter and asks me in Filipino what this is all for. Maybe it's too early in the morning for her to translate or attempt English.

Instead of answering her, I begin with my rehearsed apology. I look down at the egg in my hands and shift it around while I talk, the cool shell holding strong despite its delicate quality.

"I'm sorry for the way I behaved yesterday," I say, trying my hardest to leave any sarcasm out of my tone. "I, um, I had a fight with, um, a friend. I got home late because of that and took my frustration out on you. I didn't mean to. I'm sorry." I look up to gauge her reaction.

She studies my face, possibly to see how sincere I really am. I muster up the most genuine expression I can under her inspection. After what seems like a measured interrogation technique, the lines on her face soften and she rewards my apology with a tired smile. She walks past me to the refrigerator and pats me on the cheek. I'm forgiven.

I breathe a sigh of relief. If Mom held a grudge, it would have made my task so much harder. "I'm making pandesal," I tell her in response to her earlier question.

She opens a drawer and pulls out a milk thermometer. "Bantayan mo ang gatas," she instructs. "Make sure your milk doesn't burn." Then she hands me the thermometer.

I take it from her. She's giving me the permission I wasn't really asking for. "I will," I promise.

She leaves me to my task and goes about her morning routine. We work together in amicable silence. Every now and then, she comes over to check on my progress. She preheats the oven for me and sets out the tray I need, already laid out with parchment paper. The strong aroma of the coffee she's preparing for Dad mixes in the air with the yeast in my dough. Her company is surprisingly enjoyable and my smile is no longer one I have to work on.

The sun is up and I'm checking on the state of my dough by the time Lola comes into the kitchen. She knows right away what we're making, and she claps her hands twice in delight like a child. Mom and I laugh together.

I wash my hands and greet her properly. She tells me that she's relieved that I'm home safe because she was worried about me being out in the dark.

"I know, Lola, I know," I reassure. "I'm sorry." Today is the day for apologies. "But it's all good, right? I'm here now."

Her expression tells me I'm not as easily forgiven but because I'm also her favorite, I'm still getting away with it. I give her my most dazzling grandson smile to seal the deal. She sees right through my tactics, makes a small sound of disapproval to let me know how she feels about it, but laughs anyway.

"Thank you for the ensaymada," I tell her. "It's exactly what I needed. You have no idea how much you saved my life. I swear, you're magic."

She shakes her head and refuses credit. She tells me that Mom was the one that baked them yesterday, as a treat for me when I got home.

"Mom did this?" I repeat. It's not something Mom usually does. I can't even remember the last time she made any treats.

Lola nods, looking rather proud of her daughter. I don't know how to feel about this. It's a simple thing but I can't identify my conflicting emotions. I turn to face Mom, but she's not there. She had left the room, leaving me alone with Lola. I should follow her and thank her for the ensaymada the same way that I was prepared to do with Lola. But I don't.

And I don't know why.

CHAPTER 14

PEACE OFFERING IN THE SHAPE OF A ROLL

The paper bag containing half a dozen freshly baked pandesal I have in my hand gives me hope and anxiety at the same time. I make an effort to hold it gently so as not to crush either the bag or its contents, and it's more of a struggle than it should be. Everything is in knots: my thoughts, my stomach, my nerves.

I don't trust myself to stay balanced, so I take the streetcar to Maya's house instead of my bike. It's mid-morning and each stop has at least four lost-looking tourists, and I remember why I dislike public transportation so much. I look out the open window and focus on not sweating—as if it's in my control.

I glance at the watch on my wrist, not for the first time since I started on this operation. It doesn't help with my apprehension. I remind myself that so far, it seems luck is on my side. The HotHouse is closed on Tuesdays, so I don't have to be there. Mom was easy to deal with this morning. This batch of pandesal is the best I've ever been able to make. The morning is full of promise.

The reality is that this whole endeavor is a gamble with very slim odds. I don't know what Maya's schedule is. She may not even be home when I get there. If she's not, I can't just leave the bread. It would be a bad representation of quality. And if she is home, she may refuse to talk to me. She could accept the offering and throw it in my face. She could accept it and hate it. She might think I'm insulting her mom's memory.

The longer I have to contemplate outcomes, the higher the chances that this all fails spectacularly. I change my mind twenty-seven times before I get to my destination.

The streetcar stops a few houses away from Maya's. I get out and feel the blistering heat from the unshaded sun. I know the city has many needs but if I could, I would vote for more shade. I take refuge under the trees. It's not as effective as a solid structure but there's instant relief. I'm not usually one to really notice or care but today I'd rather not smell like a sweaty hot pepper competitive speed eater when I encounter Maya.

I don't immediately run up to the front door when I get to her house. I use the cloth handkerchief Mom always makes me carry to wipe away the visible sweat. I smell my pits to make sure I don't reek. Then, after I procrastinate as much as I can, I open the front gate.

The driveway is empty, and though that might mean that Maya isn't home, it for sure means her father isn't. Just as I raise my hand to ring the bell, the door swings open, and I'm face-to-face with Maya.

The morning sun hits her just right. Unlike the onslaught of heat burning my skin, the white light falls on her like a glow. Her hair is pulled away from her face, gathered in a low ponytail down her back. She's wearing a tank top with a low V-neck that makes her neck appear longer, like a ballerina's. A leather necklace that holds a clay pendant stamped with a unique design sits low on her chest. I've seen her wear it before; I make the effort to raise my gaze. When I look into her eyes, I forget why I'm there. I'm legitimately rendered speechless by how pretty she is.

I stand there longer than I should, with one hand poised to knock on the open door. She blinks; I must look ridiculous. I lower my hand and hold out the paper bag like I'm a delivery boy. She looks down at it with suspicion.

"I'm sorry," I blurt out without any kind of finesse. I'm as clumsy as she is graceful. The words tumble out of my mouth faster than I can think. "You have every right to hate me, I know. And never speak to me again. And how dare I show up at your place in the middle of the morning. But it has to be now because that's when it's fresh, you know? I mean, I could bring it over in the afternoon but you said you had them in the morning, so I figured it should be in the morning."

When she doesn't confirm my reasoning, I know this is going badly. Any effort to mop up my sweat was for nothing because I'm sweating so badly, I may as well be in a gross type of self-shower. I continue ranting on, filling the silence with useless babbling. "You don't have to say anything." As if she needs my permission. "I mean, you can talk if you want, of course. You can do whatever you want. I'm not trying to stop you."

I give up.

"I know I'm stupid," I finish, losing my momentum. "I know. I'm sorry." I push the paper bag toward her with both hands. "But here."

She doesn't make a move to take it. She has one hand on the door and the other by her side. She looks at me, then back at the bag, then back at me. Her eyebrows knit together slightly, enough for just a wrinkle between them, like she doesn't trust what's in the bag.

"What is it?" she asks.

I'd never said what was in it.

"Oh." I look down at the paper bag, surprised that it isn't obvious. "It's pandesal."

The wrinkle between her eyebrows is gone, replaced by a dimple in her cheek. Her suspicion is replaced by surprise. "Pandesal?"

I nod, encouraged by her positive reaction. "Yes. It's still warm. I baked it myself."

She smiles. All the effort and stress that went into making this is more than worth it for that smile. She's happy again.

"I'm sorry," I repeat, with much more resolve than I had earlier. I want to ensure she knows. "I didn't mean to make you feel bad."

Her shoulders relax, and her smile is gracious. She takes the bag of pandesal from me, a promising gesture. "Come in," she says, opening the door wider. "You're just in time for a late breakfast." She holds the bag up and shakes it. "And I know just what we're having."

CHAPTER 15

BONDING OVER BREAD

I'll forgive you if you promise to make more of this."

Maya is on her third pandesal. I spotted a jar of pecan praline sauce in her refrigerator when she went for the butter and suggested she try that instead. She seemed dubious at first but left the butter behind in favor of my recommendation. It's an excellent pairing: Manila and New Orleans in one bite. A fitting blend for her.

She closes her eyes, making exaggerated sounds of delight. Her reaction makes me want to bake for her every day.

"Take it easy," I say without really meaning it. She can scarf it all down and that would just be further evidence that I did right by her.

She laughs and wipes her mouth of invisible crumbs with a napkin. The action is largely for show, something she must've learned to do as a child. Similar to why I carry a cloth handkerchief when the rest of the kids my age don't even know what one is.

"It's so good," she says again. "I love it."

This could not have gone any better. "I told you I knew how to make it." I'm not about to admit that I had very little confidence in my abilities prior to her enjoying the first bite. I know how to make only what I've been taught but who even knows how authentic the recipe is to begin with.

"You have skills." She lifts pandesal number four up in the air like a salute.

"Oh, you haven't even tried my adobo tacos." I lean back in my chair, filled with bravado. Her encouragement is helping my confidence reach previously insurmountable peaks. I'm capable of miracles now.

Her eyebrows arch in surprise. "Are you offering to cook for me?"

Is this real life? I'm afraid to blink and suddenly wake up alone in my boxers, tangled in sheets. "Sure," I say because there is no way I'm going to deny her anything.

"If it's even close to this, I already know it's going to be incredible." She looks down at a fresh roll and her smile isn't quite as wide as it was earlier. "You know," she says in a quiet voice; she looks just as vulnerable as she had last night, and I'm grateful that she's even willing to be this honest with me again. "I can't really tell you if it tastes anything like the way my mom used to make it."

I had been afraid to ask. Afraid that I didn't do her mother justice and afraid I had dishonored a memory she holds so dear by attempting this.

"It's been so long," she admits. "I just remember being really content sitting in the kitchen and eating my pandesal before school. I haven't felt like that in a really long time." She looks up at me, and her eyes are shining. I would not think that tears and a smile could make sense at the same time but she manages it.

She drops her gaze down to the remaining rolls and absentmindedly turns the plate around slowly. "For a moment, it felt like it used to. Thank you for this."

There's nothing in my experience that can respond to this appropriately, so I say nothing. I'm awed by how much elegance she displays in the face of obvious pain. Here I am complaining about a meddling mother and an unfair existence when she faces every day knowing she may never experience the same kind of contentment she had when she was younger. She's a soul unlike any other. I'm just a child.

She takes the napkin and dabs her eyes. "Sorry," she apologizes hastily. "I'm being super emotional."

She's apologizing to me? This world doesn't make any sense.

"Tell me about your mom," I prod.

She doesn't respond right away. Her hand goes to the clay pendant hanging around her neck. She rubs the rune between her fingers, slightly tugging at the leather cord that holds it in place. She looks uncomfortable, and I'm confused. Doesn't she *want* to talk about her mom?

"She died in an accident." She begins haltingly and at once I realize what's wrong.

"No, no," I interrupt. She stops abruptly, startled. Her fingers close completely around the amulet. I'm not certain how to phrase what I want to say and stumble on my words. She's happy in the past. She's happy in her memories. That's the Maya I want to see now. "I mean"–I try to clarify–"not how she died. Tell me about *her*." I can't think of a better way to ask what I want to ask.

Maya understands what I can't seem to articulate. I know she does because her demeanor changes. She lets go of her necklace completely. She smiles.

"She was a nurse," she begins.

"So's mine." I like that we have things in common.

"Filipino nurses. Talk about feeding the stereotype, right?" She laughs. I do too, enjoying the much lighter atmosphere.

"She stayed home when I was born, though. Became a full-time mom to me for the first few years before going back to work."

"Mine kept on working. My lola was the one that stayed home with me."

Maya tilts her head. "I'm glad I had my mom at home but I think it might have been nice to have a grandparent at home too," she muses.

"Where are your grandparents?"

She shrugs. "I never met my mom's parents. I think they were gone even before I was born. When we visited the Philippines, it's extended family, who we may or may not actually be related to." She laughs. "My mom was an only child but she strangely had many cousins." She reaches out for one of the two remaining rolls. Her appetite is evidence of a happier mood. "My dad's parents are divorced and live in different states, so every other year or so, when they remember I exist, I get a card."

"My dad's folks are still in the Philippines," I offer. "He has siblings there and they all live together. I've never been there, so I don't know them. Dad says they're too old to travel." I have no real desire to get to know them. I already have more family than I need.

She nods, understanding beyond what I say. "As far as I can remember, it was always my mom and me. They say that daughters are always daddy's girls but my mom and I were the real power team." She laughs at memories I'm not fortunate enough to share. "My poor dad. He'd come home from a long shift at work and we'd pounce on him. He'd suffer through hair makeovers, nail polish, and even full face painting!"

Her eyes are closed with a hand over her mouth like she's trying to contain the emotions inside but she's shaking with laughter. It's contagious. "I say face painting because it's so much worse than makeup. There was glitter involved. He hates glitter."

"That's horrible," I say in defense of her father. "Glitter is inhumane. You tortured the poor man. He's the law, for god's sake!" I shake my head in mock pity and pretend to be disappointed in her. "For shame."

It only makes her laugh harder, wiping tears off her eyes. "He was outnumbered!" When she catches her breath again, she continues with a much more subdued smile. "Mom always made it up to him. She would cook him his favorite foods as a peace offering. Lechon kawali, pancit, kare kare … all his favorites." She picks up the last of the pandesal and holds it up. "*These* were always mine, though."

"That's a lot of Filipino food," I observe. I'm not certain what ethnicity her father is but his alabaster skin, light hair, and blue eyes suggest he's very much *not* Filipino. And I've never met anyone who had that much affinity for our cuisine who looked like him.

"Oh, he's all over it," she confirms. "I mean, there are still some things he won't eat but his favorite dishes were always the stuff Mom made."

"How did they meet?"

"Dad was in the Navy. He was in the Philippines for training or something." She rolls her eyes dramatically. "I never get a straight answer. It's always something goofy and along the lines of 'Your mom had a face that launched our ship' or 'I was there to woo your mom' or 'She was playing hard to get and I had to cross the ocean to convince her.' " She makes quotation marks in the air for every sentence she attributes to her father and speaks in a low octave. It's a bad imitation of him, which makes it extra funny. "But it was probably something boring."

She leans across the table and lowers her voice conspiratorially. "I think he was the greenest cadet on the ship and his shipmates left him in the middle of the jungle as a prank. I heard it from one of his old buddies." Her eyes narrow and her lips curl up in a mischievous grin. She's enjoying this version of the story. "Mom found him in the jungle, scared out of his mind, and saved him."

She sits back in her chair. "In any case," she continues, matter of fact, "they got married and he whisked her back here."

"Just like that?"

"Mom went to nursing school while he finished his tour. And when he left the military, she worked full time at the hospital." She shrugs. "First comes love, then comes marriage, then …" She doesn't finish her sentence and instead points to herself.

"Then the baby in the baby carriage."

"Actually, more like the back of his squad car."

I don't try to hide the shock in my expression. It feeds her delight.

"Mom gave birth before they made it to the hospital."

"You're *such* a demanding child."

"Watch out, world!" she jokes, standing abruptly and pushing her stool back. "Ready or not, here I come!" She throws her arms wide to her sides and lifts her chin.

She has crumbs on her shirt and a smear of pecan praline sauce under her chin. Strands of hair have come loose from her ponytail and fall around her face. But I don't really notice any of it. Or maybe I do but I don't see that.

I see a little girl who lost the most important person in her life at such a young age take on the responsibilities of someone much older, not because it was demanded of her but because she felt it would make her mother proud. I see the dignified, dependable teenage daughter who refuses to indulge in the foolishness of youth because she refuses to let her father down. I see the most vulnerable, strong, sweet, powerful soul.

I used to think she was pretty.

I was wrong.

I see now that she's *beautiful*.

CHAPTER 16

AGIMAT

Maya puts two glasses of ice water in my hands and sends me out of the kitchen. "Use the coasters on the table," she instructs, sounding like a middle-aged homeowner. "Be right there."

The coasters she mentioned are disks made of capiz shells, just like the chandelier, with one side backed with felt. They look more delicate than the wood. I put the glasses down like she asked but I don't sit. Instead, I take this opportunity to get a closer look at all the framed pictures scattered around the room. There are many.

Most of the frames echo the themed look of the room. Lots of capiz. The shells have a pearl-like quality about them and aren't easily found outside the Philippines. To show such an abundance of them this far away from the islands is a status symbol. I wonder if Maya's mom is from a rich family.

The woman in the photos doesn't look particularly extravagant. She wears pearl earrings but not a matching pearl necklace. Instead, a stamped clay rune hanging by a leather cord is around her neck.

I pick up one of the framed prints and look closer. The photo is old. The coloring is a little pinkish and a crack threatens the surface along the edge. While the woman's eyes are sharp, the necklace is slightly off-focus. It's the same shape and size as the one Maya wears but the picture is too small for me to tell if it's the same one.

I replace the photo when I hear Maya enter the room.

"I notice a theme to your decor," I say, making a spinning circular motion with my finger.

"It's a lot, isn't it?" she admits. "It's all Mom's doing. Dad is more of a flannel and denim kind of guy." She makes a point to look around as if she's seeing the room for the first time. "I think Dad felt guilty for taking her far away from home, so he let her do whatever she needed to make herself less homesick."

"Where do you even find capiz around here?"

She looks delighted. "Oh, you know what it is!"

I act insulted. "Listen here, Little-Miss-Philippines. You may think I'm an uncultured wastoid but remember who brought you authentic pandesal."

She bites her lip and pretends to act abashed. But only for a second. Then she rebuttals my indignance with confidence. "Oh, *excuse* me," she says mockingly. "I just remember who didn't know what an atis was."

I hold my hands up in surrender. "Fair."

She looks proud of her win and takes a seat on one of the oversized chairs. She leans back and resembles a queen on her throne. I sit on one end of the couch, closest to her. The squarish cushions are softer than they look but I don't care for the rough texture of the material.

"We haven't made a whole bunch of changes over the years," she muses, rubbing the pendant that hangs around her neck.

"What is that?"

She looks at me blankly. I gesture to the pendant she's playing with. She follows the motion with her eyes and seems surprised that it's in her hand. She lets go like it's suddenly too hot to hold. "Oh!"

I want to mention that I've noticed her wearing it before, but don't want to sound like a stalker. "Did you forget you had it?" I tease.

She gives me a sardonic look. "Sometimes." She reaches around her neck. The clasp is hidden under her ponytail and she unhooks it. Then, to my surprise, she hands me the necklace. "It's an agimat. It belonged to my mom."

The pendant, slightly smaller than a milk cap, is old and heavier than I thought it would be. Any sharp lines have been smoothed over by time and use. I thought it was made out of clay but it's a metal of some sort with a stamped image that has faded over the years. I can make out the rays of a sun on the top half of the circle and a moon on the other. The letters around the image are almost flattened and unreadable. A leather cord, not as old, is threaded through a hole in the pendant.

I turn it over in my hands. Whatever was stamped on the back is long gone. The only indication that there was anything on it is an indentation or two in what could be the shape of letters.

"What's an agimat?" I ask. I'm sure I'm not pronouncing it as well as she did.

"Like an anting-anting?"

"Using a made-up word as a definition for another made-up word isn't a proper explanation," I say, handing her back the necklace. She takes it and swats me playfully on the arm.

"It's not made up!" She puts the necklace around her neck expertly, and I'm disappointed she doesn't need my help.

"Is it like an atis?"

"Why would this be like an atis?" she asks in a tone that suggests it's an absurd comparison.

"I dunno. They both start with the letter A?"

"Does it *look* like an atis?"

"It *looks* like hardened chewed-up gum."

She puts one hand on her chest in mock offense. "Why, I never! How *rude!*" she declares in a playful deep Southern accent.

"What's rude is you not telling me what it is!"

"I'm *trying* to tell you what it is."

"No, you're not! That's like me saying a *gobbledygook* is a *wobble-wobble.*"

"That doesn't make any sense."

"*You* don't make any sense!" We're both laughing. I find that I'm not just enjoying her company but that I like who I am the longer I spend with her.

"An agimat or anting-anting is the Filipino version of a talisman," she says.

"That's more helpful. See? Was that so hard?"

"Stop it!" But she doesn't look like she means it. "How am I supposed to know what you know?"

"Let's just assume nothing. I know nothing."

"Well, that's not difficult to imagine."

I put a hand on my chest in the same manner she had just done to express her mock offense. "Why, I never! How *rude!*"

"You said it, not me!" She laughs, unapologetic.

I continue to act indignant, making sounds of derision but not quite saying any real words.

"OK, OK!" She covers her face to compose herself. When she puts her hands down, she has a much more serious expression. "This is a Filipino amulet." She over-enunciates and speaks slowly as if I'm unable to understand her if she spoke normally. "Ahm-you-let. Some might even say a talisman. Taaaaah-lis-man."

"Are you proud of yourself?" I cross my arms and lean back on the couch.

She struggles to maintain a straight face. "It's an object that people believe carries supernatural powers." She can't continue. She wiggles her fingers like she's putting a curse on me. But she's laughing so much that she snorts. She immediately clamps both hands over her nose but does not stop laughing.

I sit up straight and point at her. "See? See? That's what you get!"

Hands covering both her mouth and nose, she shakes her head.

I watch this display for a few moments, feeling happier than I've felt in a while. It's not to say I live a sad life. Not at all. It's just that she brings with her so much joy.

"What does it mean?" I ask when she finally calms down. It looks like it may start her up again but she actually answers appropriately.

"It's an image of time divided. Split into night and day." She holds the amulet with her thumb and forefinger and tilts it toward me. "It signifies a pivotal moment in one's life. Either who you were before the light or who you become when it's taken away."

There are deeper implications in what she says that I'm unable to identify. The amulet means more to her than just the imagery.

"I thought it had special abilities. What does it do?"

She rubs it and I wonder how much of the wear and tear of the object could be attributed to her. "It's more like a vessel than a source. Supposedly, you imbue it with strength that you can call upon when you need it." Her demeanor changes as she talks, more and more subdued. "This stores your light that you can call on when you're in the darkness."

She stops talking. She stares down at the amulet, lost in thought, or lost in darkness.

"Sooooo," I say, trying to lift her up from her suddenly somber state, "like glow-in-the-dark strength?"

Her eyes focus on me. She lets go of the amulet and smiles. "Yes. Like glow-in-the-dark strength."

"That's pretty cool. How does it work? How do you put that kind of strength in?"

"There's an incantation."

"An incantation," I repeat. "Like an *abracadabra* kind of incantation?" I pretend to wave a magic wand in the air. I meant to be funny but she doesn't look amused.

"Like a *prayer*." She emphasizes the last word, and I realize she takes this as seriously as my parents would. I stop myself from teasing her more. I've learned people can be very protective of their beliefs, regardless of whether or not I share them. I don't want her to think I'm making fun of her. "It's ceremonial and dependent on intention and clarity of spirit."

"Have you done it?"

She lowers her chin, suddenly shy. "I've tried," she admits. "But I think I lack the clarity of spirit."

"How do you get that?" I ask, trying to understand. I bury my initial incredulity. If it's so important to her, I want to learn.

She considers the question. It looks like she knows the answer but is trying to find the right way to phrase it. Or trying to find a way to explain it in terms I would understand.

"When I was younger, my mom used to always tell me that everything I do is a choice," she begins, seemingly unrelated.

"Meanwhile," I interject, "my mom is always telling me I *don't* have a choice and I need to do what she tells me to do."

I mean for it to be funny and she smiles. But it also fuels her argument. "You can choose to follow her or not. I mean, it may very well end your existence …"

Her sense of conviction is intimidating and I laugh to dispel some of the tension I refuse to acknowledge. "Truth. She will end me."

"That's just a consequence of the choice you make, right? But, ultimately, you choose." I nod in agreement because I don't want to argue. "Clarity of spirit is the confidence in the choices you make."

"You don't have that?"

"Do you?"

The silence that follows tells her everything she needs to know.

</br>

GOOD MOOD

Mom is in the kitchen when I get home. I greet her with a spontaneous hug and a kiss on her cheek.

"Naku! Sino 'to? I don't recognize this good mood." She laughs. "What's gotten into you?"

"The pandesal was a hit!" I declare. The win is as much hers as it is mine for all the help I received this morning.

Mom holds up a hand for an unconventional high five. I give it to her. The last time I gave my mom a high five was in fourth grade when I won the class spelling bee. It feels weird and fun at the same time. She smiles.

"Of course, it was," she says with confidence. The f's sound more like p's when she talks and is more pronounced the louder she gets. "Your lola and I know pandesal." Her hubris is entertaining, not annoying.

I go to the refrigerator for the pitcher of filtered water inside. I'm parched. When I turn around, Mom is handing me a clean glass from the cupboard. Instead of thanking her, I smile and lift my chin in acknowledgment. She does not demand anything more.

"Tamang-tama and dating mo." She takes a quilted pot holder and checks on the pot that's on the burner. "You arrived just in time. Lunch is ready."

"I'll get the table set," I offer before she can ask. Her face lights up as if I just told her I was the class valedictorian, but she doesn't say anything. I take the plates from the cupboard and bring them to the table. The room is empty. Dad is at work and Lola is likely in her bedroom praying the rosary. She does that multiple times a day. She says she prays for everyone in the family.

I set the table for three. Putting down the laminate placemats on the tablecloth before the lightweight plates. It's interesting how different Maya's dining room is from ours. While we also have a rendering of *The Last Supper* on our wall, there's not much else we have in common.

We don't have oversized wooden utensils, woven fans, or anything really that represents our heritage. Mom has large frames with collages of family photos hanging on many of the walls. Not just pictures of our family but extended family I have never met. There are graduation pictures of cousins, birthday photos of godchildren sent to her from the Philippines, and old formal photos of my grandparents. Dad's credentials are cheaply framed and hung in the living room. The only art we have on display are things I painted in primary school. And one oil painting Mom did at a paid workshop or something. Our house doesn't quite yell *we're-from-the-Philippines* as much as Maya's does.

Although I'm sure we *smell* more Filipino. I can smell the rice before I even get back into the kitchen. I guess that we're having adobo for lunch because the sharp tang of vinegar mixed with soy sauce makes a distinct aroma.

I return to the kitchen to fetch the rice but Mom hands me the large bowl that proves I'm right about lunch. There are different ways to make adobo and my family prefers the one with sauce. There is plenty of garlic and whole peppercorns floating in the liquid. I take it to the table. Mom follows me with the sticky rice.

"Kain na!" she calls, letting Lola know it's time to eat. I hear Lola call back, acknowledging that she heard.

Lola enters the room, and I see her smile widen when she sees me. Outside of greeting her the traditional way, I don't say anything else. There's this silent communication between us. Without having to say anything, I'm able to let her know that things went well with the pandesal just by the grin I give her. She lifts her chin at me, and I know she approves. Mom seems completely oblivious to this exchange. We take our seats.

With Dad at work, it falls to me to lead the prayer. When I recite the words of gratitude, I genuinely mean them this time. Mom serves me first, and I help myself to the rice and chicken before passing it to Lola.

"Are you going to try to make ube pandesal for your girlfriend now?" Mom teases, putting rice on her plate.

Ube is a popular flavor in the Philippines that I haven't seen outside of my home. It's a type of yam, identifiable by its purple color. The first time I tried it was on my tenth birthday. It was pretty radical to have purple bread to begin with but it tastes even better, a little sweeter but not in a sugary type of way.

"She's not my girlfriend," I'm obligated to say.

"Not yet." She winks at me. "Isang pandesal na lang yan! You're one pandesal away!" She laughs at her own joke, and Lola joins her.

I grin. I like the idea of Maya being my girlfriend. And I like the idea that it's something within my control. "Maybe I'll save that for asking her to prom." I surprise myself with my boldness.

Mom and Lola laugh and nod. They tell me I have the right attitude and launch into alternative food I can offer in courtship.

I like that neither of them are pressuring me. I had been bracing for the third degree but they're both respecting my privacy and letting me tell them in my own time. It makes it so much easier to participate in discussion when I don't have to protect my information.

"Ow," I exclaim involuntarily when I accidentally bite my tongue. Mom and Lola stop mid-action to look at me.

"What hurts?" Mom asks. There's concern in her voice but only behind the almost businesslike manner of her profession. The nurse is always first on the scene.

I shake my head, hand over my mouth. "Nothing," I insist, downplaying any cause for alarm. "I just bit my tongue."

A sympathetic look would have been a reasonable response but Mom and Lola laugh and jeer instead.

"Uy," Mom teases. "Someone is thinking of you."

"What?" I lower my hand. "Why?"

"When you bite your tongue, that means someone can't stop thinking of you." She shares a mischievous look with Lola, tucking her chin and bobbing her head. "I wonder who that someone might be."

"That doesn't make any sense," I protest, but I can't help smiling. What if Maya *is* thinking about me?

"Maybe you should ask *someone* if she bit *her* tongue," Mom adds, leaning into the joke. Lola agrees with more enthusiasm than is warranted.

I mumble a weak objection, not wanting to appear too enthusiastic, but I'm wondering if there's any feasible way for me to actually ask her. I don't believe in all this unfounded superstition, but I suddenly want this to be real.

It would mean Maya is thinking about me too. It would mean I made a good impression and there's a chance we'll spend even more time together. I would make more pandesal and I would see her smile.

Lola interrupts my thoughts by asking me in Filipino if this is my soon-to-be-girlfriend's first taste of Filipino food. I like the idea of having a closer relationship with Maya and don't correct her on the premature title.

"There's a lot she knows about Filipino food," I admit. "But she doesn't cook it as well as I can." I know I'm not the guy that the girls are all swooning over but I have my strengths and Maya just happens to appreciate them.

Mom and Lola hoot at my claim, both teasing and encouraging. They carry on, each claiming responsibility for my accomplishments. Mom saying I learned it from her and Lola saying that since Mom learned to cook from her first, she deserves the credit. Neither of them are speaking English but in rapid-fire Filipino. I have to make an effort to pay attention or be lost in the conversation.

It's a different vibe around the table. More jovial than I can remember it being in a long time. It's like I'm hanging with Marcus, not two older generations of Filipino women.

I'm trying to figure out what's changed. Why everything seems effortless. Mom isn't as annoying. I'm not grumpy. Lola is animated. Sure, Dad isn't around but I'm confident that if he were here, he would also be different.

I spread a second helping of sauce over my heaping rice. My appetite is invigorated and the residual ache on my tongue is a pleasant idea Maya may be thinking about me. Lola's chicken adobo recipe is one of my favorites. She boils the chicken directly in the sauce. When the meat is softened, she removes the pieces and fries them in oil so that the skin is extra crispy, before returning it to the reduced sauce. It's excellent with steaming hot white rice.

But there's something in the air that wasn't there before. Something that's making the food taste even better.

It must be Maya.

CHAPTER 18

NEW USUAL

Yo! *Daniel-san!*"

I look up. It's an hour before closing. He has his skateboard under one arm and a canary-eating grin on his face. The last time we spoke, he called me an idiot.

"I went by your place yesterday," he says, leaning his skateboard on the wall.

"I know. Mom told me."

"You weren't there."

"I wasn't."

We stare each other down. Marcus's eyebrows reach higher up his forehead, silently urging me to provide information. I think the suspense is getting to him. I like this power I suddenly have. I don't offer anything further.

"Because you were …?" he prods, walking up to the counter.

"Out." I'm overly casual with my response but intentional with my smile, letting him know that I have something to say but I'm making him work for it.

"Doing …?"

"Things."

His expression goes from eager to frustrated. He narrows his eyes. I grin. He tilts his head to one side. I raise my eyebrows.

The silent exchange goes on a few more seconds before he gives in audibly with a groan. "Come on, man," he complains. That's the closest he's going to get to begging.

"I went back to Maya's house," I admit.

He raises a fist in the air. "My man!" He spins around in a slow circle as if he's some kind of rock star acknowledging his stadium-filled fans.

"You're a dork."

"You didn't call me crying last night, so I assume you've been forgiven?"

"Shut up." He's right. Calls are for emergencies. No call means good things. "Yes, I did what you said. I went over and apologized." I roll my eyes. I don't want to give him credit because all it does is feed his ego, but he does deserve it.

He spreads his hands wide to his side, accepting the praise. "Marcus Goodman, *love doctor*."

"Never say those words again."

"You're just jealous."

Marcus winks, hops up and sits on the counter, something he wouldn't dare do if there was anyone else in the room. He picks up a plastic spoon a customer had abandoned on the counter and starts spinning it around his fingers. It's a useless skill we've both attempted to master with varied results. He's had more success and I've had plenty of dropped pens. He's now flaunting his skill to further his point. "I've got what it takes. You think you'd be grateful to be able to learn from the master."

I throw the dirty dish towel at him, aiming for his face. He catches it with his free hand but drops the spoon. That takes care of his smugness. He throws the towel back at me and I dodge, letting it fall behind the counter.

I bend over to retrieve it only when Marcus hops off the counter to pick up his spoon. I straighten up again and catch a glimpse of Maya out the window. She's never here two days in a row. It can't be her. I blink to make sure this isn't a manifestation of a hopeful heart but it's definitely her.

"How much fish fry can you have in a week before you're sick of it?" Marcus teases her when she enters. He's not looking at me so there's no way he can tell I'm inwardly yelling at him to shut up. What a failure of a wingman. He's supposed to encourage her to keep coming back, not the opposite.

"Hello, Marcus." She acknowledges him without answering his question. Her hair is still in a ponytail but gathered to the side so it cascades down one shoulder. "You're here again too."

"Hiding from the sun," he says as an excuse. She seems to accept that. He waits until she walks past him. Then he steps behind her and wiggles his eyebrows comically. He's such a goober. It makes it difficult to ignore him and keep a straight face.

"What can I get you?" I ask, abandoning the usual spiel.

"You know," she admits, "I don't think I've ever had anything here other than fish fry and potatoes." She looks up at the menu overhead, possibly considering things for the first time. Then without warning, she turns to face Marcus. Fortunately, he's recovered and not acting like an idiot. "You're here all the time, Marcus, what do you eat?"

Marcus looks a little taken aback to be suddenly included in the conversation. "Um," he begins. "I think I've had just about everything they make here."

"Whatever he can get for free," I add.

"It doesn't hurt," he admits.

"I can buy us a snack," Maya offers. "What do you want?"

Marcus, surprised again, looks at her, then at me, then back at her. "Actually," he responds slowly at first but quickly recovers when he realizes what to say, "I'm on my way out." He makes motions with his hands, pointing out the door as if we can't understand what direction out is. "So …" he continues. "You two kids …" He points to us. "You have fun." He waves goodbye, retrieves his skateboard, and is out the door.

We watch him leave, stare at the empty doorway for a moment, and then look at each other with the same *what-the-heck-was-that* expression. Then we both burst out laughing.

"I guess it's just you and me, Jay," she declares.

"I guess so, Maya."

Just you and me. I like how that sounds.

Maya sits at the table closest to the counter. She doesn't order any food but asks for an iced drink. I serve her sweet tea, wishing it could be something fancier.

"How did you get this job?" she asks before taking a sip.

"Big G is the only one that would hire me?" Prior to this, I had zero experience working anywhere. My parents believe school is my full-time job. It took some convincing to get them to agree that I should find a part-time job over the summer. "I wanted to work in the food industry but no one wanted to give me a chance."

"Planning to be a chef someday?"

I wish. I want to go to culinary school. I want to create my own signature dishes. I want my own restaurant. That's the dream I can't admit.

"I think my parents want me to be a doctor, like my dad."

She regards me for a moment then asks again, more deliberately, "Planning to be a chef someday?"

A shared look between us speaks volumes. Can she do this with everyone? See right through them and know what they're all about? Or is it just me? Is there something special between us?

I don't answer her right away. It's almost closing time and there are a few things I need to do first. I finish wiping off the most recently vacated table, drop the rag in a soapy bucket of detergent, water, and a touch of bleach. Then I go back into the kitchen and wash my hands.

When I get back out to the front, she has a chair pulled out by her. She gestures at it. I oblige, keenly aware that we're sitting incredibly close to each other.

"Big G thinks I can," I tell her. "He gave me an assignment. I have to come up with a new dish for the HotHouse by the end of the month."

Her eyes widen. "Like, something to put on the menu?"

I just nod. I like that she understands how big of an opportunity this is.

"What did you come up with?"

I bend my elbows and lift my hands, palm up, in the most exaggerated shrug I can muster.

"Oh no," she says. Her expression is an equal grimace as it is a smile. "You don't have anything?"

I repeat the action. This time she laughs.

"Jay!" She counts days off on her fingers. "That's, like, two weeks away!"

"You're one of those students who turn in assignments a week before they're due, aren't you?" I ask sardonically.

She folds her arms across her chest. "And you're clearly one of those who cram everything the night before."

"I know it's going to have something to do with fish fry." It's a weak case and we both know it. She shakes her head. "Hey," I add, digging in my heels. "It's a start!"

"Good for you, though," she says. "You're making your own destiny happen."

I wish that were the case. I grab a clean paper napkin from one of the holders on the table. I slowly rip it in little strips while I talk. I don't know why I do that. Maybe because it gives me something to look at other than her. Something to work with while I work through my life.

"As far as I can remember, I was helping my lola in the kitchen." My mind flashes back to immeasurable moments in our old kitchen before we moved. Our old house was nowhere near as put together as the one we have now and it was in a sketchy neighborhood. Probably why Lola is so paranoid about me being out after dark. I could understand that before, but it feels safer now that we're Uptown. We know our neighbors and people walk their dogs after dinner. It's a completely different environment, as far as I'm concerned. And probably the reason we moved in the first place.

"She had this stool that I could climb up on so I could watch what she was doing." I laugh at the memory of that unbalanced metal stool. "It's probably not up to any child safety standards."

"Safety standards are words not found in the Filipino dictionary," she jokes.

"I think I was told that I'd be fine as long as I didn't move around so much."

"There you go. That was your safety briefing."

"I'm not sure telling a kid to not move qualifies as safety management."

"Did you ever fall?"

"No," I admit, laughing at the ridiculousness of our conversation.

"Days since the last accident? Never had one!" she claims. "That's a pretty good safety record."

"Maybe I'm just really good at following instructions, did you think of that?"

She nods. "A good quality to have if you have to follow recipes."

"Lola never follows recipes." I lean back in my chair and hold up the last strip of napkin in my hand, looking at it but not seeing it. "I know how she makes all her dishes even if she doesn't ever write down any of her recipes or measure any of her ingredients."

"Is that a Filipino thing?" Maya asks. "My mother was the exact same way!"

I laugh. "Right?" I abandon my methodical tissue destruction and launch into a reenactment of what a conversation would be like between me and my grandmother, complete with exaggerated movements and voices.

"How much do I put, Lola?" I squeak in a high-pitched voice. "Until you have enough," I respond to myself in a feminine but deeper voice.

"Until the gods have deemed it proper and the spirits of your ancestors whisper to your soul," she adds in a silly booming voice. We both laugh. Different families, shared experience.

"It's passed on for sure, though. Because now I don't measure anything when I cook."

"Our ancestors are speaking to you."

"I think it's called *generational trauma*."

"But look at you now," she says, gesturing at me. "On your way to being the next Paul Prudhomme."

"I'm hardly the next celebrity chef of Louisiana." I scowl. "All I do is mix sauces and fry things. I have no formal training in the kitchen and no real experience."

"You make *excellent* pandesal," she points out.

I smile at the compliment. "I'm not sure I can open a whole restaurant on pandesal."

"A bakery!"

"A pandesal bakery?" That sounds ridiculous.

"That could be your specialty," she insists. "A complete bakery but with specialty pandesal! It will be so unique, you'll have no competition!"

I laugh at the novelty of it.

"No, seriously!" She leans forward on the table, her eyes alight with inspiration. She's talking faster, the words tumbling out as quickly as her enthusiasm pushes them. "Not only will you be able to corner the market on the Filipino population but you'll introduce Filipino cuisine to New Orleans like no one before you has ever done."

"There are bakeries all over New Orleans," I argue. "And there are some *really* good ones."

"Yeah, but they don't make Filipino goods. And there are so many you can offer. Think about it!" She starts counting items off her fingers. "Ensaymada, monay, puto … and that's just off the top of my head. I'm sure if I think about it, we can come up with more. And think about the varieties available for each one."

She's almost bouncing in her seat. She clasps her hands together and brings them up to her lips. Her smile has the intensity to rival the sun, bright and burning. She genuinely believes in what she's saying.

She genuinely believes in me.

I'm staggering from the purity of her faith. No one has ever looked at me the way she is looking at me. There's hope in her eyes and enough conviction that she's already made it a reality. My future self already exists. The Jay that she sees is successful. He has no insecurity. No self-doubt. He's gone through all the challenges and emerged victorious. Her Jay has everything he's ever wanted.

I see all that in her eyes. I stare at her in silence, awed by the power she's demonstrated. I'm slow to recognize it at first but then it comes to me.

This is what it means to have clarity of spirit.

I don't have the heart to tell her that my parents will probably never allow it. It's not easy to make a good living in the food industry. Especially not in New Orleans. The competition is fierce and although everyone needs to eat, everyone here is also very picky about *what* they eat. If you do well, you do really well. But failure is much more likely. Restaurants close all the time.

Mom will probably tell me that my dad never had a problem finding a job. There's always the need for a doctor. Nurses are in high demand. No matter where I go, if I'm a doctor, I'll find work. I'll make a good living. I'll be able to take care of them when they get old. Well, older anyway. They're pretty old already.

Ever since I was a kid, they've told family and friends that I'm the next doctor in the family. The first costume they put me in for Halloween was a little surgeon's outfit. I've been trained to write *I want to be a doctor* when I grow up since first grade. I never really had a choice.

But in front of Maya, I could be anything. So I smile and nod, giving the Jay she sees a fighting chance.

"What about you?" I ask, redirecting the conversation. "What are you doing with your life while I take over the baking world?"

The certainty that was so strong when she discussed my future fades. She leans back in her chair and sighs.

"I don't know," she admits. And as she's done before, she reaches for the pendant that she likes to play with. She rubs it between her fingers and chews her lip. "I'm just trying to make it to my eighteenth birthday."

"Oh, yeah. The whole debut thing, huh?" Turning eighteen is huge in the Philippines for daughters. It's a big event that involves a formal ball. The closest thing to it would be a quinceañera, the Latino celebration for girls who turn fifteen. I've never actually been in a quinceañera but I've been part of a debutante ball.

Last year, the daughter of one of my mom's friends turned eighteen. I didn't even know the celebrant at that time but she needed eighteen guys to be a part of the grand cotillion dance. My mom volunteered me. She said it would be a good experience.

I wore a barong, the traditional formal wear in the Philippines. It's made with something called piña. I don't really know what it is except that I had to wear an undershirt because the fabric is basically translucent. And supremely uncomfortable. I guess that's a prerequisite for any kind of formal wear from any culture.

As part of her entourage, I carried a rose and waited my turn to dance with the debutante. And not just any dance. It was a waltz that had to be practiced for months before the event. Every Friday night for two months, Mom would take me to her friend's house and the entourage would learn the steps out in the backyard. What I really learned was that I don't like dancing.

It's not just the guys that have a role in all this. The celebrant then has eighteen female family members or friends light a candle and say a little speech at the party. Unfairly, they didn't have to waste any of their Fridays staging that.

All in all, I don't know if I would classify it as a good experience like Mom said it would be. It felt like a lot of useless ceremonies. Maybe it's different if you're the one celebrating. At least the food was good.

If Maya is doing one, I want to be a part of it. Spending every Friday night with her would definitely qualify as a good experience.

"No way," Maya denies. "That's a lot of attention. Not to mention expensive." She shudders dramatically. "No, thank you. I'd much rather spend that on a vacation."

Where does every teenage girl want to go? "Paris?" I guess.

She shakes her head. "If I'm going to go anywhere, I'm visiting the Philippines."

I should have known. "But you've been there before. Don't you want to go somewhere different?"

"There's so much to see and I haven't seen all of it yet!" Her eyes light up. "I read that some people consider the Banaue Rice Terraces as the eighth Wonder of the World!"

"More wondrous than a dance party?"

"Dad kind of wanted me to have one," she admits. "About a month ago, he came home from work late and told me he and his buddies were talking about my mom. He said they all agreed she'd have wanted me to have a big party."

She looks sad, so I try to be sensitive. Not exactly my strong suit but I'm learning all sorts of things about myself in every conversation I have with her. I don't say anything. I just wait for her to continue.

"I think it'd be different if she were still alive," she says. "You know?"

I don't know but I nod anyway. I can't understand what she's going through but it doesn't mean I can't be a friend and listen to her. Sometimes that's all someone needs.

"Then I think the whole thing would have been fun," she continues, more to herself than to me. "It would be like a bonding experience. Something we go through together. Without her …" Her voice trails off. She plays with her amulet, sighs, then drops her hands. She looks at me, and I see the shine in her eyes. "It's just lonely without her."

"I'm sorry," I say. I can sense her isolation and there's nothing I can do about it. I wish I could hug her but I don't know if we're at that point yet. Am I allowed to?

"Yeah, me too." She reaches for her amulet again. "So, I decided, no party."

"It's a trip for sure then," I conclude.

"I won't be able to go on my actual birthday but soon. For sure, soon." I can't tell if she's convincing me or herself.

"When *is* your birthday?" There's a small thrill in the idea that I'm about to know one more fact about her.

"I was born on July fourth." She almost laughs.

"No. Seriously? Born on the fourth of July? Really?"

She spreads her arms to her sides, emphasizing she has nothing to hide. She grins. "What can I say? All the United States of America celebrates with me."

"You're such a cliché," I tease. "First generation American, born on the fourth of July. I bet your mom planned it that way."

She laughs genuinely this time and nods. "Other than the fact I arrived in a squad car, I wouldn't be surprised. Mom *was* a planner."

"And here you are, an adult in less than a month and you don't have a plan." I meant for it to be a joke, but I know by how quickly her expression changes that I screwed up again. I don't want this to be another repeat of the duck incident, so I'm quick to apologize. "I'm just goofing around. It was a dumb thing to say."

She's slow to respond and I'm scared I'll run out of chances. She eventually holds up a hand to stop my litany of apologies. Her smile is sad but it's there.

"No, no," she assures me, "it's not you. You didn't do anything wrong." Her lips tug to one side. "I mean, you're right. I *don't* have a plan." She throws her head back and groans. When she straightens up to face me, her face is all scrunched up comically. "You're all judgy just because you already know what you want to do with your life. Not all of us are that lucky!"

I'm about to tell her that knowing what I want to do and being allowed to do it are two different things when I hear the door in the kitchen bang loudly. I startle, look down at my watch, and see that it's near closing time. That must be Big G. I sweep my hand over the remnants of the napkin I shredded, the actions of a man with a guilty conscience. Maya watches me with an amused expression. She's about to say something but stops when she sees who is in the room with us. She pales.

It's not Big G, but his wife.

CHAPTER 19

FAMILY TIES

There you are, Jay." Carmelita, in a short flowy dress, walks around the counter. Her hair is in the usual ponytail but with a different scrunchie, one that's made of the same material as her outfit.

I stand right away to face her. "I'm just getting ready to close up," I lie, hiding the evidence of my guilt behind my back. Not that I'd really get into trouble for it but it feels wasteful and irresponsible.

She smiles, and there's a hint of a shared secret between us. Except I don't know what the secret actually is. "I'm sure of it." Her accent is similar to my mom's but much less clipped, so she sounds friendlier. She lifts her chin and purses her lips in my direction. "Were your palms itchy? That means money is coming your way." She holds up an envelope and shakes it. "And I have it right here! Your paycheck!"

I can't quite follow her reasoning and all I can do is blink my response. She's unfazed by my lack of reaction and looks past me at Maya.

"Good to see you again, Maya," she says, inclining her head.

I turn back to Maya and see that she hasn't moved. She looks frightened in a way that keeps her in place. She doesn't respond right away to the greeting.

"Maya?"

She averts her eyes from Carmelita and looks at me. Only then does she respond. "Hello." It's not like her at all. She stands up. "I have to go," she announces. And before I'm able to react, she's out the door.

I don't chase her this time. Without Big G present, I'm in charge of the store, and I can't leave. I look back at Carmelita, confused. She doesn't seem to have the answers either.

"We weren't doing anything wrong," I assure her, perhaps a little too defensively. "I don't know why she's acting like that."

She shakes her head, hands me my envelope, and joins me at the table. I pull the seat back for her, and she lowers herself down to it. "Hay naku." She sighs. She's more comfortable conversing with me in Filipino when we're alone. The words don't really mean anything, as far as I can tell. They're just interjections of exasperation that I hear at home from Mom or Lola whenever I do something frustrating.

"It's not your fault," she assures me. "It's hard to grow up without a mother." She lays a hand on her belly and points to herself with the other. "Ako? I cannot even imagine not growing up without a mother. I have seven brothers!"

Seven? That's too many people. I'm an only child and our house already feels too crowded sometimes. I must've made a face because Carmelita laughs at my expression.

"Naku," she exclaims again, shaking her head but smiling. "You have no idea! And boys! So magulo! At tsaka ang kukulit." She balls her hands into fists and shakes.

I think I've heard the words before but I'm not as familiar with them. I must be out of practice. So I shake my head to let her know I don't understand her.

"You know," she prods, but when all I do is shrug, she shakes her head, disappointed by my lack of proficiency. "Magulo." She looks around as if searching for inspiration. Then she moves her arms around her in an exaggerated motion. "Rowdy. Always moving. So messy!"

I smile. Oh, right. I *have* heard that before. I think Mom might have used that to describe me at some point when I was younger.

"Makulit." She tries to clarify the other word for me. "It's the same thing. So restless. Always asking questions. No rest! So annoying."

I laugh. Yes, for sure these are not new words to me. Maybe I just haven't heard them for a while.

"Are you the youngest?" I ask.

"Naku, hindi 'no?!" She shakes her head to let me know I'm way off. "I'm the panganay! The firstborn! The ate!"

Ate is what anyone calls an older sister, or sometimes an older girl cousin. I guess it works for anyone in the same generation, whether or not you're related. Now that I think about it, I've heard it used between two people who don't know each other very well. I think it's just a way to show respect by acknowledging that someone is older. The same goes for the male counterpart of the word, kuya.

"My mother taught me how to deal with all of them. I can't imagine growing up in that house without my mother. I'd go crazy!" She slumps in her chair a little in exaggerated exhaustion. Then she laughs at herself. She looks down and puts both hands on top of her belly. "It's not all that bad, though. I think I'm not afraid to be a mom because I've already had so much experience.

I already know how to handle a little boy. And a little girl would be nice."

She leans forward, and her voice lowers conspiratorially. "My mother and I, we would escape sometimes. Just the two of us. We would get our nails done together or go to the market. It was so nice." She leans back in her chair with a smile on her face that is only brought about by nostalgia.

I nod so she knows I'm listening, even if I can't relate. I would hate to have to do those things with my mom. I don't really do much with my dad. It sounds very different to me. "Maya misses her mom," I agree. I'm not breaking any unsaid rule of confidence by sharing something so broad. And Carmelita brought it up first.

She returns her hands to the top of her belly. "Yes, she must. I think maybe that's why she is so uncomfortable around me." She looks sad, not for herself but sad for Maya. "I'm a reminder of the mother she no longer has."

I hadn't considered that, and I'm kicking myself for not seeing something so obvious. It's been almost a decade since she lost her mother but maybe it hits harder now because she's at such a pivotal point in her life and her mom isn't there to throw a party for her. We were just talking about that when Carmelita walked in. That must have been hard for her to deal with.

"I don't know what to do," I admit. I want to help Maya but I don't know how.

"Do what you always do when you don't know what to do." She smiles. "Be kind."

CHAPTER 20
SAFE SPACE

I don't hear from Maya in the next couple of days. I try calling her a few times but no one picks up. Marcus tells me she gave me a fake number. I tell him he's a jerk who doesn't know what he's talking about, but I can't be too sure. I'm beginning to doubt myself.

I'm certain that Maya and I have a connection. She must feel it too for her to come to see me at the HotHouse last Wednesday. She didn't have to be there. She chose to be. She came by just to spend time with me.

But she didn't come back. What did I do wrong? Is she mad at me?

"What's wrong?" Mom asks while I wash the dishes after dinner. Lola sits in the living room having her nightly salabat, a strong ginger tea. Dad, as usual, isn't home yet.

"What?" I turn off the water and face her. I don't remember acting differently over dinner. It's actually been rather pleasant at home since I got back from my successful pandesal endeavor. I can't guess what infraction Mom is referring to.

"Tahimik ka ngayon," she declares without accusation. "You're quiet."

It's funny that she says that because I consider myself intentionally very quiet at home. The less I say, the better. That means there's less of a chance I'll be criticized. "I'm being quiet?" What does that even mean?

"Even Lola notices, you know." She nods, agreeing with her own statement like she needs a consensus with herself. "What's wrong?"

This is a weird situation. I can't remember the last time I actually talked to Mom about something bothering me. My first instinct is to claim nothing and escape to my room, but after talking to Maya about her mom, it would be doing her some kind of indirect injustice if I did that.

She doesn't push further. She puts away dried dishes and watches me, waiting for me to respond when I'm ready.

I dry my hands on the kitchen towel slung over the oven handle. Then I lean back on the counter. Where do I start? Am I really about to talk to my *mom* about a *girl*? I pick at my fingernails as I talk, just so I'm not looking directly at her. It makes it easier.

"I have … a friend," I begin hesitantly. I don't want to specify who, and I don't want her to know I'm talking about a girl. But I realize too late I sound suspiciously like I'm projecting my own problems onto a fictional character. I can't take it back, so I just swallow the cringe pill and soldier on.

"My friend is dealing with some stuff, I think, and needs someone to talk to." I'm choosing my words carefully, causing my sentences to be slow and clumsy. Mom is patient and doesn't rush me. "My friend talks to me. Sh–" I almost slip and use a female pronoun and quickly correct myself. "My friend seems comfortable enough around me but not around other people."

Mom considers this, nodding slowly. I don't know if she caught my mistake but she's not letting on. "At gusto mo siyang tulungan? And you want to help?"

"Well, yeah, of course."

"Just talk?" I don't know what she's insinuating. She's intentionally not looking at me but still giving me a sideways glance, like she's trying to catch me in the act. Normally, I'd be annoyed but right now, I'm just confused.

"What else would we be doing?"

Her shoulders lift and fall almost comically. This isn't an action she often attempts, so it looks awkward, like a bad actor playing a role. "Malay ko ba? How do I know? I don't know what you kids do these days. Maybe drinking? Maybe drugs?"

I groan. Of *course* I can't possibly have a normal conversation with her. This is a waste of time. "Forget it." There's an edge in my voice I can't stop. I'm irritated by her but more irritated with myself for thinking she would take me seriously.

"Teka muna, anak," she commands when she sees I'm about to leave. "Wait. I just want to be sure we are on the same page." She sounds too innocent to not be guilty. I don't trust her but I stay. When she sees I don't leave, her voice softens and the fake innocence goes away. "Are you asking for my advice?"

"I *was*," I mumble, still not ready to forgive her.

"I think what"–she pauses before continuing, and I can almost see the quotation marks she's not making in the air around her–"your friend is looking for, is a safe space."

"A what?" I don't know what that means but how she says it makes it sound like she knows what she's talking about. "A safe space?" I repeat.

Mom starts clearing more things from the counter. The unrelated action puts me at ease. At the very least, this conversation is becoming less uncomfortable.

"Yes," she says as she moves around the kitchen. "I see it all the time at work. Even in adults. There's a trauma they experience."

She pauses and tilts her head. "You know, like abuse or those things?" She nods at me as if prompting me to fill in the blanks. I don't actually know what *those things* are. Sometimes there *are* no *things*. She says *those things* when she can't think of the word she needs to convey her ideas.

"Takot sila. They're scared, of course," she continues. I try to keep up. "They don't know how to cope." She opens a drawer and puts away clean spoons. "But once they're in the hospital room, talking to a good nurse"—she winks at me, insinuating that *she* is, in fact, that good nurse she's talking about—"naku!" She opens her arms in a wide circle around her. "It *all* comes out. A good nurse knows how to make their patient feel safe," she concludes, her chin held high in pride for being such a nurse.

"A safe space," I repeat but no longer in a question.

She nods. "If your friend doesn't like other people, then you take the other people out of the equation!" She looks proud of herself, missing the fact that her conclusion sounds more like a mob threat than parental advice. "You can be their safe space."

I smile at her because *now* she sounds innocent. She's not trying to catch me in a lie like some kind of bumbling wanna-be lawyer who watches too many courtroom dramas. She sounds like she's just being herself.

"I think I can do that," I assure her, giving her a kiss on the cheek as thanks for her help. "I can be a safe space."

She winks at me. "Like a good nurse!"

CHAPTER 21

MEETING PLACE

Saturday afternoon, I decide I'll take my bike to Maya's house after work. I share my intentions with Marcus while I close up the HotHouse for the day. He's sitting on the counter, his ever-present skateboard by his leg.

"Stalker vibes." Marcus gives me a thumbs-up. "Not creepy at all. Good move."

"Oh, shut up!" His sarcasm notwithstanding, I'm angry because he's right. "Well, what am I supposed to do then?"

"You mean since she gave you a fake number?" Marcus isn't one to be sensitive. "I think that's a clue to how she really feels about you."

"It's not a fake number," I mumble without conviction. I stack the chairs on the table. "I don't know what I did wrong."

"You should ask her."

I drop the last chair in place. It doesn't make a loud enough bang to be satisfying, I almost want to pick it back up again. Instead, I face Marcus, unimpressed by his attitude. "No, duh, genius. That would mean I'd have to find a way to talk to her first, wouldn't it?"

He has a maddening grin on his face that tells me he's hiding something. And whatever it is, it's at my expense for sure. I narrow my eyes, which seems to feed his amusement. I know he's laughing at me but I don't know exactly why. I'm missing something.

"What?" I finally ask when he doesn't elaborate. I don't have the patience for his dumb games. Without speaking, he jerks his chin up. A gesture that tells me I should turn around.

Maya is standing at the entrance of the HotHouse, looking uneasy. Her hair, freed from the ponytail it was in the last time I saw her, falls down either side of her face.

"Oh." I had spent the last few days hoping she'd show up exactly where she's standing and now that she's here, I'm unprepared. How long has she been standing there?

Marcus slides off the counter, picks up his skateboard, and tucks it under his arm. "Hey, Maya," he says casually, but he's looking at me.

"Hi, Marcus." She tilts her head to the side.

"Well, that's my cue," Marcus announces. As he walks by, he thumps me hard on the shoulder, knocking me out of my mute state. "I'm bouncing." After he walks past Maya, he turns back around and makes faces at me again, knowing that I can't react. It's getting old. I need to get back at him.

"Hi," Maya says again after Marcus leaves. She tucks her hair behind her ears, an action that appears self-conscious.

I swallow. "Hey." This is more uncomfortable than I imagined it to be. I'm not sure what to say. "We're closed." I wince as I hear myself say that. I could slap myself.

She shuffles her feet and looks down. Her hair falls from behind her ears and conceals her face from my view. "I know, I'm not here to order."

Of course she isn't. I need to get it together. What was it that Mom said? Be her safe space?

"Oh." I'm not doing very well with small talk, so I decide the more direct approach might be a better move. "I, uh, I tried calling you."

She looks up, and I see the apology on her face. "Sorry. I realized the ringer on my phone was set really low. So if I wasn't actually in my room when you tried calling, I wouldn't have heard it."

"You have your own phone line?" I'm impressed. I have my own phone in my room but it's tapped to the same line as the rest of the house. I have to share the number, and only one person can use any of those phones at any given time. Having a private line is another level altogether and additional evidence that Maya's family is more well-to-do than mine.

"It was a birthday gift when I turned thirteen." She averts her gaze as if she finds Big G's wall decor suddenly incredibly interesting. "I don't give the number to anyone, so I don't ever really expect it to ring."

The significance of what she says hits me hard. She didn't give me a fake number; she gave me a private number. Something she doesn't give anyone else. I wish Marcus was still around to hear that but at the same time, I'm equally pleased that Maya and I are alone.

"Oh." Apparently, it's my new favorite word. I seem to have lost my ability to string together sentences. "That's good." This time, I physically cringe. "I mean, it's not good that you missed my calls, but, well, thanks for not giving me a fake number?" I didn't mean for it to sound like a question.

She turns back to me, looking aghast at the idea. "Oh, no! Of course not! I wouldn't do that to you!" She bites her lip. "I guess it was really rude of me to just leave like that. I mean, I know it was. I'm sorry. I don't know what came over me. There's really no excuse." She's flustered, looking like she doesn't know what to do with her hands. I know that feeling all too well.

I'm right. We do have a connection, and I'm not the only one that feels it. It gives me confidence, and I relax.

"It's OK," I assure her. "I know why you did."

She pauses mid-reaction, one hand frozen halfway to her face. "You do?"

"Yeah, Carmelita told me why."

Her hand falls, and she's now looking at me with a kind of dumbfounded anxiety. "Carmelita?"

I want to hug her and assure her that everything is fine, but it doesn't seem appropriate. So I just stuff my hands in my pockets and sway a little while I talk. It's to make things seem less confrontational. I don't know if it just makes me look more clumsy. "Yeah, she knows why you're uncomfortable around her, and it's OK," I repeat.

"She does?" Maya doesn't look like she believes me. "It is?"

"Yeah, and I get it."

"You do?"

"Sure." She's staring directly at me, and now I'm the one that can't look at her. The topic is so uncomfortable. What if she calls me out on it? How dare I get what she's going through when I haven't lost anyone close to me like she has? Even now, I don't have the same relationship with either of my parents as she had with her mom. There's no way I can understand her level of loss.

She doesn't look convinced. The last thing I want is to alienate her even further. At the rate I'm going, I'm just going to make her lonelier. "I mean, it makes sense," I add, hoping she sees that even if I can't relate, I'm willing to try.

"It does?"

"I think so." I sneak a peek, and she's still staring at me. She still looks like she's in between confusion and concern. I look down at the floor and shuffle my feet. "I know I'll never be able to understand but it doesn't mean I can't be your friend." I look up at her, begging her to see that I'm being sincere. I want to be her safe space. "Maya, I want you to know that you can talk to me."

Her expression changes. It's like she was lost in the whole conversation up until that point. "Oh, I know that," she responds almost casually.

"You do?" It's my turn to be surprised.

"Sure." She looks so much more self-assured all of a sudden and breaks out a shy smile. "I mean, you're the only person I *can* talk to."

"I am?"

Her smile is bigger now. "I know we've never really hung out before, and that's too bad. I get if you're weirded out. It sounds corny and cliché." Her shoulders lift and fall in the daintiest shrug I've ever seen in my life. She puts her hair behind her ears again. "But I like hanging out. You make me laugh. You're just super easy to talk to."

She might as well have called me the hunkiest guy in class. It's like I'm suddenly towering over every dude I've ever looked up to. I have a strength I've never possessed. This secret superhero power that mild-mannered Jay never knew. She likes me.

Well, she likes *hanging out* with me. That's sort of the same thing, right?

She's watching me, waiting for me to respond. I'm staring at her with what must be the dorkiest-looking smile on my face. What's the best way to respond?

"Me too," I say after clearing my throat.

What the heck was that? My eyes widen. *Me too?* Did that even make sense?

"You too?" She's giving me a chance to recover. I clear my throat again, acting as if she misheard me or something.

"I mean, I like hanging out with you too." I run my hand through my hair. I think I'm sweating. Am I sweating? Do I stink? Why is it so hot?

"I'm glad." She's smiling so wide right now, looking confident and flawless while I sweat like I'm a gym class failure.

"But maybe we don't hang out here?" I'm trying to get control back of the situation. Was I ever in control? "Like, since we're trying to avoid Carmelita and all, maybe we just find another place to hang out instead?"

She looks surprised again but doesn't lose her smile. "That's a great idea, actually." She considers something for a moment and asks tentatively, "You know where Lafayette Cemetery No. 1 is?"

I give her a sarcastic look. "You know I was actually *born* here, right? My parents are immigrants, not me." I roll my eyes. My awkwardness is gone. I cross my arms in front of my chest. Now I'm just insulted.

"That's not what I mean." She laughs. "I mean, are you OK meeting there?"

"Again, you know I was actually *born* here, right?" Maybe hanging out in a cemetery might be strange for someone who isn't from New Orleans but for us locals, it's not as uncommon as outsiders may think.

She lifts her hands in surrender. "OK, OK, I'm sorry." She shakes her head back. "Did you want to meet me there after you close up here?"

I drop my arms and smile. "I can do that." I look around me to assess how much more still needs to be done and estimate how much time it will take me to head her way. "Give me an hour?" She rewards me with dimples.

"I can do that. See you in an hour."

CHAPTER 22

LAFAYETTE CEMETERY NO.1

Cemeteries in New Orleans are a tourist attraction. I didn't understand at first but that was before I realized not all cemeteries look like ours. A typical cemetery in the rest of the country looks more like hills of green with markers on the ground. So green that they're often called memorial parks. Caskets are buried in the ground. Lots of open space. Enough to fly a kite if you wanted.

That's not how it looks here.

New Orleans is below sea level. That means there's naturally a high water table in the soil. If you bury a body, it's likely to be filled with water. There are stories of body parts rising from the ground because of it. I've never seen that myself, but the threat of it is real enough that cemeteries here are filled with above-ground tombs as tall as a small house. The tombs are made of brick and stone, sitting side by side with each other like it's its own apartment neighborhood for the dead.

It's not uncommon to find a bunch of teens hanging out by the larger tombs, hidden from view, where they can drink and play games away from adult eyes. When you're young, it's the perfect venue for a spooky game of hide-and-seek. Or sometimes, if you just don't want to be found.

By the time I get to the cemetery, Maya is already waiting for me. It's easy enough to spot her from the entrance. She doesn't have to say anything when I come to sit by her. I know right away why she picked this spot. The inlaid letters on the slab show we are in front of her mom's grave.

The tomb is gray and white, and the two stone steps leading to the sealed front are convenient for sitting. Concrete flower pots holding soil are built into either side of the steps. There are healthy plants in them, both already flowering in the summer. They give off a sweet smell. I'm not really into flowers, so I can't identify them.

"I ran away here a few years ago," I confess to Maya. The stone steps beneath me are strangely cooler than the hot air around us.

"What were you running away from?" she asks.

I lean forward so my elbows are on my knees. I start picking at the long grass growing between the cracks under my feet. "My parents told me we were moving. And I would be going to private school."

"Oh! Is that when you came to our school?"

I nod, embarrassed at how much I resisted the move I ultimately enjoyed. "Yeah, right before ninth grade. I know it all turned out fine, but I didn't know that back then."

She leans back and pulls her feet up. "I get it. It was a big change. Lots of unknowns and all that."

"Exactly." I'm glad she isn't making fun of me. "All I knew was that Marcus, my best friend, wasn't going to be in the same school as me. It felt like the end of the world." I snort at the antics of my younger self. "I was very dramatic about it."

"Why here?" She lifts her hands to gesture at the tombs around us. "What made you want to run away here?"

I remember how upset I was when my parents first told me about the move. They thought they were surprising me with good news. My reaction surprised them more. I yelled at them; they yelled back at me. I don't remember what was said. I remember slamming every door I passed until I got out of the house. Then I just got on my bike and left. I peddled furiously, powered by my emotions and not really caring where I was going.

"It was just when I ended up here that I finally stopped pedaling, I guess." I look around, trying to identify landmarks and seeing if I can remember where I hid but I can't.

"What did you do here?"

I cried. A lot. I swore and cursed and lamented about how unfair the universe was to me. But I'm not about to tell her that. "Just be alone," I say instead.

She nods. "I come here to be alone too. And cry." She rolls her eyes as if to say she knows it's a lame thing to do. Meanwhile, I'm awed by the courage she has to so easily admit something I couldn't. "I talk to my mom. Then it's like she's not so far away."

She's so lonely. The pride I felt when she told me earlier that she liked to talk to me gives way to a bigger sense of obligation. She's vulnerable in this space and she's trusting me with it. It's a greater privilege than I've ever had bestowed on me before.

"Did your parents find you?" she asks. For a moment, I forget what we are talking about.

"No." I sigh. When all was said and done, there was really nothing I could do about my situation but accept it and go home. "I was in eighth grade! Where was I going to go?"

She laughed. "Sometimes, we just need a temporary escape."

"A temporary escape goes a long way," I agree, glad I had nowhere to go back then else I might not have found myself here with her now.

We sit together, not saying anything for a while. The shadows grow longer around us as the day threatens to end. It's always cooler in the shadows. I watch a crow fly down to the ground and peck at something unidentifiable. Is it just pecking at the ground? It seems unaware of our presence. Maybe because neither of us move. I glance sideways at Maya; she's watching the crow too. It flaps its wings but doesn't fly away. It continues to peck the dust.

I don't see where the second crow comes from. It just flies down to join the first. They both flap their wings as they circle each other. For a time, the flapping of their wings is the only sound in the air. Then, without cawing, they fly away together.

"This is nice," Maya says, breaking the silence. I look at her, wondering what she's referring to. She must see the question in my eyes because she tries to elaborate. "This. Just sitting here. With you. It's nice."

I see a little red on her cheeks—she's blushing. She looks so pretty that I find myself smiling. "Yeah," I agree. "This is nice."

Above us, we hear the crows caw. It startles me. I look up; the sun is low.

"I should probably get going," I say reluctantly. "So I can get home before dark."

She stands up, and I follow suit. "Did you want to do this again?"

"Hang out here?"

"Yes."

She looks so relaxed. The opposite of how she was at the HotHouse. Here, she's less sad. Less anxious. I like seeing her like this.

"Sure," I say. "When?"

"I don't know. When?" she repeats.

"After work tomorrow?"

"Great," she agrees.

I get on my bike and wave goodbye.

"It's a date," she adds as she waves back at me.

It's a date. I don't respond. I almost crash into the ornate iron gate framing the entrance of the cemetery. I keep my eyes forward to regain balance. And so she wouldn't see the big smile on my face.

PINOY PICNIC

meet with Maya every day after work at Lafayette Cemetery No. 1. It's fast becoming our private sanctuary. We walk around the entire cemetery, just talking. Bonding over shared experiences or stories we've never told anyone else. And every day, I leave feeling closer to her than I've felt to anyone.

"Ano 'to? What's this?" Mom asks me on Tuesday morning. I'm in the kitchen, standing in front of a bunch of different things all spread out on the counter.

"I'm trying to figure out what to make," I admit.

"Para saan? What for?"

Lola walks into the kitchen carrying an old red-and-white Thermos bottle and hands it to me. She informs Mom that I'm putting together baon, food to bring with me.

"Bakit? Why? Saan ka pupunta? Where are you going?"

I see Lola bump Mom with her hip. There's a roguish expression on her face I don't see often. Lola tells her I'm meeting "a friend," and they share a look I don't understand. It feels like they're silently making fun of me. They giggle like tweens in the mall.

I look at them suspiciously, and they both suddenly adopt expressions of innocence. It's like I'm dealing with two Marcuses in the form of my mom and grandmother. I roll my eyes.

Mom asks me what I'm bringing.

"That's the problem." I groan dramatically. "I don't know."

Mom and Lola both laugh. I pout and glare at them, which only makes them laugh more. But they both step up to help me, suggesting easy-to-eat food. "Siopao?" Mom offers.

Siopao is a steamed bun with meat filling. We make ours from scratch. Lola usually makes the bao ahead of time because the yeast needs time to rise. Mom cooks the filling and lets it cool. Together we assemble them, wrapping them up ready for the steamer. It's like a savory sandwich ball. With better filling and softer bread.

We always make more than we can eat in one sitting and made a fresh batch just the other day. We freeze the leftovers to be eaten in the future. Like today.

Lola removes a batch from the freezer and prepares the steamer. Mom retrieves the homemade sauce from the fridge to be distributed in smaller individual containers for taking. I watch the women in my family move around the kitchen with perfect synchronicity I've never noticed before.

"Ano pa? What else?" Mom asks. But she's not asking me. She's asking Lola. Lola suggests dessert. They discuss options, striking the ones that won't keep well in the heat, are too difficult to make, or won't taste as good under the circumstances.

"May turon pa ba tayo? Do we still have some turon left?"

Turon is essentially a deep-fried dessert spring roll. Lola likes to caramelize overripe bananas before rolling them in the same thin pastry-like wrapper used for spring rolls. The whole thing is deep-fried and then drizzled with caramel sauce. It can be sticky and a little messy but it's one of my favorite things.

"It's not going to be crispy anymore by the time we eat it," I warn them.

Lola dismisses my concerns with a wave of her hand. She fires up the burner and puts the large wok on top. She adds oil and while she's waiting for it to heat up, tells me to wrap the cooled turon in a paper towel before wrapping it in foil. It's her trick to keep them as crispy as possible. She separates the caramel and instructs me to add the drizzle only when we're ready to eat them.

"Can we try it with chocolate syrup instead?" I ask.

She frowns, looks down at the caramel she's holding and then at my mom. Traditionally, turon uses caramel, and she doesn't like that I'm changing things. Mom makes a dismissive noise and waves her hands in the air. It's amusing to watch them argue.

"If Jay wants to use chocolate, let him use chocolate," Mom orders. "Bahala siya! Leave him alone! He's the one that has to eat it!" She smiles at me and laughs a little. "Naalala mo ba? Do you remember the first time Jay ate turon? He wanted sprinkles on it!" They both laugh.

The conversation shifts to other incidents when I had food for the first time or when I changed it to suit my preferences instead. "What about the cheese pandesal incident?" Mom reminds the room. Lola makes a loud sound in agreement while I interrupt to defend myself.

"Hey! That was really good! You liked it, right, Lola?" I put her on the spot. Lola laughs and shakes her head as if to deny her approval but agrees with me. I point to her. "See?"

"I didn't say it wasn't good!" Mom is laughing harder than I've seen her laugh in a while. "I'm saying it was expensive! Naku, anak! You used *all* my raclette cheese!" Lola howls with laughter. I'm laughing too.

"You were so mad," I remind her.

"I was saving that cheese!" She puts one hand on her hip and points the tongs she's using to handle the siopao at me threateningly. "You're lucky that pandesal tasted really good." Lola points out that Mom ate most of the pandesal herself, and Mom shakes the tongs at her. Lola isn't as easily threatened and just laughs.

"You've always been that way," Mom says over her shoulder.

"What way?" I'm almost afraid to ask.

"Straying from the traditional," she responds while picking up the softened boa with just enough pressure to hold it without making deep indentations. "Your lola and I know what we are taught but you always change something in the recipe."

Lola says something in Filipino and Mom agrees but I can't understand. I have the impression it was about me so I ask.

"Your lola says you cook exactly like who you are," Mom explains, confirming my suspicions. They share a look of mutual understanding. Lola's smile is so big, I can see all her teeth.

"What does that mean, *exactly like who I am*?" I brace myself.

She inclines her head and looks at me with a contained smile. "A product of two worlds."

Her answer is surprisingly poignant and instead of being defensive, I'm validated. And it feels so good. I smile back at Lola.

I'm having so much fun that I'm almost sad when my baon is all packed and ready to go within half an hour. Mom even added a few cookies, and Lola packed the Thermos with chilled juice made from calamansi concentrate, a bottle she usually hoards for herself.

Fortunately, the prospect of sharing a picnic with Maya helps me get over any disappointment. I leave the house with both Mom and Lola waving me goodbye.

CHAPTER 24
UNPLANNED

The summer sun is beating down on the streets of the Garden District. I don't know if it's better for me to pedal faster so I'm out of the sun sooner or if I should go slow so I'm not dehydrated and sweating. I compromise by going slow in the shade and speeding up when I'm exposed. There's not a lot of shade given the position of the sun, so I have to hug the buildings pretty close to make the most of the shadows.

I usually head straight to Lafayette Cemetery No. 1 from the HotHouse but I think I've been able to find the best route from home. It's not a very far ride at all, but the heat makes it seem longer. And I'm anxious to see Maya.

I see the white plastered brick walls of the Lafayette Cemetery, and I pedal faster, hopping over the broken sidewalk caused by the overgrown roots of large oak trees. They provide much-needed shade, so I don't mind navigating the cracks.

The ornate main entrance arc comes into view; the black iron gate is open. I dismount when I get to the end of the paved area and walk my bike in. I think I'm early, but I see Maya is already at our favorite spot.

She's sitting on a small patch of grass under the shade of one of the larger trees opposite her mom's grave. It's tucked away from the main walk. If I didn't already know where to go, I'd have missed it. We discovered that place together when we were hiding from a tour group over the weekend. We could still hear the orator's dramatic interpretation of historical events and urban legends but we couldn't see them and knew they couldn't see us. We stayed quiet, making faces in reaction to the orator's performance and trying our best to stifle our laughter.

Since then, we've spent more time under the tree than on the steps of her mom's grave. We have more privacy that way. Not just from the random tour groups and visitors but from under the watch of Maya's mom. It doesn't make sense but it does make me feel better.

"Are you eating without me?" I accuse her as I approach.

Maya looks up and smiles. She's in a tank top and lightweight overalls that end halfway down her calves. Her hair is pulled up in a high bun this time, exposing her neck. She looks cool and refreshed. I'm well aware I appear to be her complete opposite: sweaty and unrefined.

"You don't like balut." She holds up the broken eggshell. "I thought I'd spare you the experience."

I respond by making a face.

"You're such a white boy," she teases, sipping the natural soup of the egg from the opening she made.

"If that means I'm somebody who doesn't like my eggs partially formed, then yes, yes I am." I walk my bike to a nearby tree. The kickstand is useless in the uneven terrain, so I lean it against the tree instead.

She laughs and doesn't argue. She balances the cracked egg in an open paper bag on the grass. She brushes her hands on her pants, stands, and helps me remove the backpack I'm carrying. "Wow, this is heavy," she remarks. "What do you have in here?"

"Oh, wait until you see!" I grin, proud of myself. Proud of my mom and lola.

We lower the backpack to the ground. The relief from carrying such a heavy weight feels like cool water. I unzip the bag, and the first thing I remove is a thin throw blanket. I pull it out and unfold it.

"A picnic blanket!" Maya actually claps. Whenever I do something for her, I end up feeling like it's for my own sake. She has a way of making me feel really good about myself.

She helps me spread the small blanket under the tree, maximizing the amount of shade we can get.

"Sit down," I invite her. I want to be able to present the picnic to her properly.

She indulges me and sits cross-legged on the blanket. She sits up tall, hands on her ankles, looking eager. She makes the best audience.

One by one, I present the perfectly packed picnic. She claps and laughs every time I reveal the next dish. Further encouraged, I do so with increasing flourish, like we're at a fancy restaurant and I'm a maître d' with a heavy French accent. It sounds ridiculous pronouncing Filipino dishes in a French accent and it makes her laugh even harder. I hold off on the dessert, saving it for later.

When she thinks everything is set, I pull out a couple of plastic plates and solid utensils. I empty my backpack and reveal the portable CD player at the very bottom of the bag. It's not mine. It belongs to Marcus. And it was the heaviest thing I was carrying. The look on her face makes it all worth it. I hit Play and music fills the air.

I sit across from her and unwrap the food my mom and lola packed for us. When I look up, I see she's not looking at the food but staring at me. She has a smile on her face, so I know it's nothing bad.

"What?" I ask, a little self-conscious.

"How is it that it took this long to get to know each other?" There's something in her voice that I can't recognize. She's happy but also sad.

"Well," I say, acting casual, "some people, who shall remain unnamed, were just always too popular for the new kid …"

She reaches over and shoves me on the shoulder. "That's not true!" she protests. I laugh.

"Watch it! You're going to make me drop the food." I make an exaggerated show of trying to balance the containers. "So violent!"

She narrows her eyes and crosses her arms in front of her but her lips have an upward curve, and I know she's enjoying the rapport.

"We're here now," I remind her. "That's what's important, right?" I hand her a foil-wrapped siopao as a peace offering.

She looks at my outstretched hand, then up to me, but she doesn't take it. Instead, she pulls herself up so she's kneeling right next to me, so close I can smell a hint of citrus that must be her perfume. I don't know what's happening. I'm frozen in place with my hand still out in a very awkward position.

She leans even closer to me. She puts a hand on either side of my face, so light is her touch it feels like butterflies have landed on my cheeks. Her lips part, and her eyes close as she brings her face nearer to mine. Slow enough that I can see it happening but so fast that I can't react. I shut my eyes. Her lips are on mine.

I drop everything I'm holding and wrap one arm around her waist. My other hand is on her cheek, touching her as lightly as she's touching me. Her kiss deepens, and I can taste a little of the strawberry chapstick she must have and a pleasant saltiness I can't place. I have never been more glad about the fact that I brushed my teeth before coming over.

I've dreamed of this kiss every night in every conceivable situation but this one. I don't have an imagination creative enough to compare to the real thing. I'm not perfect at this. I've never done it before. Not really. Not like this. Not with someone I genuinely care about. I thought I'd be more worried about our teeth clashing, unwanted slobber, or any of the many gross things that can happen in real life.

But I don't think of any of that. Instead, an instinct takes over. Not the animalistic kind that wants to consume but a protective kind. I want her to feel safe and valued. It's not about what I can take but what I can give. I want to give her everything.

The moment is longer and shorter than it is.

When we break apart, I let her go. It's as if I've known her all my life, and I can't wait to get to know her more. I struggle to control the clash of emotions that rush to the surface. I make an effort to slow my breathing and the pounding of my heart. How can such a quick act stretch over time like this and mean so much?

I open my eyes and see all my feelings mirrored in hers. And I know. I know how a kiss can defy all things.

Because it's Maya.

CHAPTER 25

THE POWER OF A KISS

Wow."

Maya sits back on her heels, creating distance between us. She touches her fingers to her lips, smiling through them as she looks at me.

"Yeah," I agree. "That was … wow."

"Want to do it again?" she asks, a little shyly.

"All the time."

We both start laughing. Actually, it's more silly giggles but I'm not about to admit that. It's a welcome release of adrenaline.

"Maybe after lunch?" she suggests.

"Wouldn't want it to get cold," I agree because at this point, I think I'd willingly agree to anything she suggests. I pick the siopao off the blanket, grateful I hadn't yet unwrapped the foil. She takes it from me this time.

"Thank you." She's so demure, making me yearn for a repeat kiss that much more. I take a deliberate breath to steady myself.

"Had I known this would be your reaction to siopao, I'd have brought you some a long time ago," I tease. Humor is the best way I can think of to calm the heightened electricity in the air.

She nudges me in feigned protest but doesn't say anything. She unwraps the siopao. I watch her until she takes a bite. "Still warm?"

She nods. "Warm enough."

I jut my chin toward her forgotten duck egg still lying in the crumpled brown paper bag. "Better than balut, right?"

I immediately regret suggesting it because it makes her stand up and change positions. She sits where she was earlier, across from me and next to the brown paper bag. She's farther away from me, and there's a ripple of irrational sadness, like I miss her.

"Actually," she says, seemingly unaffected by what I perceive as an unnecessary distance, "I think the two go really well together." She takes her plate and breaks up the egg completely. I never liked the sight of balut, so I intentionally avert my eyes and watch her instead. She takes alternate bites from the balut and the siopao.

We eat in silence for a while. It's not uncomfortable, but I think we're lost in our own thoughts, processing what just happened. When I finish my siopao, I crumple up the foil and toss it to the side to be collected later. I pause before moving on to anything else.

"Maya?"

She's not yet done with her food but she pauses too, as if she was waiting for me to say something all this time. "Yeah?"

"What does this mean?"

She lets the question hang in the air between us. She tilts her head a little and smiles. "What does what mean?"

Is this all in my head? Am I the only one with questions? I hesitate to continue, but she completely stops what she's doing and waits.

"You know," I prod, unwilling to put it into so many words. I chew on the side of my lip, so if it wasn't obvious what I was referring to before, it should be now.

Her cheeks redden slightly, and she averts her eyes. There's a dimple. Her smile is coy and shy at the same time. "It means I like you."

I exhale. "Oh." I can't help myself. I know I must have the goofiest smile on my face. "Good."

Her eyes snap back up to mine, and she raises both eyebrows. She looks uncertain. "Good?"

"Yeah." Her admission gives me the confidence to say what I never thought I'd ever admit to her. "I like you too."

The uncertainty is gone. Her smile deepens her dimples. I'm already elated but her reaction pushes me over the edge. There's a physical response to all this joy. I'm about to burst, and for a panicked second, I'm afraid I may throw up.

"Soooo?" she asks, adding a sing-song tone to the extended vowel. She wiggles a little in place but leans closer to me.

"Soooo?" I mimic, leaning forward and bobbing my head slightly from side to side.

"Does that make you my boyfriend?"

That's it. I can't take it anymore. I close the short distance between us in one move and take her in my arms. I hear her laugh into my shoulder, and she wraps her arms around me. My arms do the same, one hand on her back and the other by the nape of her neck. I squeeze, removing any space between her and me.

She leans back a little so that our foreheads touch. I don't release her. We sit there, nose to nose, too close together to open our eyes. And for once, I don't mind the heat so much. She runs her fingers through my hair. It tickles.

"You're my boyfriend," she repeats in a whisper.

The only proper response I can think of is to kiss her again. So I do.

151

CHAPTER 26

OFFICIALLY JAY AND MAYA

I've never had a girlfriend before," I confess.

Our picnic lunch is long over and packed away. The backpack is safely corded to my bike and locked up around the tree. We're walking hand in hand around the cemetery, not concerned by the thin layer of sweat between our palms.

"Really?" She's surprised and for a split second, I regret telling her. She must see it in my face because she squeezes my hand and tugs a little. "I've had a boyfriend before but not, like, a *boyfriend* boyfriend."

I laugh. Before I can elaborate why I'm laughing, she tugs my arm again, this time in protest. She pulls me to a stop. "You know what I mean!"

I shake my head, thoroughly amused by what seems to be embarrassment on her part. She pulls her hand away and crosses her arms. I want to apologize because I like holding her hand but her expression is so petulant, I can't help but laugh some more. When she stamps a foot, I'm certain this is all an elaborate act, and I hold up my hands in surrender.

"I genuinely don't know what you mean," I insist, holding out one hand to her, palm down, like I'm trying to calm a feral animal.

She doesn't look convinced. "No, really. What's the difference?" I do my best to control my laughter and look sincere. She's still clearly suspicious but she takes my hand again.

"You know, like in middle school? Where you're in a relationship"—she uses her free hand to make quotes in the air—"when you sit at the same table for recess." She tilts her head toward me. "That kind of boyfriend."

"Right." I swing our intertwined hands between us. "Then maybe I have a confession to make."

Her eyebrows raise. "Oh? Have you had many girlfriends, after all, Richard Gere Jr.?" Richard Gere? Recently named sexiest man alive by *People* magazine. He's fifty. Yuck.

"I was married."

She looks at me sideways, and her eyes narrow. I keep my expression as neutral as possible. "I'm listening," she says slowly.

"I was young." I shrug. "You know how it is."

"I don't think I do." She must know I'm up to something. "Tell me how it is to be married young."

"It was a cool fall afternoon," I begin, spreading my free hand in front of us like I'm inviting her to picture the scene with me. "She was a little older than me, actually. More mature." I wink at her, and she rolls her eyes. "She wore a white dress," I continue. "With lace. She had ribbons in her hair."

"Oh, she did, did she?"

"She sure did. I think it's what held up her pigtails."

"Her … pigtails?"

"I had on a striped shirt and shorts." I'm grinning openly now. "I was five. I think she was six. It was an innocent time." Maya started laughing. "Some other kid was the officiant. He had green and purple Mardi Gras beads around his neck so you knew he meant business."

"Did you kiss the bride?"

"Gross." I shudder dramatically. "Don't you know that girls that age have cooties?"

She bumped my hip with hers. I pull her closer to me and smell her hair. Then I give her more room as we walk. It's still hot, and I'm trying to minimize sweating all over her.

"But, alas." I sigh dramatically. "The relationship didn't last."

"How sad," she responds appropriately. "For her, I mean. Lucky for me." I smile. She acts like I'm the most popular boy in school and there's all sorts of competition for my attention. "You're my boyfriend now, so no more kissing other girls," she warns me playfully.

"I didn't even kiss that one!"

I'm excited to tell Marcus that Maya is my girlfriend when something occurs to me. "Are you going to tell your dad?"

"Sure." She's not bothered by this at all. "We've already had dinner together, so it's no big deal."

Everyone jokes about the girlfriend's father and hers is a cop. What will he do if he doesn't like the idea of me being Maya's boyfriend? The anxiety must show on my face because Maya asks me what's wrong.

"Was I supposed to ask him first?"

"Ask him what?"

"I don't know? If you can be my girlfriend? Is that something I'm supposed to ask him first?"

She lets go of my hand and watches me for a moment, confused. It looks like she's about to say no but then doubts herself. We stand there, staring at each other, both inexperienced and clearly unprepared.

"I don't think so?" she finally says, but without the confidence that she seems to want to have. "I mean, it's not like you're asking him to marry me or anything." She laughs a little uncomfortably, and the atmosphere is suddenly weirdly charged. "And like I said," she hurries on, "he knows who you are already."

"But he doesn't know my family." I may as well put everything I'm worried about on the table if we're discussing this. "Is that a problem?"

"Actually, he knows your family."

That's a surprise. "Wait. What?"

She nods in emphasis. "Yeah, I think he's actually met everyone."

I'm dumbfounded. "How?" Was my dad pulled over? Was my family arrested? Did he put out a BOLO on us? Asking other officers to be on the lookout for us? Are we being followed?

She shrugs. I should be reassured by her casualness but it feeds my anxiety. "Must be through Mom," she offers reasonably. "I mean, your mom is a nurse too, right?" She lets that sink in.

"I guess that makes sense," I admit, calmed by the explanation. Her dad isn't out to get me. Not yet, anyway. "Trust the Pinoy Network," I mumble. "It's Asian voodoo. If you're Filipino, they will find you." I wiggle my fingers at her. She laughs and takes my hand again.

"How come your dad didn't say anything about knowing my family over dinner?" I ask suddenly. My mind is running two trains on the track of thought and they are about to crash.

Maya bites her lip. "That's my fault," she admits. "Mom used to say that Dad always interrogates our guests, so before we have anyone over, I remind him not to give them the third degree." She slouches and exaggerates a tired expression. "And I mean *everyone*. One time, my sixth-grade teacher was walking past my street and we just started a conversation with her, right? Like, normal people."

She waits for me to nod before she continues, waiting to reveal the plot twist. "Then Dad starts asking her all sorts of questions. Like work history, personal history, family history"—she ticks it off on her fingers—"what she bought at the market last Friday." She throws her hands up in the air, frustrated.

"Wild," I agree. I'm a little frightened.

"Yeah, I think he just doesn't know how to make regular conversation. So I have to warn him to not be all, I don't know, cop-like with people." She makes an impression of a stiff person with a funny face. She's so cute. I love that she's not afraid to be silly.

"Thank you. Your dad is intimidating enough as it is. I don't think I'd have survived that." I wipe the real sweat off my forehead and upper lip.

"He told me that your family name was familiar. Like, there are so few Filipinos to begin with, right? What are the chances?"

I'm feeling better. "So you don't think he'll be violently opposed to me being your boyfriend?" I ask, looking for further assurances.

She isn't quick to reassure me. She considers my question more thoughtfully, then smiles. "Maybe bring him some ensaymada, just to be sure."

CHAPTER 27

LIFE IS GOOD

take her advice and Lola helped me make ensaymada to bring to her dad. He eats it and doesn't throw me out of the house. I'm invited back to dinner a couple more times. I even help her feed her ducks. I see Maya every day. Everything is going well.

The next step is to introduce her to my family.

I hesitate because Mom and Lola have been giving me advice … and food to help me woo my dalaga, the young single lady I'm courting. If I tell them the girl I like is already my girlfriend, they might stop.

"The way to the heart is through the stomach," Mom declares with authority. She walks into the living room, where the rest of the family is, dressed for a late dinner out with Dad. This doesn't happen very often but when it does, she's always wearing her diamond earrings.

It's Friday evening, the sun is already down. Dad is ready to go, slouched on the couch in his dress socks and indoor slippers. "It worked on me," Dad agrees, patting his stomach. He's not a big man but has developed the rounder belly of someone who spends more time behind the desk than in the gym.

The house smells of garlic and shrimp paste from the dinner Lola made for herself but when Mom walks by me to stand in front of Dad, I can smell her floral perfume. She stops with her back turned to him. She doesn't say anything but he knows to stand and help her with her necklace. She rewards his assistance with a kiss on the cheek. He puts a hand on his heart in response and falls back into the couch like he's fainted. Mom laughs. They're acting like a couple of kids.

Lola, sitting on a chair by the defunct fireplace we never use, juts her chin at me and tells me in Filipino that this is my fault. "They're like this because of you."

"Me? What did I do?" I'm standing by the door frame, watching the scene. I'm happy to take the credit because I like the atmosphere at home better when they're like this.

Lola makes a harrumphing sound, dismissing my innocence and acting like I know what she's talking about. I don't know but I don't mind. "Nakakahawa ang pag-ibig," she says knowingly.

I only understand half of what she's saying and look at her quizzically. Mom translates for me. "Love is contagious," she says, winking.

I don't argue. Things have felt different.

"Naku! Kailangan na nating umalis!" She playfully slaps Dad's knee. "We need to leave now or we'll lose our reservation!"

Dad doesn't move from his splayed position. "Ikaw!" he says, pointing at her. "You're the one that's not ready!" Mom pretends to act offended.

They launch into rapid Filipino banter. It's difficult to follow but it's clear they're teasing each other and flirting. Lola and I may as well not even have been in the room. Lola shares a private look with me, lowering her chin and raising her eyebrows. She's just as amused as I am.

Mom and Dad head out through the kitchen. Mom is rattling off last-minute instructions that no one is really listening to, and Dad is making motions with his hands behind her to shoo her forward. Lola and I follow behind in a mini procession.

They open the door, and Marcus is standing right outside, one hand raised. His eyes are wide; he's just as startled to be discovered as Mom is to discover him.

"Naku, Diyos ko!" Mom exclaims, grabbing her necklace to her chest dramatically. "Marcus! I thought you were a ghost!" She makes the sign of the cross as if the mere mention of the supernatural is enough to summon evil spirits. "What are you doing skulking out there in the dark like some kind of ghoul?"

"Sorry, Mrs. Abayani. I was just about to knock."

"Come in! Come in!" Mom makes room for him to enter. "Have you eaten?" She fusses over him. "Jay's father and I were just about to leave for dinner, but I'm sure Jay can find you something to eat. Jay! Your friend needs to eat!"

"Thank you, Mrs. Abayani. That sounds great!" Marcus grins at me. "Dude. Feed me."

I roll my eyes. I'm about to respond with something rude that would probably get me in trouble but Dad saves me.

"Time to go, 'Ling. We don't want to lose our reservations." 'Ling isn't my mom's name. It's short for darling, a term of endearment that they sometimes use. I don't hear it very often, so I know Dad is being intentional as he gently but firmly leads her out the door.

Mom raises her hands in surrender. "Yes, yes, we're going." But before the door closes behind them, she yells over her shoulder, "Be good!"

The door closes with a distinct click, and it's quiet again.

"I'm not feeding you," I tell Marcus matter-of-factly.

"Your mom said you should feed me." The tone of his voice means he reads between the lines. He enjoys giving me a hard time. "And she said, 'Be good.' You don't want to disobey her, do you?"

I open the cupboard, grab an open bag of Sunflower Crackers, and toss it at him. "Here. Eat this."

He catches it without effort and isn't insulted at all. He digs in right away. "Why so grouchy?" he asks, bits of yellow crackers falling off the side of his mouth in his haste. "Did you and your girlfriend have a fight or something?"

I reach into the top cabinet to grab a glass. I give Marcus a hard time but I'm not a bad host. Mom would have a conniption if she thought I was being less than hospitable. "Shut up. Things are great." I fill his glass with some chilled calamansi juice from the fridge. Marcus loves calamansi juice. This is a treat, and he knows it. I hand him his glass.

He takes it from me, jerking his chin up as thanks. He washes down his mouthful of crackers with a large gulp, then wipes his mouth with the back of his hand.

Lola is sitting on a stool by the kitchen table. She watches him and shakes her head. She makes a disapproving noise and hands him a paper napkin. Lola is used to having Marcus around and treats him like another grandson. Another grandson who doesn't understand Filipino. She never bothers to actually talk to him but communicates just fine using exaggerated expressions and mannerisms to express ideas.

Marcus takes the offered napkin and makes a show of using it, however unnecessary. "Thank you, Lola." His voice is a fraction too loud, and he speaks slowly.

"Have you *just* met?" I ask him sarcastically. "How many times do I have to tell you? She *understands* English, you nimrod. And she's *not* deaf. You don't have to yell at her." Granted, he hasn't come around the house in months. When we were little, he was always over. We spent so much time together back in elementary school that if we didn't look so different, people would've assumed we were brothers.

I think he's only been here a couple of times since the move. We're older now anyway, and it makes more sense to hang out somewhere else.

He puts a hand over his mouth. "Yeah, yeah, right. Sorry." Then to Lola, "Sorry, Lola. My grandmother *is* deaf, and I'm always yelling at her, so I forget."

"Everyone in your house is constantly yelling," I point out, unimpressed. One of the reasons he was always at my house and not the other way around. That and my parents are way more overprotective than his mom.

He shrugs. "It's our love language." He grabs another handful of crackers and stuffs his mouth. He acts like he hasn't eaten all day but I'd bet a week's pay that he's already had dinner at home, a Po-Boy on his way over here, and maybe even someone else's beignet. It's also why I don't take the responsibility of feeding him very seriously. Eating is his natural state of being.

"Speaking of loooooove …" He adds vowels to the word and wiggles his eyebrows comically. He's speaking to Lola, not to me. "Can you believe little Joshua here is all grown up? Huh? Huh?"

Lola laughs at his antics, which only encourages him, so he moves closer to where she is sitting and makes kissy noises. He takes the stool across from hers. "With a girlfriend and everything!" Lola reacts with surprise.

"Shut up!" An oven mitt is the closest thing in my reach, so I grab it and aim for Marcus's head. He ducks, and the mitt hits the curtains behind him. He laughs. I look for something else to throw at him.

Lola waves her hand at me and makes disapproving noises. Her eyebrows are knitted together, and all the folds of her skin are turned down in a frown. It's her cross face. Her way of telling me to stop.

Marcus continues to laugh. Now he's just taunting me. I make another move but Lola warns me off, so I stop and content myself to just scowling at him.

Lola turns to Marcus; her expression changes to one of delight. Her eyes are wide open and she's smiling so big you can tell that she has false teeth. She's making motions with her hands, encouraging him to tell her more.

"Oh, you don't know?" He's loving this. His enjoyment is directly proportional to my discomfort. I know because he keeps eyeing me, and the more I growl at him, the happier he is. "Jay has a girlfriend." He says the last word in a sing-song tone and bats his lashes excessively. He makes more kissing noises.

Lola actually starts clapping. I groan and cover my face. This isn't how I wanted to tell Lola. Now I regret not introducing Maya to them before Marcus could ruin everything.

Marcus starts singing. "Jay and Maya sitting in a tree. K-I-S-S-I-N-G …" He's looking at me, gauging how much torture he's inflicting. He doesn't see Lola's expression change.

"Maya?" she interrupts in a flat tone.

Marcus stops suddenly, likely more startled that she had said anything than the tone of her voice. It's entirely possible that this is the first time he's ever heard her speak. "Uh," he stutters, looking at me. The smile is gone, and his cheeks sag with uncertainty.

I also don't know what's going on or what triggered Lola's sudden mood change. I shake my head slightly at him. I'm just as confused as he is.

"Maya?" she asks again, more insistent. "Mayaari Hebert?"

Marcus and I stare at her a few moments first and then each other, uncomprehending. Maya is not an uncommon name; how does she know exactly which Maya I'm dating? And why is she acting so weird?

She grabs Marcus's arm, forcing him to look at her. He nods dumbly. She pushes her stool back with such force that it slams against the wall. Marcus and I jump at the sound. She's moving so fast I don't know if I'm supposed to help her or hide.

"Get out!" she orders Marcus in Filipino. He may not understand her words but there's no mistaking her intention. She's pushing him toward the door and talking loudly.

"Lola!" I admonish. "You're being rude. Stop it!"

She tells me to be quiet and continues to urge Marcus out the door. Marcus, one hand still in the bag of crackers, looks legitimately worried. His mouth is agape, his eyes darting between me and Lola, but he allows himself to be led out the door.

Am I supposed to stop her or help her? I don't remember this being in Mom's etiquette handbook. I watch helplessly as Marcus is pushed past me. I give him an apologetic look, but he looks just as apologetic. Neither of us knows who is wrong in this situation.

I open the door because Lola looks like she's about to slam him against it. He leaves without saying a word. She doesn't quite bang the door shut after him but makes sure it's locked before turning slowly to face me.

When she does, her stare is so intense, the world closes in on me. When she speaks, gravity itself bends to listen. Her words aren't angry but there's an ultimatum that is not used to being defied. I can't even process if she's speaking in English or Filipino. The language doesn't matter because the message is the same.

"Mayaari Celeste Hebert is a monster."

CHAPTER 28

THE FAMILY CURSE

Lola tells me about a night, almost a decade ago, when I was so young I barely recall the time my mother was pregnant. I vaguely remember something but not clearly enough for me to distinguish between a real memory or a dream.

She was having a boy. I was going to be a kuya, an older brother. Everything had been progressing well; she was in her final trimester, and everyone was preparing for his arrival.

My mother went to the corner store to pick up paper plates for the church potluck. Lola was home with me. Dad was at the hospital.

It was still early in the evening when she left the house. And because she wasn't going far, she decided to walk. She said it was good exercise for her and her baby. She had done this before, and she was a nurse. There was no reason for concern.

Neighbors had seen her on her errand. Some had stopped to have a conversation with her, talking about the baby on the way. One of those people was Maria Hebert, Maya's mom.

Our moms knew each other. From work and from church. They were friends. So when Maria saw my mom at the store, it was natural for them to connect. Mom hadn't yet gone on maternity leave but she had voluntarily cut her hours at the hospital, so the two friends may not have seen each other as often. They had some catching up to do.

The mystery is what happened on the way home. Mom had spent too long at the store but she didn't mind. The streetlights were on by the time she was on her way. Some say Maria was with her.

Somewhere between the store and home, Mom lost consciousness. Doctors speculated a spontaneous rupture, but Lola thinks it was something more nefarious. Because when a neighbor saw her lying on the sidewalk, she was bleeding. And by the time the ambulance arrived, she had lost the baby.

The same night, Maya's mom was killed in a questionable accident.

Lola took me with her to the hospital, but I wasn't taken into the room where my mom and dad were grieving over a lost child. I stayed in the nurses' breakroom with some of Mom's colleagues, watching TV and being fed unhealthy vending machine snacks. It wasn't that unusual for me to be lounging in the breakroom as a kid. Every now and then, when there was some scheduling mishap or something, Mom would leave me in the room to wait until another adult could take me home. I don't remember the reason for being there that night. I remember the Dunkaroos and Planters Cheez Balls.

Mom, devastated by loss, was never the same. Dad became reserved, often absent. Lola prayed more often. I noticed but also didn't. I was six, almost seven. There were other things that mattered more. Like *Teenage Mutant Ninja Turtles*. I had my parents, my lola, a tummy full of junk food, and my favorite blanket waiting for me at home. What did I care about the rest of the world?

It was a pivotal night for everyone in my family but me.

I'm older now. I have a better understanding of how such a loss can impact a family, a deeper compassion for my mother I didn't have before. What does it mean to me to almost be a kuya? I don't know. There's a hurricane happening in my head as my past and present collide, but one thing still doesn't make much sense.

"What does this have to do with Maya?"

Lola looks aghast, like I'm asking the obvious. "The Hebert women are cursed," she tells me in Filipino, with the drama of a Shakespearean stage actor. She leans forward, bridging the space between us and wagging a finger at me. "Maria Hebert might have been a good Filipino nurse to people here who don't know any better. But Maria Paniqui, before she married a white man, was a manananggal. And her daughter, Mayaari, is too." Lola's face crumples in disgust, and she goes as far as to spit into the kitchen sink.

I must look like a Black Moor Goldfish the way I'm gaping at her. The word means nothing to me except the way she says it suggests that it's something ungodly. And whatever it is, she just called my girlfriend one. Had it been anyone else other than Lola, I might have punched them in the face for the perceived insult.

"A *what*?" I blurt out when I've sorted through my initial bafflement.

She repeats the word. Manananggal. It's a monster, she explains. She describes an unbelievable creature that splits in half at night. Leaving its bottom half behind, the torso grows bat-like wings and flies into the darkness in search of a victim: a pregnant woman. It has the power to transfix its victims, like a vampire. Then with a horrifying long hollow tongue, it sucks out the fetus for food.

It's hard to follow because I'm out of practice and she's using Filipino words I don't hear often. It sounds disturbingly made up. Like something kids invent on the spot in a darkened room with a flashlight under their chin and surrounded by other kids they're trying to scare. Not something a grown woman, someone I respect, genuinely believes.

"You think this *thing*, a manananggal"–I struggle with the word, making it sound more comical than the horrifying image it's supposed to conjure–"was responsible for Mom's miscarriage? You think that Maya's *mom* was one?" I'm trying to make sense of it all but the pieces just don't connect for me.

This is Filipino folklore. Not real life. It's one thing to believe in good luck and prayer but this? She can't possibly really believe this.

Lola nods emphatically. She's reeking with prejudice. For a fellow Filipino, no less. So much for solidarity. She points out that Maya's mom had contact with mine that same night.

"So what?" This is incomprehensible. "You said she met loads of people that night! You said she spoke with more than one person! Why would you single *her* out?!" My voice rises in volume, and it doesn't even register in my head that I've never, in my entire life, spoken to Lola with such disrespect and anger.

She doesn't acknowledge my tone. Her accusation grows more outlandish. Saying that James Hebert knew all along. And that he was the one who killed his wife to prevent her from hurting any more people.

I'm done with this. She's reaching for far-out explanations that are damaging to reason and sense. She's the kind of person who makes Maya's life harder. The people that abandon a hurting family at their most vulnerable. Gossipmongers that toss out superstition instead of lifelines. How can I possibly be related to someone like her? How can this be someone I actually respect?

I'm disgusted. The more she talks, the more I see her as a crazed, provincial, uneducated savage. She's speaking so quickly

I can barely understand her anymore. I can't bridge the language barrier and my emotions. She's just an ignorant babbling old lady to me all of a sudden.

I swear at her. Loudly and repeatedly.

She reels back like I hit her. It's a ridiculously dramatic reaction but maybe it isn't. I'm so angry that I'm radiating violent energy. Maybe my words have actual physical impact, powered by the storm raging in my head. I'm not even sorry. The room feels smaller, like all the lines deepen and thicken, tightening around me. I need to get out of here before I start punching walls.

I throw open the door with such force that it bounces back on its hinges, making an alarmingly loud noise. I hold it open while I fumble into my sneakers, hating the fact that I have to stop instead of storming out like I want to.

Lola is yelling, but I've erected an invisible force field behind me and her words are muffled. I don't hear them. I don't want to. I can block her out.

She doesn't follow me when I finally get out of the house. I push my bike through the gate, leaving it open behind me. I refuse to acknowledge the angry tears that block my vision. I'm not crying. I'm too angry to cry.

I get on my bike and pedal furiously. I'm not paying attention to the streets or the turns. In a few minutes, I'll be lost. I don't know where I'm going but I know where I'll be.

With Maya.

CHAPTER 29

MAYA THE MANANANGGAL

I've never been to Maya's house so late. When I arrive at her gate, I get off my bike, panting from my efforts. My muscles are so tense they hurt and I'm sweating through the house shirt I didn't bother changing out of. I look up at her house and I suddenly question what I'm doing.

What am I supposed to say to her? Hi, Maya. *I had so much fun on our date earlier, I had to bike over in my worn-out Teenage Mutant Ninja Turtle shirt to see you again. By the way, I just found out that my grandmother believes your mom was a vampiric winged monster from the provinces of the Philippines that ate my baby brother?*

I understand that Lola is from a different time and different environment. But the whole thing is outrageous. It's one thing to believe in spirits and a higher power. But a flying half human that eats babies through a tubed tongue? Unreal.

I've never even heard of such a monster before. Vampires, sure. There are places all over New Orleans that obsess over them. Witches? That's a thing. Zombies, everyone has heard of them. But this? This manananggal can't really be something my people are afraid of.

I'm embarrassed for my family. I'm embarrassed for the entire Philippines.

I'm about to turn around, maybe try to find Marcus instead, when the door opens. It's not Maya who stands at the doorway but her father.

"Jay?"

I look up at his imposing figure, silhouetted by the hallway light behind him. I see him differently now. Does he know what people say behind his back? What *my family* has been saying? He's a cop. Of course he knows. What does that say about me?

"Good evening, sir." I swallow, trying to steady my voice. I'm well aware of my subpar attire. "I'm sorry," I apologize right away. "I know it's late. I can go."

"You can't go if you haven't even been in yet." He smiles gently, the opposite of Lola's hysterics, and steps to the side to invite me in. "You look like you could use some company. Maya is in the backyard."

His kindness is so undeserved, it's a physical gut punch. At the same time, my muscles unclench. I'm safe here. There's no need to run.

"Thank you, sir." I park my bike inside the gate, careful to latch it behind me. I climb the stairs with my head down, humbled by the kind of hospitality that people say Filipinos are known for. And it isn't from a Filipino.

He closes the door behind me and leaves the room. "You know the way," he says over his shoulder. He returns to the couch where there's half a glass of something alcoholic he had been clearly nursing before I arrived. He leaves me where I am, giving me the space I didn't even realize how much I needed.

I remove my shoes and carry them with me. I duck a little when I walk by him, and he lifts his chin slightly in acknowledgment. Then I slip my Nike Airs back on before I leave through the kitchen door where I know Maya will be.

The moon isn't quite full so if it weren't for the string of lights that run along the house to the duck pen, it would have been too dark to see much. I didn't notice the lights before but this is also the first time I've been here at night.

Maya is sitting on one of the benches, bending down to indulge some of her pet ducks. She looks up expectantly when the door opens but the sudden smile on her face means she's pleasantly surprised to see me.

"Jay!" she exclaims, standing up quickly and startling her fowl friends. They quack and waddle away from her. "What are you doing here?" She makes her way to me.

She's wearing the same oversized T-shirt and denim shorts I saw her in earlier today. Her hair is in a low ponytail held together with one of her many hair ties. Loose strands frame her face. The night air and the glow from the lights make her seem ethereal. She moves with dignity and grace beyond her seventeen years. But more beautiful still is the gentle soul reflected in her eyes, enduring despite any pain and loss. She is a strong and brilliant diamond forged under unbearable pressure.

How can anyone see her as a monster?

I meet her halfway and engulf her in a hug, squeezing her so tightly I feel her breathing. She wraps her arms around my waist and leans her chin on my shoulder. I hold her there for a moment, lost in this feeling I'm desperately seeking. I belong here. With her.

After an undefined amount of time, she whispers, "What's wrong?"

I don't know how to tell her. I shake my head a fraction and squeeze her again. I'm unwilling to let go. I bury my face in her neck, breathing her in.

She returns the hug to let me know it's OK. "Oh, Jay." Her voice is gentle and soothing. She can't possibly know what turmoil I'm feeling but she knows I'm not fine and she's letting me know I can count on her. It's almost enough to reduce me to tears.

I let go only because I'm afraid if I don't, I may start crying. I look down at our feet and see one of her ducks, Papan, squeeze between us like an attention-seeking puppy, its feathers brushing against my bare leg. It makes me smile.

Maya touches my cheek, urging me to look at her. I allow her to guide me and when I meet her eyes, they're deep pools filled with concern. "Talk to me," she implores.

I take a deep breath and let it out slowly through my nose, still not certain I can control my voice. I try to smile to let her know that I'm making an effort so she doesn't ask again. She nods, takes me by the hand, and leads me back to the bench I found her sitting on. She pulls me down to sit beside her.

Papan flaps its wings to get her attention. It struggles a little when Maya picks it up but is happy to be noticed. She straightens its feathers for a bit until it settles. Then she hands the duck to me.

I expect the duck to protest, but Maya has sufficiently calmed it, and its eyes are halfway closed, barely noticing the change in hands. I mimic her actions, stroking the feathers. The rhythmic motion helps calm my tangled emotions.

"I yelled at my lola," I confess between strokes, looking down at the duck and not at her. "She was saying really stupid things about you … about your mom." My hand trembles a little. I'm not as calm as I thought I was. I don't want to accidentally hurt Papan so I put the sleeping duck gently on the ground before continuing.

I look back at Maya; she doesn't look shocked or angry. She looks sad. She reaches out to my empty hands and holds them in hers. "What did she say?"

I shake my head. Am I really going to repeat that drivel for her? I can't possibly admit that my family is that ignorant. That my lola was probably the one that started the rumors about her father and damaging her childhood. Will she forgive me?

She waits for me to respond, and when I look into her eyes, I'm tempted to lie. I can make up a believable fight. Certainly more believable than the load of crap Lola actually told me. I'll invent the argument to explain why I'm upset, and she'll never have to know.

But at the same time, I also know I can't lie to her. She deserves more. She deserves the truth and my promise to make things better. She'll know I'm not my family. She'll know she can depend on me.

"She said your mom was a manananggal." I figure that if I use the unfamiliar word, it will confuse her and sound ridiculous. Maybe minimize the impact of the insult.

Except she knows what a manananggal is. Her reaction says as much. She pulls her hands slowly away from mine and wraps them around herself. She's a rose without water, wilting in front of my eyes.

"How did she know?" she asks in a small voice.

I can't comprehend what's happening. I thought she might be righteously angry. Possibly insulted and indignant. Best-case scenario, she'd laugh it off. Of all the reactions I had been anticipating, shameful acceptance wasn't one of them.

"Maya?"

She turns her head away from me, like she can't handle seeing my face.

"You can't be serious," I demand, hoping this is her idea of a tasteless joke. "Do you even know what that is?"

She nods and squeezes her eyes shut. She looks afraid. Does she think I'm going to yell at her? Hit her? I look down at my empty hands, checking to see if a pitchfork had somehow materialized in them. But they are empty.

I reach out to touch her gently on her elbow. She flinches but doesn't move away. "I don't understand," I admit. "Help me understand."

She starts to cry. Her shoulders lift and fall in an unnatural rhythm, and tears chase down her cheeks. I don't know what to do. I look toward the house in near panic, afraid that the door will swing open and her father will see his crying daughter with me. I look back at her. I want to help but don't know how.

"Stop," I plead. "Don't cry. I'm sorry."

My appeals only make her cry harder. The ducks in our immediate surroundings begin to ruffle their feathers, likely affected by Maya's emotions. The near panic I was feeling is now full blown. I stand, look around us as if I could find some kind of garden tool that would stop the floodgates of tears. There are none, of course, made for this emergency.

I shoo the ducks away, trying to make an empty space for us to be alone in. I kneel in front of her, my hands on her arms and hoping she'll look at me.

The whole world of mythology and monsters is forgotten. The immediate concern is Maya. And she's crying.

"I'm the monster and you're the one apologizing," she hiccups.

"Stop," I plead again. "Come on, Maya. Please?"

It's irrational for me to ask that. I should know that tears aren't always something you can control. I just experienced my own tearful assault and here I am asking Maya to manage her emotions like she's some kind of failure for not being able to. I'm such a hypocrite.

But she nods, accepting my double standard. Demonstrating much more control than I can claim for myself, she regulates her breathing. She wipes her eyes. They're red and puffy but the leaking stops. Her cheeks are still tear-stained, and I reach over to wipe them gently. I have very little to offer but what I have is hers.

She smiles and puts a hand over the one I have on her cheek, so much more generous than I can possibly be. And in an act that further proves she's a better person, she kisses my hand and holds it to her heart.

"Your grandmother is right. My mom *was* a manananggal."

"I've seen photos," I say, attempting to lighten the heavy mood. "Your mom doesn't have bat wings."

The joke is a lame one, but she rewards the attempt with a wan smile. I reach over with my other hand and hold hers in silent apology. She puts our intertwined hands on her lap, accepting the offer, and continues. "It's an old curse on my family. From all the way back in the province where my mom is from. No one even remembers how it started or why. But as far as I know, every woman on my mom's side is afflicted with it. And there's no cure."

"A curse?" It sounds like a fairy tale, not real life. But Maya's emotions and fear are very real. And so much more credible than Lola's.

She nods. "It starts the first night of adulthood. Then every occurrence of a blood moon."

"A blood moon?"

"It happens a couple or so times a year." She shrugs. "It's called a blood moon because the full moon turns a reddish color."

"What happens?"

"I've never seen it myself," she admits. "But I remember learning about it as a child." She bites her lip. I can't imagine how difficult this conversation is for her. I shift in my position so I'm sitting cross-legged on the ground. I don't let go of her hands.

"My mom said at first it'll feel like a really bad period cramp. And when that happens, to find a safe place." Her voice shudders. "That means the change is going to begin. Like werewolves, I guess. Except manananggals grow wings." She sighs. "And not pretty angelic wings, mind you. Of course not. I'm supposed to sprout grotesque veined skin wings."

She pulls her hands away to cover her face. I reach over and stroke her bare arms, trying to comfort her during this unthinkable confession of sorts. I don't say anything.

"And while that's happening," she continues, her voice has the edge of anger, "my body is going to rip in half. Divided right in the middle. Entrails and all just hanging there." She makes a motion with her hand, slicing across her stomach. "Then, supposedly consumed by some kind of unholy hunger, I'm going to leave my bottom half, exposed to the elements, and go searching for a … for a …" She can't continue. She puts both hands over her mouth, trying very hard not to burst into more tears. Whether for my benefit or hers, I can't tell.

"An unborn child," I complete for her in a dead voice. Because it needs to be said and she can't do it.

She closes her eyes tightly and nods. She doesn't cry but releases a guttural howl from the depths of her soul. It's a horror that she's had to deal with all her life. And since her mom's death, all by herself.

"Or anyone that might get in my way," she adds, her words strangled. As if there's a need for clarification. "No one is safe."

"That's what happened to your mom," I deduce, still void of any emotion. "It was a blood moon and the curse took her. She turned."

I let her cry. I'm stunned dumb. Lola told me an outrageous story that seemed straight out of a nightmare. I couldn't believe it. But here is Maya, a girl my age, from my world, telling me the same thing. How could that be?

"How did she die?" Maybe it's insensitive. Inappropriate. Unfair. How can I ask this of her? Because I'm looking for a way out. I'm looking for a reasonable explanation that debunks all this superstition.

We live in the modern United States of America. We're halfway to the year 2000. We're living in the future. The monsters here are supposed to be corporations and faceless bureaucrats, men who take away the hopes and dreams of families in need. Racism. Inequality. Injustice. Those are the monsters here. Not mythical beings with wings and fangs.

Maya swallows. She looks away from me, toward the house where her father is sitting, blissfully unaware of the world that is shifting between her and me. "My mom lived this double life in the Philippines. It was about survival. It's not her fault that she's cursed." She bites her lip before continuing. I'm afraid she'll draw blood. "She became a nurse, you know? Not for the money or so she could find her next victim." She spat the words out in disgust. "She did it because it was her way of repenting for the … stuff she had to do." Her eyes fill with tears. "She was a good person."

What a thing to live with. I could call her a monster, condemn her to hell, and pretend that I would have been more noble in her shoes. It's easy to pass judgment. I can't even stop myself from crying, I'm supposed to claim that I can do better? So I don't. I don't form opinions or make any judgments. That's not what Maya needs from me right now.

"She tried everything she could to stop the change. There's no cure," she repeats. "But she found ways to control it." Her fingers close around the pendant she always wears. "She tried so hard."

"And when she got pregnant, it stopped. For a while. That's the reprieve, apparently." She looks down at the pendant between her fingers, tracing the edges of a talisman that may have aided her mom's cause.

"Maybe our bodies are so busy passing a curse and damning the next generation, we take a vacation from attacking the rest of the world." Her sarcasm is a coping mechanism. Something I'm familiar with but not something I've seen her display before.

"But then it started again." She drops her hands to her lap and stares at them, palms open. "And this time, stronger than before."

I reach over and clasp my hands over hers again. I want her to know I'm still with her. I'm still listening. She looks up at me.

"So she tells my dad, right? Gives him the ultimatum. Tells him she doesn't want to be a monster." Her eyes fill with tears again but she doesn't move to stop them, and I don't let go of her hands. "She tells my dad that if it happens again, he has to stop her. For her."

I swallow, unable to comprehend that kind of responsibility. Her mom literally put her life in the hands of her husband. And asked him to end it.

"There's one way to kill a manananggal," Maya says in a deadpanned tone. "You find the bottom half after the divide, and you pour a whole bunch of salt on the exposed organs."

In spite of myself, I wince. Literal salt on a wound. The pain of that must be unbearable.

Maya sees my reaction and nods. "Yeah. It cauterizes the organs, making it impossible to merge again. Garlic works too."

"Garlic?"

She shrugs and doesn't provide any further explanation. "Then, when the sun comes out, the manananggal dies."

She raises her face to the stars. "So that night, my dad realizes the divide happened, right? He goes looking, and sure enough–" Maya closes her eyes. She doesn't open them again when she speaks. "Dad doesn't just find her but also a prepared bag of salt." She opens her eyes again to look at me. "She had it ready for him, Jay."

The dread settles in my stomach. I want to vomit. "Your dad did it. He killed her."

She looks back toward the house and nods. "She didn't want to be a monster, and he loved her enough to listen to her."

"I thought it was a car accident," I mumble, an admission that this was talked about behind her back. She isn't fazed by it. It's like she's already accepted everyone in town already knew.

"How else was he supposed to explain it?" It might be unnerving how matter of fact she talks about murder and death but considering all that she's had to endure and survive, the trauma might have otherwise destroyed her. "He dumped the salt and when she returned, she full-on attacked him."

Her voice gets smaller. "So he shot her. Then burned the body. Staged the whole thing to look like a bad car accident."

I swore under my breath, envisioning the scene. Was it heroism or was it murder? Or can it have been both? I can't imagine the man inside, so in love with his wife, having to destroy everything in horror and lies. It's like a bad movie.

"When did you know?"

"That I'm the next one in a cursed bloodline of monsters?" Her voice is sharp with pain. "When I was six. And my mom left a journal, like an everything you need to know about being a manananggal manual." She sighed. "Like, she knew."

"I mean," I ask hesitantly, "when did you find out about what your dad did?"

"Oh." She looks down at our hands. "I was fifteen. It was her death anniversary." Her lips tug to one side in something that isn't a smile. "I think he was a little drunk."

"That must've been so hard," I offer lamely. Everything about this is hard but I'm not eloquent enough to think of something better to say.

"I hated him for a while," she admits. "Blamed him for everything. But what was I supposed to do? Report him to the police? Then what? I won't have a mom *or* a dad."

The unfairness of her life leaves a bitter taste in my mouth. I had no idea. No one does. She's been so alone all this time.

"I wouldn't have believed any of this if it weren't for Mom," she confesses, her voice mellowing into one of nostalgia. "I spent a lot of time rereading her journals and looking at her pictures. And one day, it just hits me. I realized that the burden was all on him."

She looks back up at the stars. "And if you believe in heaven and hell, he condemned himself to hell for her. Because she asked him. And he did it. Because he loves her."

She looks back at me; there's more in her eyes than memories of the past. I can't identify what it is, but it looks suspiciously like yearning.

"We'd be lucky to find that kind of love."

CHAPTER 30

THE UGLY DETAILS

There is too much information for me to absorb and an onslaught of memories she's reliving, so it takes several silent minutes for us to collect ourselves. In the silence, I move to sit next to her on the bench, and she shifts so that her head is leaning on my shoulder. What a couple of messed up kids we are.

The ducks seem to know we need our space, or perhaps they're just tired because most of them are back in their roost. The night has quieted, and the summer air doesn't even have a breeze enough to sway the lights.

"Is this what's going to happen to you?" I ask. "At the next blood moon?"

She shakes her head, and the sadness threatens to gurgle back out as a wail. "Sooner," she manages to say softly. "On my eighteenth birthday. Supposedly."

My blood runs cold, and I intentionally fight the urge to shiver unnecessarily. I've been able to hold all this information out at arm's length, an outside observer looking in. But the upcoming deadline feels like an oppressive ultimatum.

Will my sweet, smart girlfriend turn into a bloodlust monster?

"Helluva birthday gift, huh?" She sighs heavily, the weight of a generational curse pressing down on her. There's been a shadow lurking behind her all her life, counting down the years until it completely engulfs her. What a solitary experience.

"Who else knows about this?"

She has little patience left, and I don't blame her. Her expression is a mix of disgust, frustration, and sarcasm. "This isn't exactly an icebreaker topic. Hi, nice to meet you. My name is Maya, and when I turn eighteen, chances are, I'm going to divide and prey on vulnerable pregnant women for a little hors d'oeuvres before dinner." She sits up straighter, spitting the words out like they taste vile. "I've had enough people cross the street when Dad and I are on the sidewalk because of all the conspiracy theories surrounding my mom's death. I'm not about to add supernatural occult stories to the fire."

I recoil without meaning to. I know the hate isn't directed at me, so I lean toward her and squeeze her hand so she knows.

She doesn't apologize, nor should she, but her voice softens. "Other than Dad, no one knows. I didn't think so anyway." She faces me and searches my eyes. "But your grandmother knew. How?"

Suddenly, the focus isn't on Maya and her curse but on me and my ill-gotten information. It's like the time Marcus and I ended up in the principal's office when we were eleven for passing notes. I got into trouble because Marcus sent me something. I didn't instigate anything, I just received it, but I was guilty anyway. I'm just as guilty now.

"My mom had a miscarriage that day your mom died," I admit reluctantly. My voice is just over a whisper, and Maya leans in to hear me. "My lola blames her for it."

Maya's hands are suddenly cold in mine. Her mouth falls slightly open, and the horror reflected on her face is the look of someone who sees nightmares. My heart hurts for her even more.

"Oh, Jay," she wails, her voice breaking and tears filling her eyes. "I didn't know."

I let go of her hands and wrap my arms around her shaking shoulders. I pull her into a tight hug, as if I can smother the cries with an embrace. She sobs against my chest, her tears soaking my shirt, and I don't care if she ruins it. I only care about her.

"I've got you, Maya," I promise her. I make this vow quietly into her hair. I don't know if she hears me through her tears. It matters but it also doesn't. I say it aloud so the universe knows what's in my heart. I say it aloud so it's out there and cannot be taken back. "I've got you."

You aren't alone.

CHAPTER 31

PERILOUS PASSIONS

It's rare for my parents to go out, so when they do, they're usually home late. I'm home well before they are. Lola had closed the gates sometime after I left and had locked the door. I've had a key to the house since we moved in so it isn't a problem for me.

She's still awake when I enter the kitchen. I know because the glow from the other room tells me she's staying up. Probably saying a few rosaries for my irreverent soul. I know she can hear me but I'm not calling out a greeting. Nor do I go out of my way to see her.

She wants an apology. I'm always the one apologizing, regardless of who is at fault. That's how things are in this household. Lola, Mom, or Dad, it doesn't matter. I'm always the one that's wrong because they're my elders. They'll never apologize for anything.

She might have been unbelievably right about the manananggal part but she's wrong about everything else. Maya isn't a monster. She's the victim of circumstances beyond her control. She can't help being one any more than I can help being Filipino. If Lola is going to condemn her for what she is, it's no different from being profiled because of the color of my skin.

She's wrong.

I kick off my shoes, leave them where they are, and go straight to my room. I collapse on top of the covers, not caring that I'm dressed in clothes that probably still have a duck feather or two stuck to them. I never get on my bed until after I've showered but tonight was draining on both a physical and emotional level.

I would have thought I'd fall asleep right away, given the circumstances, but I'm still uncomfortably awake when my parents get home. I don't know what time it is but judging from their hushed tones, it's probably really late. I can't make out the words but I can tell from the tone of Mom's voice that she's complaining about the shoes I left in front of the door. She probably tripped on them. Some part of me I refuse to entertain hopes she did or that it causes them some level of inconvenience.

I'm prepared to feign being asleep if they try to call me out on it, but they don't. If it's as late as I guess, they probably assume I'm deep in sleep already.

The muffled voices are between Mom and Dad as they walk through the house. That must mean that between my arrival and theirs, Lola had gone to bed. My stomach drops a little when I imagine the conversation they'll have about me in the morning but I'm resolved to remain unwavering in this.

I lie awake, staring at the ceiling but seeing past it. I'm replaying the events of the evening in my head, seeing them as an outsider. I'm experiencing it all over as if it had happened to someone else. In this way, maybe I'm not as emotional.

Before I left Maya, she had calmed down, and we made our way back inside the house because her dad seemed unhappy about the amount of time we were outside on our own. Maya saw his silhouette at the kitchen window a few times and took the hint.

She had excused herself to the bathroom to freshen up, likely more for her dad's benefit than mine. I was alone with her father for a few minutes. He didn't say anything other than offer me something to drink. His face and body language were unreadable. Not because he kept them neutral but because it was as if he was rotating through a wheel of emotions. Was he suspicious? Sad? Guilty? Hurt? I couldn't tell.

I was nervous. I didn't know him well enough. Or maybe I was being extra sensitive with what I knew. He couldn't know what I knew. He wasn't outside with us. How could he?

But he carried on like he did and didn't know what to do with that information. To be honest, I didn't know what to do with it either.

Maya and I shared a more intimate connection than I had been prepared for. At school, they talk about being careful when entering a physical relationship with someone. They drill into our impressionable, hormonal adolescent heads the risks of physical intimacy. Yes, there are steps to take to protect yourself but it's never perfect. You always leave your body vulnerable to all sorts of medical, scientific risks. Best to be avoided altogether.

They don't talk about the risks involved in a relationship like this. They encourage friendships. They celebrate a chaste kind of love. But they don't prepare us for the vulnerability involved in the emotional investments we make and the intimate coupling of hearts. Maya is vulnerable. But so am I.

How can I protect myself?

CHAPTER 32

UNINSPIRED

The city always seems loudest at night, but in the dawn hours, the late-night crowd is on its way home, and the day workers are just getting up. I leave home extra early, avoiding any chance I'd encounter anyone in the family. By the time I get to work, it's bright enough to legitimately be morning. The HotHouse looks sleepy but welcoming. I imagine that if it were alive, it would be yawning.

I hit the switch, and artificial light floods the kitchen. Even that temperamental bulb behaves. Outside the hum of the faulty fluorescent light, it's quiet. I could use quiet. My thoughts are pretty loud on their own.

I go about my duties mechanically. I'm itching for some physical exertion to release this increasing tension so I prep the dining area first. I don't need to, but I do a top down cleaning before I flip the chairs and do a surface clean. I've done this only once before and only because Big G insisted. Today, I find a strange kind of calm in the activity. It's mindless but productive. And it's something I know.

The unknown is terrifying.

By the time I return to the kitchen, the dining area is cleaner than I can remember it ever being. What is there left to do?

I go down my mental checklist and with a pang of panic, realize I still have to come up with a HotHouse special. I hadn't been thinking about it with everything going on but the Wednesday deadline hasn't changed. I've got the time now and the entire kitchen to myself.

I open the refrigerator door and stare aimlessly inside, looking for inspiration. If I'm to make a HotHouse special, then the main ingredient must be the fish fry. Otherwise, it wouldn't really be a HotHouse special. I tap my finger on the top of the open door, staring at the recycled bottles labeled with painters tape.

Sauce. Big G's sauce is what makes the HotHouse so desirable, but in this summer heat, maybe we can offer a different option. One that cools the palette instead of heating it up. My gaze lands on a jar of mayonnaise, one of the standard ingredients in the original sauce. I'm not a big fan but mayonnaise can be cold. That might be a good starting point.

I grab the jar and close the refrigerator door. I put it on the counter and stand back a little, waiting for it to speak to me. Nothing.

I find a small bowl in one of the cabinets and take a spoonful of the mayo to put in the bowl. I return the jar to the refrigerator and resume my pointless staring at a clump of white condiment. The texture is just too lumpy. It needs a little thinning.

When I was four and a half years old, I took it upon myself to make Lola merienda, a light afternoon snack usually eaten a few hours before dinner. I had seen her make tuna fish sandwiches before and thought it was something I could do on my own. The ingredients were easy enough to reach as long as I pushed the stool close to wherever I needed to be.

Except instead of mayo, I used sour cream. They were both white and found in the refrigerator. And I wasn't really reading very well yet.

Lola knew what had happened on her first bite. She didn't hide her surprise very well, and I cried because I knew I'd screwed up. But she added mustard to it with a couple of powdered spices and I thought it ended up tasting better than before. We've made tuna fish sandwiches with sour cream ever since.

I dig for the sour cream in the back of the refrigerator. I take a bit of that and whip it into the mayo. It's a much better consistency. Inspired by the memory, I continue to add other things: a little mustard, pepper, and salt. I smile as I mix, remembering not just the serendipitous sequence of events but also the innocent happy emotions conjured along with it.

How different life was back then. Easy to tears but easy to laughter. And I could always depend on Lola to catch my mistakes and make them better. My heart sinks when I remember how we are now, no longer speaking to each other. If it weren't for that explosive argument, I'd be home right now. Lola and I could be in the kitchen conspiring together for this big culinary opportunity I've been given. Instead, I'm alone.

It's not just Lola I miss. I miss my mom, too. I miss the back and forth of conversation in the kitchen during prep. I miss the barking orders, the loud chatter, and even the ribbing I originally thought was annoying. I miss all of it. In one evening, my entire life was turned upside down and I don't know if I'll ever get it back.

I thought I'd like the quiet but it's deafening in the silence.

I stop mixing. Maybe it's all for the better. I leave for college next year, and I'll be on my own then, right? So what does it matter?

The only dependable thing in life is that everything changes. I think I read that somewhere. I remembered it when we moved four years ago and I had to leave everything I thought I knew behind. Except for Marcus. He didn't care that we weren't in the same neighborhood. He was a constant from my previous life during that change.

Are things going to stay that way after graduation? A neighborhood away is one thing but what about different states? What are relationships going to be like then?

And what about Maya?

I fall back on a stool, landing heavily from the weight of an uncertain future. I stare at the mix on the table. I can't taste it. The idea of it is suddenly unsavory. Not because of a screwed-up recipe but because of my screwed-up life.

I want to pick it up and throw it against the wall. I want the satisfaction of seeing the bowl splinter into powder and its contents splattered everywhere. I want to scream irrationally and rip my clothes off. I want to punch things.

Instead, I pick up the dish, scrape the untested mix into the garbage, and take it to the sink to wash.

Because that's what's expected of me.

CHAPTER 33

BEST FRIENDS WITH ROMEO

Marcus walks into the HotHouse twenty minutes before we open. He looks annoyingly well-rested.

"Well, aren't you a ray of sunshine." There's an unfair edge in my voice. I know Marcus is here because he wants to know what last night was all about.

His eyebrows arch up and his lips form a straight line. Not because he's upset with me but because he knows I'm stressed. "You good, man?"

I shake my head. "Nah."

He doesn't say anything at first. He just looks at me with an expression of deep sympathy. He lowers his chin, balls up a fist, and hits me lightly on the shoulder. Not hard enough for me to even move. "I'll hang out here today," he says.

And that's why he's my best friend.

He sits in his usual spot, leaning his skateboard against the wall. Seeing him there, a fixture in my life, is comforting in a way only Marcus can manage. I'm not so alone anymore. The weight of the new truth I carry is halved. And it doesn't even matter to him what the load is.

The day isn't much different from other days. Nothing particularly notable. Which makes it all the more strange because so much has shifted under the surface.

I vacillate between silence and the small talk I abhor. Marcus navigates my changing moods expertly, giving me just enough rope so I don't fall off the edge. He only offers stories when I initiate, telling me how he finally achieved a kickflip flawlessly at the skatepark. When I lapse into silence, he does too, not needing to fill the space with anything but his presence.

Every so often, I look at Marcus and want to tell him everything. I know he's trustworthy and will keep every secret I tell him. We've kept each other's secrets for years. Even when we fight, which happened a lot in our preteen years, I'm never tempted to break his confidence. And in turn, he's never betrayed me.

But this isn't my secret to share. And Maya deserves the same respect.

An hour before closing, Marcus attempts a deeper conversation. "I take it that your grandmother isn't a fan?"

My stomach muscles clench involuntarily, and my first instinct is to say something rude. But I want to talk about it just as much as he does, without giving up any of Maya's secrets. I need this too. I worry about giving away too much, so all I do is shake my head and sigh.

"That blows," Marcus agrees. "Is it because she's only half Filipino?"

"What?" The question surprises me, throwing me off.

"Like, is it a race thing?"

"No!" I respond a little too aggressively, so I make sure to take it down a notch when I elaborate, scoffing a little for show. "I actually think Filipinos, in general, are on the other extreme end of that racist ruler."

He tilts his head, asking me without asking me.

"I think being part of a country that's been colonized by Spain for over three hundred years, immediately followed by American occupation for almost fifty years gives us some kind of inferiority complex."

"Shouldn't it be the opposite?"

"You'd think." I can't really explain definitively why I think this. It's not like it's a rule of some kind. More like something I've extrapolated over time. I think back to the many examples of this behavior I've witnessed in my life and hope that one can be enough of an explanation. "My dad made a comment before that as long as you've got some mestizo blood in you, you can be a movie star in the Philippines. You don't even need talent."

"Mestizo?"

"I think it's a term used back when Spain still colonized the country to mean anyone with Spanish blood, but it's basically used now to mean anyone with some foreign blood. Preferably the kind that lightens your skin a little."

We both roll our eyes at the same time; it would've been comical if the subject wasn't so serious.

"So Maya is a mestizo?"

"She's a girl, so, technically, that makes her a mestiza."

"So by that logic," he says slowly, attempting to put two and two together in real-time and finding it doesn't equal four, "shouldn't your grandmother be stoked that your girlfriend is mestiza?"

"I thought she might be." I'm careful with what I tell him, trying to avoid giving away too much. "But I think there's bad blood—specifically between my family and Maya's."

"How do they even know each other?"

At the same time, we both say, "The Filipino Connection." In spite of the distasteful conversation, I grin at our impromptu chorus.

"Lemme guess," he says, pointing at me like he's in some kind of game show. "Church."

I make a loud *buzz* noise. "Oooh, so close," I joke, playing along. "Hospital."

Marcus groans dramatically, slapping his open palm on his knee. "I almost said nursing. I knew I should have gone with my first instinct." He leans back on the stool, his elbows on the table behind him. "It's always one or the other."

"You had a fifty-fifty chance," I admit. The temporary levity is quickly passing, and I see in Marcus's expression that he knows it too.

"Hey, look"–his voice is gentler, free from ribbing–"you wouldn't be the first couple in history to deal with feuding families."

"I wouldn't say our families are *feuding*," I argue, bemused.

"Whatever." He dismisses my objection without really considering it. "I'm just saying it's not a completely unique problem."

"If only," I mumble. I want to say more but that would also give away more than I'm willing to share.

He leans forward and puts a hand on my shoulder. "Listen," he insists, "you'll be a full-fledged legal adult in less than a year. At that point, no one can really tell you who you can or can't date."

He isn't wrong about that. But that isn't the real issue. I nod anyway because I can't argue.

"So just suck it up, tell the old folks what they want to hear but don't let it change how you feel about your girl. Get it?"

I raise an eyebrow, my expression sardonic. "Your advice is to lie?"

He grins at me, sticks both hands in his pockets, and lifts his shoulders in a half shrug. "My advice is to keep the peace until then." He relaxes his shoulders. "You don't have to lie. Maybe just be creative?"

I roll my eyes. Marcus is a master slacker capable of getting away with half-truths, an acquired skill from being the baby in the family. I, on the other hand, not so much.

"Not everything in life is black and white, Jay."

"I know, I know." I raise a hand to stop him. "Some things are gray."

"Well, in your case, some things are mestiza."

I hope to make him fully understand how bad his attempt at a joke was by the twisted expression on my face. I don't even want to dignify it with a verbal response. He just winks, which leads me to believe I failed.

Satisfied that he's accomplished his best friend duties, he picks up his skateboard and tucks it under his arm. "You'll be OK," he promises me as he gets ready to leave. "Better that it's your family that's giving you issues instead of hers."

I agree with him. Maya's dad already makes me nervous just because he's Maya's dad. I don't know how I'd be able to handle it if he hated me.

"Oh," he says at the door, turning around like he forgot something. "I know the whole star-crossed lovers thing is a romantic notion and all but promise me you'll avoid the Shakespearean ending, Romeo." Then he calls out behind him as he walks out the door, "Don't die."

I'm glad he's gone before I can respond because I'm not sure I can promise him that.

CHAPTER 34

BETTER TOGETHER

I bike directly to Lafayette Cemetery No. 1 after work. I don't see Maya right away. I look for her at our favorite spot. When she's not there, I make a couple of lazy rounds inside the cemetery. She's still not anywhere I can see, so I check the perimeter outside the walls. Unlike the rest of the Garden District, the sidewalks around the cemetery are broken. No amount of patching would help this as the strong roots from the well-fed trees that surround the park easily break the concrete from underneath. I ride on the road, which is a slightly better option.

Finally, sweating from the afternoon sun and my futile search, I visit her house. I ring the bell without much confidence. An afternoon of failure has lowered my expectations. When she answers, my spirits rise.

I don't imagine her to be in the best of conditions, given what we both went through last night, but the Maya that answers the door surprises me nonetheless. Her hair is a mess of loose strands; I wonder why she even bothered trying to pull it back in a ponytail. Her eyes are red, and the thin skin beneath them is dark and swollen. She's been crying, but I see no evidence of tears on her cheeks. Her lips are pressed together in a straight line, the edges downturned. A frown is so unusual on her that it's the most significant factor that makes her less Maya than anything else.

I look down at my shoes, studying the scuffed sneakers like they hold the secrets to making this less uncomfortable. "I looked for you at our tree," I mumble. I don't mean for it to sound accusatory but hearing the words spoken aloud makes it seem so.

Maya apologizes. "I didn't know if you still wanted to see me."

I look back up at her, intending to search her eyes but they're downcast. Apparently, her house slippers are just as fascinating as my sneakers.

"Why wouldn't I want to see you?"

She meets my eyes, and I see her eyebrows curl toward each other. It's an expression that looks somewhere between uncertainty and despair. "Because I am who I am."

I tilt my head to the side. I don't know why this should surprise me. She has always had such empathy and concern for others; of course she would worry about me even before herself. There's an ache in my chest more painful than the anxiety in my stomach.

"Because of who you are?" I echo. "You mean my girlfriend?"

I meant for that to sound lighthearted, hoping to ease her sadness but instead, she bursts out crying. I don't look to see if anyone is around to witness this. I take her in my arms and let her cry—not so daintily—on my shoulder.

"Why are you so nice to me?" It takes her longer than usual to finish that sentence because she sobs in between.

I kiss her on the top of her hair. Her hair doesn't smell like her usual shampoo but more like the ducks in her backyard. "We covered this," I say, trying to lighten the mood. "You're my girlfriend."

She sobs louder. I look around, and I'm grateful there's no random person walking their dog or a gaggle of tourists taking pictures. I don't know what else to do. I think I'm failing in my objective but she finally pulls away from me and wipes her eyes. She grabs my hand, leads me inside the house, and closes the door behind us. Her hand is unusually cold, not fresh-from-the-air-conditioning cold but more lack-of-circulation cold.

"I'm sorry," she apologizes, trying to pull herself together. "I'm a mess. I need to wash up. Meet you in the kitchen?" She doesn't wait for my answer and turns toward a part of the house I haven't seen yet, her bedroom.

I remove my shoes, put them away neatly, and head to the kitchen. I peek out the window and see that her ducks are corralled in their pen, hiding from the sun. I've never had a pet but I would never have considered ducks. They are her little feathered support group, keeping her family secret and rallying for her. I telepathically send them my thanks.

I know where most things are by now and set out glasses for the two of us. I'm in the middle of extracting ice from the tray when she returns, hair in place, face washed. There are still signs that she'd been crying but as long as she doesn't burst into tears again in the next half hour or so, that will probably go away too. She is wearing a tank top and loose overalls instead of the oversized shirt and shorts she had on when she opened the door. She smiles, not enough for dimples but a valiant attempt.

I put down the ice tray, take her face in my hands, and kiss her gently on the lips.

She giggles. "Your hands are so cold!" She pulls away from me. "And wet!"

I wanted it to be a sweet gesture. I clearly failed but it's good to hear her light, silly laugh. I grin. "Count your blessings," I say, returning to the ice tray. "It's better than hot and moist."

"Ew!" She shudders. "That's such a gross word."

"What is? Moist?"

She shudders again. "Yeah. There's something about it. Like, just, ew."

I didn't know this about her and I like that I have new information. Information that can be exploited. "What's wrong with … *moist*?" I say the word slowly and with exaggerated emphasis. She dances in place, shaking her head and puckering her face. She makes a show of putting her hands over her ears, overextending her elbows in the air to make a point.

"Stop it!" she demands, but she's laughing.

"How are you so affected by this?" I laugh. "It's just a word."

She lowers her hands. I pretend that I'm about to say it again, and her hands are back on her ears. She glowers at me. "Don't you dare!" she warns. She's adorable, like a little angry kitten trying to threaten a Rottweiler. I can't resist. I hold a hand up in promise. She's suspicious but she releases her ears. "Words have power," she claims defensively.

"I don't think that's what they meant."

"It applies."

She's no longer crying. That's what matters. I don't know what she sees in my expression but hers softens, and she leans against me. My hands are occupied, so I lean my head on hers as a gesture of communality. "You OK?" I ask quietly, as if I'm worried about being overheard.

"Not really," she admits in the same quiet voice. "But better that you're here."

I know Maya would rather be outside with the ducks but it's too hot, so we stay in the kitchen. There are stools on either side of the island, just like in my house. We sit across from each other, our fingers brushing as we nurse our glass of sweet iced tea.

"I didn't think you'd want to be with me anymore," she repeats. I brace myself for more crying but she seems more stable now. "This is heavy stuff."

I get it. I stare at our hands. Every now and then our knuckles brush against each other. "Yeah," I agree reluctantly because we don't need to sugarcoat things right now. We need to be honest. "It's deal-breaker territory."

I see her fingers tighten around her glass and I almost regret my honesty. But I hear her exhale a slow, deliberate breath, and I know we're on the same page.

We're not talking about an acne breakout before prom or a secret crush. This isn't a dumb typical teenage problem. You won't find this kind of conflict in an afternoon sitcom with canned laughter. This is in the impossible-soap-opera domain. And not even like a family secret involving a twin sibling back from the dead and an illegitimate baby. It's more like finding out your girlfriend's family is in the mob. And your girlfriend is the one that's taking over.

"Well, you haven't changed yet, so it's not like you've hurt anyone," I say. No one should be judged for what they're capable of doing, only what they decide to do. I'm trying to find the loophole in a contract with the devil.

Either what I said or how I said it rubs her the wrong way because she pulls away slightly so that there's a little space between our knuckles. I know her well enough to notice the tension in her shoulders.

"*Yet*," she repeats, her voice tinged with bitterness. "And it's not as if it's something I can control when it happens."

"I know that." I'm taken aback by her tone. I don't understand. "That's what I'm saying."

She looks frustrated. Her shoulders slump, and she lets out a heavy breath. She stares at her drink and fidgets with her glass. "My mom was a good person," she insists as though I had said otherwise.

"I didn't say she wasn't."

Maya doesn't look at me. It's as if she doesn't even hear me. "When she lived in the province, that's just the way things were. It's not fair to hold her to a different standard." I don't say anything because she's not listening anyway. "That's like saying soldiers at war shouldn't hurt anyone because that's not something you do when you're not at war."

She looks up at me, her eyes burning with defiance. She's daring me to argue. "That's not fair," she says again. "There are different circumstances."

I nod. I'm not challenging her.

"She did her best not to hurt anyone when she came here. Different circumstances." Her voice is smaller now. She sounds as fragile as she did last night. She's repeating the same things she's already told me. "She was a good person. She chose death over hurting anyone else. She was *not* a monster." Her grip on her glass tightens.

I reach out to her, laying one hand gently over hers. "I know," I assure her. Her grip relaxes.

"What she did was so horrible, Jay." The sudden change of tone from defensive to tortured is a glimpse of the conflict that she's dealing with. This is a conversation she's had with herself before. Many times. "When she was a manananggal, she must've devastated so many families."

My mind flashes to the image of my mom bleeding on the sidewalk like Lola had described, and I'm sick to my stomach. Maybe I imagine it to be much more dramatic than it had really been. And before I can stop, I'm thinking of an alternate reality in which I'm an older brother. How would it have been to really be a kuya? Would my family be happier? Was my family one of the casualties?

Maya must see the change in me because she goes from introspective to concerned. It's not about her family anymore. It's about mine. "I'm sorry."

I don't know what to say because I don't know how to feel. Should I be angry? Isn't this an affront against my family? And if it is, why am I numb and confused? When I look back at her, the rest of the world melts, and all I want to do is make it all go away. I want us to be together.

Star-crossed lovers, Marcus had called us. The idea of an ill-fated future stirs a greater emotion in me than the *what-ifs* of my imagination.

"It wasn't *you*," I insist, perhaps for my benefit as well as hers. "Maybe that was your mom's struggle but it isn't yours."

"Not yet, anyway." She's pessimistic, and I won't have it.

"You're a mixed kid," I remind her. "That changes things."

"I still have my mother's blood," she reminds me. I hate that she's arguing with me about this but at the same time, maybe it's a good thing. I can convince us both.

"But you're also your father's daughter." There's a confidence in my voice that surprises even me, and I think it's what makes her pay attention. "Your blood *is* diluted. I mean, scientifically, doesn't that make a difference?" I actually don't know. I did well in my chemistry class but only because I turned in all my assignments and know how to take tests. I didn't actually retain much of it. Maya doesn't argue, so I press on. "And it makes a difference that you're *here* and not in the Philippines."

"That doesn't change anything."

"Different circumstances," I parrot back to her. "You see it all the time. People like us, immigrant children, born here, grow up differently." I can see I'm not making a convincing case. "I mean, I'm already the tallest one in my family. Lola says it's the hormones in American milk." I roll my eyes and see Maya react positively to that. "Or maybe it's the fluoride in the water. Or the kind of allergy-inducing pollen in the air." I make wild motions with my arms because I see that it makes her smile.

"My point is," I continue, "environment *is* a factor. Whether it's the hormone-injected cows or something like water and air quality, it matters where you are. Not just culturally. Everything changes."

"Everything?"

"Think about it," I challenge her. "We're like fish out of water. We weren't physically meant to live here, right? Like evolutionarily, we were meant to be on the equator or something."

She laughs. On one hand, she may think my ideas are foolish but on the other, she's not crying. I'm onto something, and I can't keep the excitement from making me talk even faster. I grasp at every idea and say it aloud before they're gone. "Or … or … like orchids!"

"Oh, first we were fish but we're *plants* now."

"Well, we're all living things, aren't we?" I dare her to argue. She doesn't. "And orchids, they need to have a specific environment to even survive. We take them here, and they struggle. So we put them in greenhouses, special soil, and measure how much water they get. All just to simulate an environment they were meant for."

"Orchids. How do you know so much about orchids?"

I give her a sarcastic look. "Like there's a Filipino grandmother in all of America that isn't trying to keep one alive?" She bites her lip to keep from laughing again. I'm on a roll. "All I know is that trying to keep orchids alive is a pain. But that proves my point. Your mom grew up in a completely different environment. Then she comes here to have you. You're changed."

I start counting things off with my fingers. "You're only half Filipino, you were born in a different environment, and raised in different conditions. There are so many factors in our favor here."

"You sound like some kind of scientist." She is teasing me but appears more receptive to the idea. "Like you're presenting a paper in front of a panel of your peers."

"I don't know if you know this about me yet." I cross my arms in front of me and lean back a little, trying to exude a confidence I don't have. "But I'm *very* smart."

"Oh, are you now?"

"I am," I say, raising an eyebrow intentionally like I see suave men in suits do on TV. "You should listen to me."

There's a shift in the tone of the conversation, it's in the air. She's searching my eyes, and her thin, wavering smile dips a little. I wish I could give her what she's looking for. "What is it you're trying to tell me?"

The question is heavy with implication. It hangs in the air between us like a marker, defining everything before this and everything that happens next. I lean forward and put both my hands over hers.

"We can beat this together."

She doesn't react immediately. She looks down at our hands, and I wonder if I was a bit too forward. But she doesn't move. I squeeze. When she looks back at me, her eyes are brimming with tears, but there's a braver smile that wasn't there before. Hope fills my chest before I identify what it is.

When she removes her hands from under mine, it isn't to retreat. She reaches under her hair to unhook her mother's pendant and remove it. She cradles the medallion in her hands, looking down at it with an expression I can't translate. Then she stretches her hands to me like a formal offering.

"Here," she says with a confidence she has not demonstrated recently. "Take it."

Her mother's agimat? An heirloom from a homeland on the other side of the world. She wears it all the time and constantly turns to it for comfort. It's too big of a present to be given so casually and for no occasion. This doesn't make any sense.

"Why?"

"Because you have such clarity of spirit. You're the only one who can get me through this. And you'll need all the help you can get."

CHAPTER 35

REBELLIOUS AVOIDANCE

By the time I bike home, it's well after dark. I had dinner at Maya's house with her and her father, intentionally delaying the inevitable. I see a figure at the window and judging from the height, it's Mom. I know I'm walking into a fight when I walk into my house.

My hand closes involuntarily around the pendant Maya gave me. I've only been wearing it a few hours and I'm already acting like Maya, as if it had been with me all my life. I smile, feeling like a little part of her is with me.

I don't agree with her. Everyone *but* me has this clarity of spirit she claims she sees in me. The agimat feels heavier when I let go of it, like it's also ladened with the responsibility of what it represents: Maya's faith in me.

I brace for the yelling I'm sure to receive when I open the door but Mom just looks up from washing the dishes and asks me in a surprisingly calm voice if I've eaten already. "Kumain ka na ba?" She doesn't bother translating.

I nod, waiting for the lecture that's sure to follow. But she doesn't say anything else. She shuts off the water, dries her hands on the dish towel, and leaves the room. That's it. No other conversation.

It's not that late yet, and I can hear Dad's muffled voice in the other room. He's asking a question, and Mom answers him with a single word. They lapse into silence. I can't tell if Lola is with them or in her room. I stand there, one hand on the ladder leading up to my room, wondering what my next move should be.

This is unusual. The quiet throws me off. I know I've broken so many of the cardinal unwritten house rules. I left this morning without a goodbye. I stayed out after dark. I didn't call to let them know where I was. I didn't even greet Mom properly. She didn't say a single thing about anything.

Is this the silent treatment? Some parenting ploy they picked up from a weekly family sitcom on TV? I look up to the entrance of my room and wonder if they had done something there. What kind of punishment awaits me there? Did they go through my stuff? My suspicion quickly turns into anger, and I haul myself up the ladder.

Nothing is out of place. Even the new items I added to the pile of laundry on the floor are exactly where I left them this morning. I stand to one side, surveying the room with a more discriminating eye. Nothing is different.

I'm stumped. I slide into a sitting position on the floor, my back to the wall. My shoulders slump, and I hang my head. It's been such a long day. I don't think I have the energy left to process what's happening at home after a full day of work and the emotional tightrope walk with Maya. I want to throw things and yell but at the same time, I just want to curl up inside an invisible shell and hide from reality. I'm so done.

I don't think I can handle the loaded atmosphere around my parents or face Lola's self-righteousness. I take the coward's way out and wait until I think they're either all asleep or at least in their rooms before I go back down and shower.

As usual, the rhythm of the spray puts me in a contemplative mood. A moment of reflection might often inspire but tonight, it's a downward spiral, much like the soapy water circling the drain. I stare at my feet and think about how things have gone from being perfect to how they are now.

Two days ago, I was in the ideal relationship with the ideal girl. I was making delicious creations in the kitchen. Opportunities at work were opening up. Mom wasn't even annoying. It was the peak of a perfect summer.

I was able to avoid confrontation for the most part today. I wonder how long I can contain things before tensions hit critical mass and explode in my face. I have no doubt that it will. There's no coming out of this unscathed.

It's like knowing I failed the quiz but still having to wait for the paper to come back showing me how badly I failed. Degrees of failure. That's what my future looks like at this point.

I'm only vaguely aware of the motions I go through to dry off, dress, and brush my teeth. My physical self is doing all these things but I'm mentally in the future, berated by the actions of my past self.

I study myself in the mirror between brushing and rinsing. My hair, still damp from the shower, needs to be cut. I've let it grow too long. There are dark bags under my eyes that weren't there before. And I'm pretty sure those are five new zits on my forehead. At least none of them are smack in the middle of my nose like on the first day of freshman year.

My options are limited. I hold my breath when I open the door. When I recognize that I'm acting like a scared mouse checking to see if predators are waiting for me outside, I let my breath out. I try to convince myself I'm braver than vermin.

The hallway is empty. I practically run to the safety of my room. There's no victory when I make it without being seen. I hang my towel up and fall back on my bed with an audible groan. I press the palms of my hands over my eyes. I'm such a coward.

I'm clearly not ready to deal with consequences just yet.

CHAPTER 36

ON THE SEVENTH DAY

Just like yesterday, I arrive to work earlier than usual. We open later on Sundays, so this would have been the best time to sleep in, but I wasn't going to do that. Most people would balk at having to work on a Sunday but it's one of my favorite things about this job. It pays time and a half and it gives me a bona fide excuse to skip church.

Church is a verb for my family. It involves more than just a weekly visit. Mass is a one-hour service that involves readings, lectures, singing, and a sip of wine. I used to love attending. I didn't know what was happening for the most part, but we were there so often that at one point, I was allowed to pass the offertory basket around. It let me think I was grown up and involved. I didn't have much else on my schedule when I was ten years old.

But as I got older, it was less a covenant with God and more like losing my Sunday morning. It's not that I don't understand things. I know all the basic Bible stories and even the not-so-basic ones. I aced my religion education classes and breezed through the requisite sacraments appropriate for a good Catholic of my age. I get all that. No problem.

My spiritual journey is probably stunted. It's all in my head but not in my heart. I see the rest of the family commit but I'm just going through the motions. As far as the world can tell, I'm a devoted Catholic. I think my family sees my heart isn't in it but no one calls me out on it. Maybe Lola prays a little extra for my soul but my dad and I share an arrangement of sorts. He looks at me with understanding but also with a hint of *you'll understand when you're older.*

Today, everyone was up early. We follow the tradition of not eating an hour before mass in preparation for the Eucharist, the commemoration of The Last Supper. Breakfast is earlier to accommodate the required fasting time. Since I wasn't partaking today, I took bread from the pantry and threw it in my backpack for a later meal. I can have breakfast whenever I want.

I heard them all in the other room but I wasn't just skipping out on church today; I was also skipping out on any kind of confrontation. So I ducked out of the house before anyone called out to me. I felt guilty, but not enough to change directions.

At work, I'm alone again. That's better. Breakfast for one. I make myself some eggs Benedict sans the bacon but add some of our signature spices to the hollandaise sauce. Is it even still considered eggs Benedict? It would be better with a muffin but I've learned to be adaptive. I toast the bread on the grill and add an unhealthy amount of butter. Butter makes everything better.

The first bite is good but I miss having the extra protein. It's not my first choice but you work with what you've got, right? I keep the dish next to the grill in hopes it will stay warm while I deep fry a few fish sticks for my makeshift dish.

It would have been better with bacon, in my opinion, but the HotHouse fish fry brings something to the table that can't be found elsewhere. I pull a tall stool up close to the prep counter. I'm not dining at some fancy restaurant or by the water but this suits me well. I welcome the solitude. I'm never as comfortable anywhere as I am in the kitchen. And on a Sunday morning with my world in turmoil, this is my church.

My communion in this meal isn't with a higher being but with myself. Here, alone, I can shed all the roles I have to play for everyone else. I don't have to be the responsible son, dependable friend, approachable boyfriend, or conscientious student. I don't have to prove myself.

I can admit frustrations, fears, and my latest anxiety. Here, I can celebrate personal accomplishment, righteously earned or otherwise. I don't have to defend my feelings. I don't have to worry about coming off like I'm a poser. I can be full of myself and there's no one around to tell me it's not a good look.

I obviously like being with Maya. And Marcus knows me more than I know myself sometimes. But there are days when I'm convinced that if they really knew me, they wouldn't like me so much. There are days when I don't like myself.

I'm not particularly proud of my current self. I don't have direction. I just react to things that happen and hope for the best. Granted, this isn't your typical weekly teen drama dilemma, but I still think I'm not handling things as well as I should.

What I need is a plan. It's like cooking; I need to first envision what I want the product to be and then figure out how to get there. I almost never strictly follow a recipe unless it's for work. And I often wing it on my way. But there's always that end goal, and that's what I need to identify now.

In a perfect world, everything we're worrying about turns out to be nothing. Maya doesn't inherit her mom's condition. My family meets her and adores her. Lola and I are speaking again. I graduate with honors and go off to whatever college or university my parents want me to go to, which means Mom will get off my case. I don't care where it is as long as it's far away from here.

Maya comes with me. I'm an adult and have the kind of freedom I've been waiting for all my life.

I still have one more bite left on the plate, but I put down the fork. I don't live in a perfect world. I never have.

I unclasp the agimat from my neck and flip it over and over between my fingers. There isn't much on the back but the stamped image in front taunts me. *A pivotal moment in one's life*, Maya had said. *Who you were before the light or who you become when it's taken away.*

What happens if Maya does turn into this monster on her eighteenth birthday? Do I break up with her? Go off to college and forget I know what I know? I mean, it won't be my problem anymore, so I shouldn't care. And who am I kidding? Even if I go to whatever college or university my parents want me to go to, I'm almost one hundred percent sure that they'll still be on my case, if not more so. I'll be an adult, sure, but I'll also always have to answer to someone for something.

My shoulders slump. I can dream all I want but there are so many things out of my control that will just screw everything up, no matter what I do. Was there ever really any light in my life to begin with?

I sigh aloud, return the medallion with everything it represents back around my neck, and dump the last bite of food into the garbage.

Unlike the church my family goes to, there's no worshiping in mine.

And sometimes there's no hope either.

CHAPTER 37

GARLIC, THE MAGICAL ROOT

What are you going to do?"

Kitchens have been my default setting the past few days. If I'm not at work, I'm at Maya's. Today the HotHouse is closed. Maya is sitting across from me, peeling a balut egg for herself. She offered me one, but I declined.

"I don't know." I frown at the partially formed chick. Even though I know theoretically every egg could eventually be a chicken, or in this case, a duck, it's still unsettling to see the embryo. "I think that one has feathers." My stomach churns.

Maya turns the chick, still attached to the veiny yolk, over in her fingers. "It's not my favorite," she admits. "But it's supposed to help. That's why my mom raised ducks. So she'd always have fresh eggs available."

"Oh."

"You thought I just really liked ducks, huh?"

"I mean, yeah." There's no point denying it. "Lots of people keep ducks as pets. Sure." I'm not very convincing, and the ghost of a smile deepens.

"It's a plus that they're darlings," she agrees. Knowing that she eats it out of necessity and not enjoyment makes it a little better for me. "I'm surprised it's such a delicacy in the Philippines."

"Maybe the Philippines has more manananggals than we think." I regret saying it right away, wondering if my glibness offends her. But she's unfazed.

"Honestly, I wouldn't be surprised." She sprinkles freshly chopped garlic on one end, dips it in the rock salt she has on her plate, and takes a bite. Her face contorts, puckering and grimacing. Setting aside the aesthetics of the meal, I know balut actually tastes good. She's not reacting to the taste so much as the burning sensation she experiences when she eats garlic.

Garlic is universally considered to be a vampire deterrent. It's also historically been used to ward off evil spirits and monsters. A lot of people would consider raw garlic to be spicy. If the legendary properties of garlic are true, and there is any trace of the monster in Maya, the sensation must hit differently.

"I think when Spain colonized the Philippines back in the fifteen hundreds, they called every powerful woman a manananggal," she continues after she swallows. "Propaganda to subjugate the women and control the population. It's like the Salem witch trials, the Filipino edition."

"But without the trials part," I point out. "Or witches."

"I have a theory." She repeats the ceremony of garlic sprinkling and salt dipping. She does not continue until after she takes another bite and swallows. As she speaks, one eye is closed so tightly that future crow's feet lines appear on her face. The other eye is so wide open her pupil is a small island in a sea of white. I stifle a laugh at how silly she looks.

"A theory about what?"

"So, here's what I think. Listen," she demands. "The Spanish accused every woman they couldn't handle as being a manananggal. And after taking all the abusive and false accusations, the albularyos–"

"What's an albularyo?"

"Oh, sorry." She tilts her head and looks off to the side as if the answer were pinned to the refrigerator. "A witch doctor? I guess the equivalent of a voodoo priest or priestess?"

It makes sense in context after she explains. I nod to show her I understand.

"I think the albularyos helped *create* manananggals. I mean, if these big, bad invaders are going to accuse you of being something you aren't, let's see how they like it when they actually get what they want, right?" There's a glint in her eyes, and she doesn't wait for me to respond. "I bet the women all had enough of the lies. I bet they wanted revenge."

She flashes me a triumphant grin, then takes another bite of her quickly disappearing daily dose of anti-manananggal. "I bet manananggals developed in the province as a measure against colonization."

"I thought you were *born* into the curse."

"Well, yeah, *now*. But centuries ago. According to the Spanish, there was a sudden rise of them. It's got to be an army. A manananggal army!"

"What's that recruitment brochure like? 'Fly amongst the birds.' " I fanned my hands in front of me like I'm performing a magic trick. " 'Be a manananggal. It's only one of the perks!' "

"Shut up. You're such a dork."

I laugh. "I mean, how does that even happen? From a bite? Like rabies? Or like from the blood of another manananggal?"

"You're confusing a manananggal with a vampire." Her tone is almost an admonishment. "No, I personally think the vampires have it easy. According to what I could figure out, a *new* mananaggal is created by eating the blackened chick created from the throat of an existing mananaggal."

I physically recoil at the idea. "That's so gross!"

She laughs without humor. "You think? But it tracks, right? I mean, *being* a mananaggal is gross." A sadness descends on her like a shadow, darkening her face.

"What is it with the chicks and eggs?" I keep my tone light, hoping it will pull her away from the shadows. "You have to eat a chick to become one or you have to eat many chicks to *not* become one."

The darkness retreats. "Maybe because it has wings?"

"It could be worse, you know," I remind her. "You could be eating bugs."

Her laughter is less stiff now. She polishes off the last of what isn't a bug, piling it on with the remaining chopped garlic. "That probably wouldn't taste as good. I'll say this for balut, it's like chicken soup—a hearty comfort dish."

"With lots and lots of garlic."

She clears away the dishes. "Also yummy." She throws the egg pieces and the hard white part of the egg in the trash. "Even if it burns."

"How bad does it hurt to eat it?"

Her back is to me as she washes the dishes but she answers me without turning. "It's like eating the hottest hot sauce as it goes down but the moment it's down my throat, it stops hurting. Not like hot sauce, that just burns no matter how much water you drink."

"You're supposed to drink milk, not water."

She turns her head to look at me, checking to see if I'm serious. When I don't volunteer more information, she asks, "Milk? With hot sauce?"

"It's not because they taste good together," I clarify. "There's something in the milk that helps smother the spice."

She considers this, finds no reason to argue, and returns to washing dishes. "It's probably stupid but I like to think that every time I have it, it kills a little of that monster in me."

Hope is a fragile thing but it's also the force that holds our spirit together. I'm not going to let her give up on that. I've never believed in good luck charms or magical cures but if it gives Maya hope, I'll preach it like it's the truth. "Garlic is a manananggal inoculation."

She's done washing the dishes, and she turns around with a smile. "Yes, exactly!" As always, her smile is contagious, and I find myself mirroring it. "But garlic is so much yummier than a shot in the arm."

I'm hit with a sudden inspiration. "Garlic," I say without any other explanation. I half rise from my seat, and I know my smile is even wider. She sees my wild expression and must know there's something going in my head that she can't interpret. She looks surprised and a little wary.

"Yes"–she nods–"garlic."

"That's it!" I exclaim, pushing the stool back and closing the space between us so I can kiss her. "You're a genius!"

She doesn't shy away from me but looks bewildered. "Of course I am." She laughs. "But tell me why?"

I let her go and rummage through her kitchen without permission. I'm comfortable enough not to ask and confident that I'm welcome to it. "That's what's missing from the sauce. Garlic." I gather all the same ingredients I had the other day at the HotHouse kitchen and quickly mix them together. She hands me a bulb of garlic. I take it from her, loving the way she knows what I want before having to ask for it.

When the white dip is fully incorporated, I use the same chopping board she had used for mincing her garlic earlier and proceed to mince the entire bulb. I add it to the mixture and blend it together.

"That's a lot of garlic," she comments unnecessarily.

I grin. "Yes, it is." Our eyes meet, and she grins as well. "This will taste better if I let it sit for a while, but …" I grab a teaspoon and dip the tip of it in the sauce. Then I have her try it.

She doesn't hesitate. As soon as she tastes it, her eyes grow wide but she smiles. "Wow," she exclaims. "That tastes great! And, strangely, not as spicy."

I hadn't intended on it being a more palatable way for her to get her inoculation but it's a win regardless. "It's the sour cream, I think. It functions like milk."

"This is going to taste great with the HotHouse fish fry. I may like this even more than the sawsawan you brought before."

"Probably because it doesn't burn as much," I point out. A ridiculous idea pops into my mind, and I say it without giving much thought to how insensitive it sounds. "It's funny that you can defeat a manananggal with spices."

Her smile drops a little, but I can see she's making an effort to catch it. "It's not actually the spice that kills us. It's the sunlight. The garlic or salt prevents the joining but it's the sunlight that actually kills."

It was a tasteless joke on my part, and I regret saying it. Every time I'm finally winning the race, I step into something smelly.

"It makes sense, actually," she continues, talking to herself aloud more than she is talking to me. "A manananggal is a product of darkness, so light will always be able to defeat it."

I lean my hands on the kitchen island and hang my head,

ashamed for ruining a good moment with my thoughtlessness. The pendant she gave me swings away from my chest. I stare at it in the long stretch of silence that follows her hopeless revelation.

"Clarity of spirit," I mumble.

She looks at me but her eyes are still out of focus. I look back at her with renewed determination.

"Clarity of spirit," I repeat. When she doesn't react, I stand up straight, my hand on the agimat. "You said there's a spell or a ceremony or something that can imbue it with powers."

She nods, still confused by my sudden change in attitude. "Yes, strength that can be called upon in the future."

"Let's do it."

"Do what?"

"Imbue it with strength or whatever." I remove the cord from around my neck and let the pendant hang between us. "Let's do it."

"What, now?"

I walk around the island so I can be closer to her. She stands up to meet me and I take her in my arms and lean my forehead against hers. She closes her eyes instinctively, and I do the same.

"You said the one thing that was needed to make this happen was clarity of spirit," I whisper, feeling an intensity I need to properly convey. "I have that, Maya. Take it. Let it be your strength. You know how to perform the ceremony. Let's make that happen."

I lean back so I can open my eyes and see her. She opens her eyes to meet mine, looking vulnerable and hopeful. It's fuel for my resolve. I narrow my eyes and lick my lips, ready to win whatever battle needs fighting.

"Maya, together we can beat this thing."

CHAPTER 38

TOURISTS IN OUR OWN TOWN

The ceremony requires a few items that Maya doesn't have readily available. We take the two streetcars we need to get to Decatur St. in the French Quarter to shop. I don't know the first thing about tribe magic but I'd have thought shopping for ingredients at tourist traps would be near the bottom of the list.

The store is on the first floor of a three-story brick building with Mardi Gras paraphernalia still hanging from the iron balconies. Full-length painted shutters frame three large windows the same size as the door. An A-frame chalkboard leans against the entrance, and incense smoke ribbons from a small dish behind the sign.

We squeeze by loudly dressed tourists in large sunglasses and even larger hats. It smells like sunblock and sweat in the crowd, peppered with a bit of spiced smoke. Maya knows exactly where to go. She grabs my hand and pulls me behind her when we're threatened to be separated by a midwestern couple with matching shirts. Her hand is a little sweaty but strangely cool. I squeeze to let her know I'm behind her.

It feels like we've walked into a kitschy Halloween store, heavy on the candles and jars. It's packed from floor to ceiling, as if they have too much inventory to fit in one place. An old mirrored bureau is used as a makeshift altar of sorts with a bunch of different photos and offerings. Whether they are sincere or for show, I can't tell.

A soundtrack of spooky sounds plays from hidden speakers. I look up to see if I can find them but instead, there are mirrors, masks, and idols. The chaos is everywhere. It's an onslaught to the senses. But that's exactly the sort of thing that attracts the tourists with all their vacation money.

Maya isn't fazed by this. She continues past the wooden brooms and novelty voodoo dolls. Near the back of the store is a shelf of raw materials: rocks, leaves, feathers, and spices. The goods are loose in baskets, kept in jars, or wrapped in cloth. The tourists don't go this deep into the store. They stay close to the cashier, asking questions about the little hex bags segregated by color.

No one asks if we need help. I see the cashier, probably the owner's college dropout kid, give us a suspicious sideways look through his long unwashed hair. He's possibly gauging if we are the type of teens to steal the low-hanging fruit merchandise. But the items on the shelf are all fairly inexpensive, however odd they might be.

I study a jar of dried bones without touching it. I can't identify what animal they are from. The jar is generically labeled. Maya is looking at the herbs. "We need white sage," she tells me. "It's the closest thing to guava leaves around here."

"Guava leaves?"

"You know what a guava is, right?" She asks me without judgment. She tilts her head to the side and waits. I've been put on the spot.

"A fruit?"

It sounds like a dumb answer but it's the right one. She nods. "It's pretty abundant in the Philippines, and the leaves are the preferred medium used in ancient Filipino practice to cleanse the spirit and environment."

The sage isn't in a jar. It's rolled together with twine in bundles and left loosely in a basket. Sage is a spice, and it smells rather pleasant. I bring it close to my nose and inhale. It has a strong fresh, earthy smell. "I can cook with that," I tell her, handing her a bundle.

"No," she corrects me. "You cook with regular sage. This is white sage. It's stronger and doesn't work the same in dishes but it's what we use for incense." She turns her attention to the bowls of rocks.

"What are we looking for?" I ask, scanning the collection of colorful stones.

"Alum."

I purse my lips. "Yeah, I don't know what that is."

"In the Philippines, it's called tawas and used as deodorant." She's studying a random rock too intently, and I know she's baiting me.

"Are you trying to tell me something?" I make a show of smelling my armpits. She grins, the dimple a deep imprint of delight. It's exactly how she had hoped I would react.

"If the shoe fits?" She's openly teasing me, a favored change from her previously hopeless mood. I'm happy to take any bait for her to remain happy.

"Oh, really?" I wrap my arms around her and pull her close to me. She stifles a squeal but doesn't attempt to break away.

"Ew! So sweaty and stinky!" she protests, laughing.

I lean my face close to her neck. Her hair tickles and smells of flowers. It's pretty and well-suited to her. The heat from her breath warms my neck and sounds louder in my ears.

"Get a room!" a voice admonishes us.

I break away immediately. It's the cashier, shaking his head and giving us a bad look. I lift my arms up in surrender and look down.

"This is a store, not the back seat of your dad's car," he adds in a grouchy tone.

"Sorry," I say automatically and share a look with Maya. We both try not to laugh. We're failing at looking sincere.

"Whatever," he grumbles, turning to the new customer who comes up to the counter. His angry expression instantly changes into an obviously practiced customer service smile. We're no longer worthy of his attention.

"That's what you get," Maya says, swinging her hip to bump mine. I don't retaliate.

"We really need deodorant for this?" I ask instead.

"It's also widely used as an astringent and to heal open wounds and sores," she says. She picks up a clear crystal that looks like a large rock salt. "There are many uses for this."

She collects a few other things, including a small jar of long matches. When we bring it to the counter, the cashier's stage smile falls, and he rolls his eyes. Unlike the purchases of tourists, ours don't add up to as much. I hand him cash before Maya opens her bag.

We don't try to win him over. He puts our items in a paper bag and hands it to me with my change. I pocket the coins but hand the bag over to Maya. She has her little backpack already open and stuffs the items inside. We thank the cashier, and he grunts a response. For some reason, this makes me want to laugh. I peek at Maya, and she has a similar expression. This shared moment just makes me adore her.

We escape from the confines of the shop and stand out in the middle of the street, unconcerned about oncoming traffic. The streets are too tight for any cars to come barreling down at high speeds, so it's easy to step away when we see one coming. People stay on the sidewalk more for the shade than for safety.

"Do we have everything we need?" I ask.

Maya turns her face up to the sun and squints. "Almost. Now all we need is the moon."

CHAPTER 39

STORING THE LIGHT

I thought we would perform the ceremony in her backyard but she takes us to the cemetery. Something about being under the watchful eyes of her mother's spirit and the strength of generational blood. She sets up on the steps of her mother's tomb, laying down a small dish the size of a dessert plate with great purpose. She mumbles something as she does this. Whether it is to herself or to the spirits, I don't know. I look up at the clear moon, giving her a little privacy.

"Oh, cool, a full moon," I observe.

"No, it was a full moon yesterday. This is a waning gibbous. It comes after a full moon. You can see a sliver of light missing right off one side." She doesn't look up from her task but doesn't seem annoyed by the interruption. "It's always better with a full moon but there's still plenty of light for this to be effective."

Candles are set up on either side of the small dish, where strips of paper look like they've already been burned. She lights the candles with one of the long matches we bought at the shop, and when she touches it to the center of the dish, the strips of paper flash a bright flame, then die almost instantly. The suddenness of it startles me but I cover up my surprise with a cough. Maya doesn't seem to notice.

She puts one end of the sage to the flame of the dying match until the end turns black and starts to smoke. By the time the match dies completely, there's a strong ribbon of smoke coming from the wrapped bundle of dried leaves. She drops the entire bundle into the dish.

The burning white sage tinges the air with an unusual scent. In addition to the pungent smell of burning there's also a kind of sweetness that mixes with the summer smells of the other plants around us. It's not entirely unpleasant.

Maya grinds the alum with a small marble mortar and pestle. We have a similar one at home that we use to crush spices for our food. She does this with surprisingly little effort. What looks like solid rock breaks into a fine powder, reflecting the candlelight when it hits it at just the right angle. She sprinkles the powder all over the steps around the dish.

"Ancient Filipino albularyos would burn guava leaves to clean the slate," she tells me unprompted. "It's like starting to write on a clean sheet of paper."

"Starting with a clean cutting board," I offer.

She nods without letting my interruption disturb her motions. "The tawas heals any wounds that may interfere with the ritual." When she is done, she moves everything to the side so that all that is left on the steps are the smoking dish, alum powder, and burning candles. She turns to me and holds out her hand, palm up–asking for the agimat without words.

I remove it from around my neck and hand it to her. I don't know if it's the stage she's so successfully set or this sense of heavier purpose, but the casual motion feels ceremonial. I let the pendant land on her palm first and then slowly bring the rest of the cord down until our hands touch. She closes her hand around the rune, and I let go.

"I'll say the incantation, then I'll give the agimat back to you. We'll take three deep breaths together, and I'll ring this bell."

She holds up a tiny clay bell on a red ribbon. In the dim light, I can't make out any of the marks on the bell's surface. "Then you'll have to hold on to it tightly and repeat the incantation."

"I'm not going to remember what you say," I confess, already anticipating failure.

"I learned them from my mom. I don't actually know what the words mean," she admits. "I just learned how to say them."

"I think as long as the intent behind them is sincere, it should still be OK, right?" I shrug. "I learned so many prayers before I learned what half the words even meant. How old were you when you learned what *hallowed* means?"

She smiles at my reassurance. "If I can say them, you can say them. But when you repeat them, you have to concentrate really hard," she instructs. "Empty your mind by imagining you're floating in a white fog. You see nothing else. Then with every deep breath, imagine the fog disappearing until there's nothing left but the clarity of your spirit."

I nod but don't say anything. She studies me carefully, like she's searching my eyes for something. I make the effort not to blink, hoping she finds what she's looking for.

"This is where I always fail and where you'll know if the ceremony is successful or not." She looks anxious. "Your intent can't be clouded with fear or any kind of negative emotion. The purity of the intent is what imbues the talisman with strength."

That's a big ask. I'm already anxious about saying the wrong thing and messing this whole thing up. How do I let go of all that in three breaths? But when I look at her, I see she's trying to mask the hope she doesn't want to rely on. She wants it to seem as if this is a burden all her own but I see she's grateful for assistance. She's hiding more than the appearance of weakness. And suddenly, I see her differently.

Every smile she's ever flashed hides a heartache. Every dimple hides the grief. Even when I make her laugh, I see that it's a thin veil over a deeper well of anguish. Because how can she be happy when she's always afraid? When she's always alone?

My heart breaks but it also reinforces my determination. I want to do this for her. At the very least, I am going to try.

I nod. "I got this," I assure her with more confidence than I feel.

I got you, Maya.

We begin the ceremony just as she described. I don't recognize any of the words. They sound vaguely Filipino but not familiar at all. It's not really surprising. The Philippines is a country with over a hundred different languages and dialects. When you're made up of over 7,500 islands, I guess it makes sense.

I do my best to follow along, becoming more and more apprehensive as we get closer to the part when it all falls on me.

The bell rings. The sound is tiny and tribal, nothing like the deep gong of the St. Louis Cathedral bells. But it's surprisingly poignant.

I imagine the white fog as she instructed. She takes a deep breath; I follow suit, finding that it helps. I let go of the first breath; I let it blow away the fog until, in my head, I'm floating in an empty space.

Success with the first breath! There is nothing but white space. I breathe in the second time, and Maya's image forms in my head. I make a conscious effort to try to let that image go. She wavers in place and as I breathe out, the form morphs into a shadow of something larger, something more sinister. I catch my breath sharply, holding it as the black form grows wings and looms over me. I can only make out shapes, not features. I'm confused until the shadow breaks in half, its winged top half rising away.

This is the Maya I'm afraid of. The monster in her we may not be able to stop. I understand why she always fails at this stage of the ceremony. My eyes snap open, and I break the ritual.

Maya must sense the change, and she opens her eyes. Disappointment is etched on her face, visible even with the limited light.

"It's OK," she assures me. "Thank you for trying."

I grab her wrist before she can turn away. "No," I insist, much harsher than I intend. "No," I repeat more softly so she isn't alarmed. "I just … wasn't prepared."

Her lips part like she's about to protest but she sees something in my expression, and she stops. She closes her mouth and nods, conceding to my request. I let go of her hand.

We begin again.

I dismiss the fog even easier than I had the first time. But instead of basking in the victory of a successful step, I brace myself for what's to come. And just as before, the image of Maya wavers in the space in front of me. But before she changes, I imagine wrapping my arms around her. As I breathe out, I imagine that I'm holding her together so she can't shift. The image twitches but I don't let it stop me. I'm doing this for Maya.

I'm not afraid.

I let go of the Maya in my dream. Her form twists and turns to grow into the monster. I watch the shadow morph into the exact image it had before but when I breathe in for the third time, I'm acutely aware of filling my lungs with the summer air tinged with sage smoke.

The same summer air we shared when we picnicked together. Where we laughed together, held hands. The same summer air that blew through her hair when we first kissed.

A brighter light starts to form in the center of the shadow. As I let go of that last deep breath, the light grows. It's not blinding, like the sun, but like the light of the moon, a tempered reflection of a much stronger power. It grows large enough to clear all the shadows.

Maya starts reciting the words, and I repeat; an energy swirls around me. There's a sound, like the last note of the ringing clay bell caught in time and stretched until it becomes white noise.

A buoyant kind of peace lifts me up, light and unburdened.

As I continue to recite the words aloud, I sense a pressure building inside me. The agimat in my hand feels hotter. Not so hot that I have to let go but hot enough that it radiates energy in my closed fist.

I've raised my hand higher. I hold my closed fist above my head like an offering to a greater power. The energy from it spirals around my arm toward my chest.

I try to recognize these emotions I'm feeling. To affirm their existence and let them be present. There is nothing negative in my thoughts, so I'm confident it will only be good. And with every emotion I identify, I'm stronger and more capable.

There's joy right on the surface, dancing around me like a carefree child. It's comfortable. There's a confidence I didn't think I had. And on its heels, inspiration. There's gratitude, faith, optimism, and even a healthy sense of pride. All positive. All strengthening. And they swirl in the space around me, a tornado of good.

Just as Maya rings the bell to signify the end of this ritual, the most powerful of convictions explodes from my chest, and I almost stagger at its might. I'd have been rattled but I'm determined to face everything with acceptance and without fear.

The sound of the last note fades. All the energy we manifested funnels into the tiny artifact in my palm. And right before it disappears completely, I identify that last emotion.

It's love.

At the end of the ceremony, I open my eyes. It takes a moment to adjust to the light but as I focus on Maya's face, I'm filled with a certainty I have never felt before in my life.

I love her.

CHAPTER 40

STANDING OPPOSITE

I return the agimat to Maya. She puts the necklace back around her neck. Whether it's the way the moonlight hits or the aftermath of the ceremony, the talisman looks like it's glowing. Maya is equally empowered. She smiles.

I, on the other hand, don't feel so good.

It doesn't make sense. After all that positive energy, I should be just as strengthened as Maya, if not more so. Admittedly, I didn't go into this thinking it would really be a magical experience. I was just finding a way to break Maya out of the slump she's in. I was just trying to give her more hope. And it worked. More successfully than I anticipated. Maya looks more relaxed now than she's been in days.

Why don't I feel good about this?

I watch her extinguish the sage, making sure the smoking stops. She collects all the items we brought with us, leaving nothing behind. I should help her, but I'm rooted to the spot, watching her like I'm watching television. I'm having a stranger out-of-body experience than I had during the ceremony itself.

My hands are clammy. A sense of dread bubbles in my stomach like bad egg salad. I'm at the top of a rollercoaster ride, terrified and regretting the decisions that brought me here.

This can't be normal. Love is supposed to be happy and light. I should be taking her in my arms and kissing her passionately like in the movies. We should burst into a duet, singing the joy in our hearts because words aren't enough.

What if she doesn't feel the same way?

I'm in over my head. She's more than a teenage crush. More than a summer fling. If I was supposed to find ways to protect myself from being hurt, I failed miserably. All I did was risk even more.

It's such a rookie mistake. I should have seen it a mile away. Boy who has never had a girlfriend before falls head over heels for Girl. Girl breaks his heart and goes on to date the prom king and live a perfect life. Boy is never the same again. Classic eighties teen movie.

And like the idiot that I am, I walk right into it.

Then again, our story may very well take a different turn. Boy who has never had a girlfriend before falls head over heels for Girl. Girl breaks his heart, turns into an ancient monster, and kills unborn babies. Boy is never the same again. My life is a psycho horror movie.

Either way, I'm screwed. And just like the rollercoaster ride, the only way to go is down. At high velocity.

I walk her home in silence. It's not as if there isn't anything to say. Quite the opposite. There are so many things I want to talk about but I'm too overwhelmed and too scared to try. She reaches for my hand but I claim I'm too sweaty. It's not a lie but it's also an excuse. It's too late to distance myself but the physical separation helps me from spiraling. Maya doesn't seem bothered either way.

"Good luck tomorrow," Maya says when we're in front of her house.

I stare at her, blankly. I'm too swallowed up by what's happening now to think about tomorrow. I don't want to think about the future. I'm not even comfortable with the present. I want to backpedal into the past and stay there. Before I was pulled into this unbelievable world of real superstition. Before I knew monsters existed. Before I fell in love with one.

"I know you won't need it because everyone will love your new dish," she continues and I remember tomorrow is the end of the month, the day I find out if my kitchen skills are any good. My stomach drops even further. I see nothing but failure in front of me. Am I doomed to fail there too?

She's so confident. I'm suddenly unsure about everything in my life. The difference is a gigantic wedge between us only I can feel, pushing me further away from her.

I wait outside with my bike until she turns at the door, says goodnight, and closes it. I stare at the closed door for a minute before getting on my bike and heading home.

CHAPTER 41

THE CHEF CHALLENGE

It's strange that I'm energized in the morning. I get up with a sense of purpose. Today is the day I flex my culinary skills. The outcome no longer seems as important as it was yesterday. The opportunity is what matters today. Anything else, mixed emotions over an ancient ritual and possible emotional impacts included, would have to wait on the sidelines until I can spare them attention.

I leave the house as early as I have been doing all week. It's my new normal. But I also empty the kitchen of all our garlic just in case there isn't enough at the HotHouse for my use. I figure if I end up using it, I'll swing by the store on my way home and replace it. If not, I'll just return it, no harm done.

Big G is already there, sitting in his office. He's leaning on his elbows with his face in his hands. He doesn't raise them when I come inside to greet him.

"The wife was craving a burger in the wee hours of the morning," he complains, his hands still on his face, muffling his voice. "And not a burger I can make, nooo, that's too easy." He lifts his head to face me. "I have to *buy* one. From a *restaurant*. For it to *taste right*." He makes quotation marks in the air at the last two words.

I grimace. No one who works in the food industry ever wants to hear that their food isn't good enough.

Big G stares at me with dead eyes but is satisfied I can empathize with his frustration. "I know, right?" he says in response to my reaction. He sighs. "So I decided after dropping off a *fast food burger*"–his voice increases in volume and he stops for effect; I bite my lip–"I would just come here. Before she asks me to go *buy* her some fish fry." He grumbles the last sentence, clearly still nursing a bruised ego.

I can't think of anything to say. Big G sighs heavily at my silence, possibly thinking it is no longer an appropriate response. "Why are you here so early?" he asks.

He must not know I've been coming in this early all week. I don't think he needs to know I'm using his restaurant as a safe house. "Featured Dish of the Day?" I say instead, hefting my backpack up as if he could see what was inside. "I figured out what to make."

This gets his attention. He sits a little straighter in the chair and turns so his whole body is facing me. "Oh? What is it?"

Encouraged, I eagerly rummage through my backpack for the large jar of dip I made with Maya yesterday. It's still cold from sitting in the refrigerator and will have settled for a more balanced flavor overnight. I set it on the prepping counter in front of me.

Big G stands up for a closer look. I open the jar for him and he takes a compulsory whiff. I interpret his expression as one of curious optimism. He waits for me to show him more.

In order to receive the proper experience, I tell him that it needs to be served with our house fish fry. He acquiesces and preheats the fryer while I prep the fish. I appreciate that he doesn't demand immediate answers. Big G is a man of patience and it serves him well.

It takes twenty minutes to get everything ready. When it's almost done, Big G sits back on his stool and waits for me to serve him the finished product for judgment. I lay the freshly fried fish in one of our standard paper trays and spoon my homemade garlic sauce carefully on it. It's important to get the ratio right. Too little and it won't complement the fish properly. Too much, even of something as delicious as this sauce, isn't good either. It'll drown the flavor and change the crisp texture that makes the HotHouse fry so delectable. And to finish it, I sprinkle some finely chopped scallions on top. The green rings stick to the sauce and complete the look. Plating matters.

When I serve him, he raises his eyebrows in what I've learned to accept as grudging approval. Even though it often comes with a slight downward tug of his lips, it is combined with an encouraging head nod. He forgoes the plastic fork I offer and picks up one end with his fingers. He takes a good bite, almost putting the whole thing in his mouth. He closes his eyes and chews deliberately, focusing on just the flavor and allowing the food to hit every taste bud.

The anticipation is killing me. Now I understand why every challenger on those cook-off shows always stands with their hands behind their backs, sweat beading on their foreheads, when they're awaiting the judges' comments. Because I know if I didn't stand this way, I'd be pulling my hair out. I rock on my heels and chew on the inside of my cheek.

Finally, Big G opens his eyes. He throws the remaining piece in his mouth and claps his hands twice. Loudly. He approves. I exhale.

"That has a completely different bite from our house sauce. Still a kick but mild and flavorful," he observes. "If you don't mind, we can add a bit of Cajun powder to the top for the initial flavor."

That's a great suggestion. I'm disappointed I didn't think of it myself but it's a relatively small thing in comparison to creating this from scratch. The seasoning would also be a way to unify the sauces under the HotHouse banner.

Big G takes a tasting spoon and dips it into the sauce. He licks it, trying it in its pure form. "What's in it?"

"Well, that's *my* secret, right? You have your sauce, and I have mine!" I grin, feeling rather proud of myself.

He looks taken aback at first but then laughs aloud. "I like the spunk. It's well deserved, and that's the sign of an entrepreneurial spirit." He winks and points at me. "But that means you're going to have to make batches of it all on your own." He lifts up his hands and, with an air of manufactured innocence, declares, "I wouldn't want to spy on your methods or anything."

I laugh. "Fine, fine. There's a lot of fresh garlic in it," I confess. It's not really that big of a secret. The flavor is strong and identifiable.

"You gave that up way too quickly!" he says, but he doesn't sound disappointed. I'm certain he could distinguish all the ingredients I used with his experienced taste palate. "We might have to use every single garlic bulb we have in the kitchen!"

I pointed to my backpack. "I brought reinforcements from home."

"Well, let's get to it then," he says, getting to his feet and wiping his hands on his apron. "Grab the mixing tub and use the machine if you have to." He points at the industrial-sized Kitchen Aid we use to make batter. "We're going to need a lot of it. I have a feeling it's going to be a hit."

CHAPTER 42

FEATURING CHEF JAY

While I slice green onions into scallions and crush cloves and cloves of garlic, Big G takes a roll of form feed paper from his office printer and with thick colored markers crafts a handmade banner: Featured Dish of the Day. I tease him for being cheesy but it builds my internal excitement.

My dreams of a long line of customers waiting to try my new dish are dashed when the first customers arrive and opt for items off the regular menu. I don't want my insecurity to show but I think Big G can sense it. He makes a pitch to the next set of customers but they politely decline as well. My spirits sink even further.

An hour into opening and I've lost all enthusiasm for this venture. Of course it would fail. I should've known. It was a dumb thing to be excited about. Why would anyone want to take a chance on me?

A group of teen boys arrive shortly before lunch. I recognize them as students from my school but not much more than that. I greet them with a sullen spiel.

"What's the Featured Dish of the Day?" one of them asks, reading the banner Big G hung across the counter.

"It's just a new sauce," I respond, downplaying what I had been so eager to unveil earlier today.

"It's more than that." Big G steps in, salvaging my awful marketing strategy. "It's a tantalizing blend of New Orleans fire and the cool breeze of Manila on our signature fish fry."

"What's a Manila?" the kid asks, looking genuinely curious. One of his friends hits him on the back.

"It's the capital of the Philippines, dipstick. We learned that in middle school." His friend elbows someone else in the group. "Well, at least some of us did."

"The Philippines is in Asia," the other one adds. "In case you forgot."

"Oh, shut up! I knew that!"

They shove each other, low key laughing and jeering. I want to sink under the counter. Can the day please be over already?

"Sure," the first teen says after an unsuccessful attempt at smacking his friend on the head. "A cool breeze sounds fantastic right about now anyway. We'll take four."

Big G smiles at me encouragingly but I'm afraid of how this group of kids my age will react to what I've created. I go to school with them. If they hate it, they'll surely remember how they wasted money on me. I'd have to endure a new level of taunting for it. Every muscle in my body tightens in anticipation as I watch them take the first bite.

They finish the food. All of it. And just like the teenage locusts they are, they order again.

By the time the usual lunch rush arrives, the buzz of this new dish has spread down the order line. Customers rave about it as they walk out of the restaurant, prompting casual bystanders, who may have passed us on the street, to see what the fuss is about.

The general public lives in fear of missing out.

And just like that, we sell out.

Outside of Ash Wednesday, Big G declares the HotHouse had never had such a successful Wednesday before.

"Look at you, Chef!" Marcus teases me as I hang up the chairs. He stopped by thinking he would keep me company on a slow day. We were so busy, he ended up unofficially recruited to assist in the kitchen. "How does it feel?"

I hadn't been able to wipe the smile off my face. Even in the thick of things when our standard order calls turned into urgent yelling, I felt like I could keep going. I could go all day. It's an adrenaline rush. It's empowering. I feel alive.

"Here's a little something for your help today, Marcus," Big G interrupts before I can respond. He hands him an unsealed plain white envelope, which Marcus receives with a little surprise. His face may as well be a large question mark but he doesn't ask anything aloud.

Marcus opens the envelope and sees the cash inside. "Wow!" he exclaims. "Thank you, Big G!" He doesn't show me how much is inside but it must be significant because he waves the envelope in the air and grins. "I'm the man!"

This adds to the great vibe of the afternoon. Big G wasn't expecting Marcus to work for free and Marcus wasn't expecting a monetary reward when he thought he was just doing a favor for a friend who needed him. They are both generous people and I'm reminded how lucky I am to have them both in my life.

"So burgers are on you?" I quip.

"Don't mention burgers," Big G growls, still smarting from his early morning experience with his wife. He hands me my paycheck, also in a plain white envelope. "I'm boycotting burgers."

Marcus looks at me for an explanation but I shake my head. He doesn't press the issue. Sometimes Marcus actually knows when to be prudent.

I don't open the envelope. I fold it in half and put it in my back pocket. It's my wages from last week's work. I'm more interested to see if I get a bonus in next week's check. Though even if I don't, this experience was so incredible, I'd have paid *him* for it to happen.

"This was a successful launch, Jay." Big G walks behind the counter to put more things away. "And now you'll have one full month to think of what you'll do next. Are you up for the challenge?"

I don't remember ever smiling so much for so long. I think I may pull a cheek muscle. Is that possible? I feel so good about myself I have confidence that Future Jay can commit that far ahead. "You bet," I assure him, feeling every ounce of that promise.

"It's too bad your folks weren't here today," Marcus laments. "Or your grandmother. Did they know it was your launch day?" Sometimes, Marcus doesn't know when to shut up.

My spirits plummet at the mention of my parents. I hadn't thought about them all day, which suited me just fine. Now he brings them up and it's the splash of vinegar on my dessert plate. My face sours.

Big G must've picked something up from my expression because he interjects. "It's Wednesday," he reminds Marcus. "I'm sure they're probably working." He throws Marcus a stern look but my best friend isn't taking any hints.

"His grandmother doesn't work," he argues. "She could have been here."

"They don't know, alright!" I blurt out. It probably came out angrier than I intended because Marcus looks startled. Normally, his reaction would have been enough for me to stop right there but I just don't care anymore.

"It's not like it matters to them anyway," I add, growing more and more bitter as I'm saying the words aloud. "Who cares? Nothing important to me matters to them. What I want to do, who I want to date … none of that matters to them. It's all about what *they* want *for* me and not what *I* want. I mean, why should it matter anyway, right? It's not like it's *my freaking life* we're talking about."

"Jay–" Big G's voice is far more gentle than I deserve. He doesn't say anything past my name but it's enough.

I close my eyes because angry tears are threatening to surface. I refuse to admit I care about this. I intentionally stretch my fingers when I realize that I've had my hands in such tight fists, balled up and ready to fight. This turmoil inside me has been festering for years and on the shoulders of such a victorious achievement in my life, it's deciding to come out. I can't even have one good thing happen without my family ruining it for me. It's not fair.

I open my eyes. No one is angry at me. I catch them exchanging a sympathetic look before looking at me. That just makes everything worse.

"We can finish up here," Big G assures me in the same tone of voice he used to help me get myself under control. "You did a great job today. Why don't you go see Maya and celebrate?"

I know it's an excuse to get me out of there. Maybe because I'm making them uncomfortable acting like an out-of-control toddler who can't process anger issues. Pride urges me to brush it off and assure him I can handle things. But I'm tired and I accept the exit strategy he presents to me.

"Yeah, thanks," I mumble. I don't even get to the backroom before I'm already untying my apron. I can't look either of them in the eye. "That's a good idea. I'll do that."

But I don't.

CHAPTER 43

THE GOOD SON

I don't go to Maya's house. That's another complication in my life and I'd rather not add to the mix.

Now that the adrenaline of a successful launch is over, the heavy weight of yesterday's events descend on me. It manifests itself physically, making me really work on pedaling. Or maybe it's the heat. It doesn't matter.

I'm inclined to go back to the cemetery. Almost like going back to the scene of the crime to help me process everything. But the chances of bumping into Maya there are high, and I'm just not ready to see her.

I go home instead, thinking it should be safe enough with Lola not speaking to me anyway and Mom and Dad at work.

It is, of course, the wrong move.

Mom is home. I see her in the kitchen when I park my bike, and I contemplate going out again. But I'm hot, tired, and thirsty. Escaping into the sanctity of my bedroom seems like the ideal situation.

"Maaga ka ngayon," she comments without looking at me. It sounds like an innocent observation but her tone is laced with sarcasm and heavy with negative insinuation. "You're early today."

I grunt in response, not wanting to start a conversation. I go straight to the refrigerator for water.

"Did you get fired?" It's a mean-spirited joke and she doesn't even bother with the Filipino. She thinks she's being funny.

She's picked a bad time to antagonize me. Any other day, maybe I'd just roll my eyes but I haven't fully come down from my angry high horse and I need to get right back on that saddle. I spin around so abruptly that water spills from the pitcher I'm holding.

"No, *Mother*, I did not get fired." My words may as well have been bullets the way I was shooting them out. "Actually, *Mother*, I had a *fantastic* day, not that anyone in this damn house cares!"

She recoils. "How dare you speak to me like that!" If she had been wearing pearls, she would be clutching them. That's the kind of pretentious outrage she's exhibiting.

"Why not?" I yell, jerking my hands up so more water spills from the pitcher. "Nothing I say or do is right anyway, so I may as well say whatever the hell I want!"

I never would have envisioned myself speaking like this to anyone in my family but I'm not considering repercussions anymore. I'm tired. I'm angry. I just want to yell at the world and my mom is a very convenient target right now.

"You're so disrespectful!" she sputters. If stating the obvious was an Olympic event she would be the reigning gold medalist. Her eyes are wide with surprise. This barely registers with me. My vision is narrow and all I see are transgressions against me.

"What is it I'm supposed to respect?" I take a step toward her. She involuntarily twitches but does not back down. "You don't respect *me*, why should I respect you? Or anyone in this house? I'm not a person here! I'm just your slave!"

"So selfish!" Her initial surprised outrage is replaced with quickly rising anger. She's never been good at playing the victim.

"We provide you with the best we can and this is how you repay us? Such an ungrateful child."

"I'm *not a child*!" I roar. I don't see the irony of the tantrum I'm throwing as I say those words. "Stop treating me like a child!"

Her eyebrows shoot up. She has righteous anger on her side and she isn't backing down. "Maybe if you stop acting like a spoiled brat, you'll earn some of that respect you keep talking about!" She may as well have slapped me in the face with that argument. It's a classic reproach I should have seen coming. I've been missing a lot of obvious signs lately so it shouldn't be a surprise to me anymore.

"Wala kang pakialam kundi sarili mo!" she continues, straightening all of her five-foot-one frame to meet me head-on. She's back to speaking Filipino. I have a difficult time following but I don't dare ask her to translate. I can't process fast enough to respond.

"All you think about is yourself! You just take, take, take! You don't even ask!" She throws open the cupboard next to her. "Like today, you just take *all* the garlic and leave nothing for the rest of us!" She slams the cabinet door. "And you have the audacity to say that *you're* the slave here? Everything everyone does here is always all for you!"

I forgot about the garlic but it seems like a losing debate to defend. The argument is escalating to a point I'm not prepared for, but my pride refuses to acknowledge that. There are tears in her eyes and I know it's not part of her drama. She's furious.

"Your father and I?" She's picked up her momentum, and she's barreling me down with it. "We're always working! We're old and we're tired but we're always working! Why? So we can give you things that we never had! So you can have a better future! You think you're *our* slave?" She thumps her chest hard. "*We're* your slaves!"

I'm not done either. "For *me*?" I yell back, refusing to fall for her dependable guilt trip tactics. "This isn't for *me*. This is for *you*!" I slam the pitcher on the counter. If it were glass, it may have cracked but the plastic just bounces. It doesn't tip over. "You don't care about me! You don't even *know* me!"

All the resentment I've been harboring over the years, unable to offload because a good son would never think this way, much less act this way, comes spilling out. I'm done being the good, responsible son. Done doing only what's expected of me. There's more to me than this.

"How are we supposed to know you?" she shoots back, unaffected by my outburst. "You leave before breakfast. You come home after dinner. You don't talk. What do you want from us?" She throws her hands one way and then the other, large movements that make her look larger. "Are we supposed to read your mind?"

My hands are balled back into the same tight fists they were at the HotHouse. I'm aware of them but this time, I don't want to release the anger. I want to use it. I want to punch a hole in the wall. Instead, I swear at her. The same way I swore at Lola a few days ago. With the same vengeance.

She swears right back at me. In Filipino. I don't know the exact translation but I know she's swearing. Her intonation is crisp and sharp. I can't say she's treating me like a child anymore because she would never say those words if there were children present.

"Are you on drugs?" she asks incredulously, her anger seemingly spent on her cursing. "Is that why you're acting like this?"

It's further infuriating that even as I'm telling her point blank that I'm not who she thinks I am, she's still trying to explain my anger away like there's some kind of external force causing it. Like it can't possibly be her fault. As if the only reason I'm not the perfect son I should be is because I'm on drugs. Not because of her failure as a parent.

"No," I seethe through gritted teeth. "I'm acting like this because you suck at being a mom."

It's not a response she's expecting, and it visibly drains her. Her arms hang limply on her sides like her puppet strings are cut. She stares at me, not saying anything, but with her mouth gaping. The only sound is her heavy breathing.

I smack the pitcher so it tips over and spills water on the counter, dripping into the sink. Mom jumps. It's so satisfying that I sneer. Then I climb up to my room, once again wishing I had a door I could slam in her face.

CHAPTER 44

LEAVE A MESSAGE

My phone rings. There isn't a single person I want to talk to. Not my parents. Not Marcus. Not even Maya. I let it ring a few times, and when the caller doesn't take the hint, I yank the plug out of the wall.

It's blissfully but painfully silent again. My fan is on high, vainly trying to cool the hot air in the loft. I can't tell if the air is on. My parents are too cheap and at this point, would happily see me suffer, I'm sure. But even with the humming of the fan, I can hear the muffled conversation downstairs. Not enough to make out the words but enough to know it's not a happy one.

Mom hasn't tried to get my attention since I stormed out of the kitchen. It's been hours since I heard her moving around. I assumed she was cleaning up the mess I made. It was a juvenile move, I know, but I'm not sorry I did it.

Not yet, anyway. I suspect it will eventually come back and knock me on the side of my head but at the moment, I'm indulging in this victory.

Dad is home. The conversation is nearing the kitchen and his voice is clearer. Mom must have been giving him the commentary. That would explain the very angry tones. The facts are most likely embellished with all sorts of dramatic additions suitable for an opera.

"Jay?" Dad calls from the bottom of the stairs.

I'm lying on my bed, on top of the covers, staring up at the ceiling joints of my room. I don't move. I have no intention of dealing with any of the fallout from this.

I hear someone coming up the ladder, and I assume it's Dad. Lola isn't capable and I'm certain Mom isn't the one to make the first move. My suspicions are confirmed when I hear my name repeated.

"Jay?"

He must have his head above the ladder. I don't know because my eyes are closed and I'm feigning sleep. I'm not a very good actor, so it's a pretty flimsy way to avoid confrontation but unless Dad decides to climb all the way up and poke me, I'm not moving.

He gives up sooner than I think. He's probably not any more excited to have this conversation than I am. I hear him go back down the ladder and tell Mom I'm sleeping. He'll talk to me when I come down for dinner.

I don't come down for dinner. I'd rather not eat. I'm not convinced there would have been a welcome spot for me at the table without having to jump through hoops anyway, so I don't try. Instead, I stay in bed for hours just staring at the ceiling wondering how many more things I can screw up in my life.

I don't think I'm done failing yet.

CHAPTER 45

ADORING FANS

When I leave my house to escape to the HotHouse in the morning, I notice there are bread rolls wrapped in shrink wrap sitting on the kitchen table, almost like they were intentionally left for me. I couldn't tell who left them. It doesn't seem like something Dad would do but both Lola and Mom are mad at me so they wouldn't do that. Or maybe they weren't meant for me at all.

I almost take them. But then it feels like I would be compromising something if I did. So although my hungry stomach makes an argument for bread rolls, I leave the forbidden buns behind and take a bag of cereal from the pantry instead.

I'm in a lousy mood even by the time Big G arrives. He can tell right away but he's smarter than Marcus, so he doesn't press the issue. We work mostly in silence, forgoing small talk and just getting through the work.

Near the end of the day, the same group of high school kids from yesterday return. The tallest kid in the group of four boys walks right up to the counter. He raises his right hand in a high five.

"Yo!" he says. I instinctively return the greeting but instead of the quick contact, he grabs my hand and pulls me in to bump shoulders. He smells strongly of Axe body spray. Then he lets go and leans back so that the other three can step forward one by one.

I repeat this greeting four times in total. There's an identical "Yo" one with a "Hey," and the last one comes in with a "my man." Why am I having a ritualistic greeting with kids I don't know? What their names? Is one of them Mike? He looks like he could be a Mike.

It's another hot day, and they're all just wearing large shirts and long shorts. None of the shirts are the same but they still look similar. Except one of them is wearing a cap. They loiter at the table Marcus would have occupied if he were here. Before I can recite the standard HotHouse spiel, the first kid starts talking again.

"Excellent eats yesterday, man," he says, probably because he also doesn't know my name.

"Thanks." I'm further surprised by the accolades but genuinely thrilled to hear it. "Glad you liked it."

"Oh, for sure. I mean, Big G's grub is always top-notch but you brought it to another level yesterday." The other three boys nod in agreement. "Is it going to be a regular on the menu?"

The idea that I'm bringing in repeat customers who are specifically looking for my creation fills me with prideful accomplishment. I'm standing taller.

"No," I tell them, ready to explain how the end of the month special is going to work. But they burst into disappointed protests, which only makes me smile wider. I lift my hands up in the air as if to try to rein them in but I'm grinning so wide that it only encourages them.

"What's going on?" Big G steps up behind me, presumably to deal with any unhappy customers in a way only the owner can.

"Your boy here is telling us there's no more featured dish?" The tallest kid still has to look up to Big G. Instead of looking like he's trying to cause any trouble, he looks like a homeless orphan begging for oatmeal. He pouts and wrinkles up his eyebrows.

"Tell us it isn't true, Big G!" one of the other boys calls out, and the other two echo the chorus. "We want the special!"

Big G looks down at me and raises an eyebrow. I realize belatedly he suspects I staged this commotion to make myself look good. I shake my head to deny it but can't stop smiling.

"I promise," I protest when he doesn't look convinced, "I had nothing to do with this."

He rolls his eyes and addresses the group. "It was a trial run," he announces, and they continue to whine. "And later on this month, we'll have a different special." He gives me a sidelong look and sees I'm still grinning. I shrug. "Or the same one. We don't know yet. But don't worry, your best friend here will handle that, and I'm sure he'll come up with something for you boys to come back for." He pats my shoulder once and turns to go back to the kitchen. I see him roll his eyes.

"I swear!" I call out to his retreating form. "I didn't ask them to come here!" Big G raises a hand to acknowledge he heard me but he doesn't turn around. I know he doesn't believe me. "I don't even know their names!"

"I'm offended," the tall kid says, putting a hand on his chest dramatically. "You don't know me, man?" The other boys release a low hoot, like a friendly warning, and I suddenly have an understanding of what it means to have a pack mentality.

I give him an apologetic look. "I mean, I know we're in school together …" I let my voice trail and shrug, that's the extent of what I know. His friends laugh and holler.

"I know who *you* are!" he says, still acting offended but smiling.

"Oh, I doubt that," I counter, but there aren't many Filipinos in our school, so maybe there's a chance he does actually know me.

"You're James, right?"

Before I can tell him he's wrong, he's bombarded with jeers from his friends. He turns his back on me to face them. "You dipstick," one of them yells at him. "That's not James!"

"Shut up!" he yells back, defensive. "You thought he was James too!"

"Bogus!" his other friend yells, throwing his cap at him. "Yo, Mitch, James is Vietnamese! They're not even the same people!" The whole group is laughing at his mistake. The kid they called Mitch looks properly chastised. He has one hand behind his neck, and he's shaking his head. When he turns back to me, he actually looks embarrassed.

"Man, I'm sorry. I thought you were James." He rubs the back of his neck and bites his lip. "I guess y'all look alike to me."

"I'm not Vietnamese," I say, slightly uncomfortable.

"Oh, yeah, yeah, I know. For sure." He takes his hand out from the back of his head and spreads both hands in front of him in apology. He's not trying to be offensive.

"But I mean, y'all both Asian, right?" He tilts his head to the side questioningly. He looks like he's afraid he might be wrong. I nod. He's looking at me like I'm the one holding all the answers but I'm feeling trapped. "And y'all like rice too, am I right?" He nods as if doing so will encourage me to follow suit.

"Yeah, we do love our rice," I agree, and he relaxes.

He grins and points at me. "I knew that, though, right? I mean, I got your name wrong but I knew that!" As if he's in a game show and gets credit for partial answers. He turns to his friends, hands up in the air like he won some kind of boxing match. They all jeer at him and make jokes.

He turns back to me and looks like he's about to finally place an order, when I look past him to the door and catch a glimpse of someone standing there.

Maya.

When she catches my eye, she shakes her head slowly, then turns around to leave. I have to blink to make sure I'm not imagining it. Maya hasn't been back to the HotHouse since encountering Carmelita. Why is she here now?

I'm so focused on Maya I completely miss what the order was. When I look back at him, he's reaching for his wallet. I look back out the door but she's gone. I practically jump over the counter to follow but stop when Mitch calls my attention.

"Yo, you aren't just going to, like, leave, are you?" he asks, wallet in hand. I look back at him, then around the room. They all stare at me in silence, confused.

I run back to the counter and yell. "Big G! Can you please man the counter?" I look back out the door, wondering how far Maya has gone in the time I'm wasting. "Big G?" I call again, a little more loudly. A little more desperately.

His head comes into view, looking annoyed. Am I really ordering the owner around? I have too much on my mind to worry about that. "Please?" I beg. "There's, um, an emergency of sorts. I, um, I have to deal with something real quick."

His eyebrows scrunch together to form one squiggly line. He doesn't look happy but he nods once. I don't wait for him to change his mind. I yell a thanks and run out the door.

CHAPTER 46

BIG WIN

I catch up to Maya easily. One, because I'm running, and two, because it doesn't look like she's really trying to get away from me. But when I call out to her, she doesn't turn. I'm certain she hears me but refuses to acknowledge I'm there. Not until I physically grab her by the arm.

She shrugs my hand violently off, and I let go right away. She doesn't say anything but she stops, looks at me and frowns. We're standing under a cluster of trees, and the shade from the summer sun makes her expression look more severe.

"Hey! What's your problem?" I ask, annoyed that she had me running and angry at being ignored.

"I don't have a problem," she responds, her voice level and cold. "But maybe you do."

I bristle at her tone. "What's that supposed to mean?"

"I heard you in there." Her voice is soft and quiet. "Laughing with your friends. Making fun of Filipinos."

"First of all, they aren't my friends. They're customers. Customers who came back today because they happened to really, really like the special I made yesterday!" My voice gets louder and louder the more I talk. Where does she get off judging me like that? "You know, yesterday? It was a big day for me, but you wouldn't know because you weren't there!"

I didn't expect her to be there. I know she's uncomfortable being at the HotHouse. Not when there's a chance Carmelita might turn up. Truthfully, I wouldn't have wanted Maya there anyway because she'd just have been a distraction. But it's a guilt card I can play, so I play it.

"I thought you were coming by after–" she begins.

I talk over her before she finishes her sentence. Her defense is reasonable, so I'm not giving her a chance to make it. "Second, I *know* what it's like to be made fun of. You don't think I know? I know!" I thumb my chest as if there's any doubt about who I'm talking about. "I've been made fun of all my life. My *entire* life! I probably know more than you'll ever know. In case you forgot, I've been to public school. We were just joking around."

"It doesn't have to be a racist joke to be racist."

"You don't know what you're talking about. They weren't being racist. They just don't know any better."

"But you do. And all you did was make it worse."

Her accusation makes no sense, and all I can do is shake my head. I don't get why this is even bothering her. When she realizes that I really don't understand, her attitude changes. Her voice softens, and she steps closer to me. "Don't you recognize the microaggression?"

"No one was being aggressive."

"Microaggression isn't the same as physical aggression," she explains. "It's subtle things like what happened earlier when they made comments about all Asians looking the same. Or that we all eat rice."

"So what?"

"When you, a Filipino American, laugh along with comments like that, then they think it's OK to continue making those comments. And then it escalates. They might not know they're being jerks but it's your responsibility to educate them or else they'll always continue to act that way. And not just to Filipinos but to all minorities. Think about what they'd say about Marcus."

I blink at her, trying to clear the sudden haze that blurs my vision until I realize the haze is my building fury. This sheltered kid thinks she knows what *that's* like? She's going to tell me how I should process this? "Are you seriously giving me a lecture on how to deal with being Filipino?" I'm not yelling anymore. I'm too angry to yell. "You?"

I shake my head, remembering all the occasions I've been made fun of for my dark skin and flat nose. How I was shoved against lockers because I was too small and too short to defend myself. How the kids in school made comments about my lunches or pretended to shield me from their pets, and I think she can't possibly understand that kind of abuse.

I'm always watching how I speak. Watching how I move. I have to fly under the radar of attention. I've had to worry about making it through the day untraumatized, and now it's also supposed to be my *responsibility* to educate the same bullies that make my life more difficult than it needs to be? What about *their* responsibilities to minorities like me? What about their responsibility to decency?

"You have no idea what it's like," I say. "I have to constantly prove myself over and over again because people make judgments before they even speak to me. Telling me I don't belong here. I don't belong anywhere. I've walked past full-grown adults telling me to go back to where I came from. As if I wasn't born in this country. As if I know any other home."

I step away from her, and instead of this girl I've had a crush on, all I see is a privileged brat who thinks she's better than me, and I'm disgusted. "You talk a big game, standing on your soapbox like a self-proclaimed champion of the cause. What can you possibly know about what it's like to *be* Filipino? You don't even *look* Filipino."

I gesture at her face. "People look at your half white features and pointed nose and they don't see Filipino. All they see is how beautiful you are. You're not Filipino. You're *perfectly tan*." I throw quotation marks in the air as I sneer the last two words.

"I'm proud to be Filipino." She raises her chin, daring me to counter her claim.

I know she is. She knows more about our history and culture than I would ever care to know. But I'm not about to give her that. I'm sick of being told I'm always wrong. Nothing I do is ever right. For anyone. And anytime I'm finally winning at something, I still lose. No more. She's not winning this argument. I'm done losing.

I step so close to her that our faces are almost touching. She stays defiant. Here I am, falling in love, fighting her battles, risking everything to help her, and she's telling me I'm still doing everything else wrong. *Screw it.*

"What does being Filipino mean to you?" I ask in a voice dripping with disdain. "Other than make you into a monster?"

She steps back, her eyes fill with tears. I stay in place, watching all her arguments fall apart. Watching *her* fall apart.

The stoic expression she's struggling to maintain crumbles. Her once defiant chin quivers. She shakes her head slightly from side to side, whether because she refuses to believe I said what I said or if she refuses to admit I'm right, I don't know. And I don't care.

She backs up a few more steps, almost trips on the broken sidewalk, catches herself enough to not fall. Then, when all her emotions wash away and leave nothing but a look of absolute betrayal, she turns and runs away.

I don't follow.

I don't move from my spot at all. I watch her figure get smaller until she turns the corner and is out of sight. Only then do I slump my shoulders, look to the ground, and turn to walk back from where I came. It's over.

I won that argument but I may have lost Maya in the process.

CHAPTER 47

WHEN WE CHOOSE THE DARK

Five pairs of eyes turn to me when I walk into the HotHouse. Big G isn't behind the counter but Marcus is standing near the door looking unsure of himself. He doesn't have to speak to communicate complaint and suspicion with his eyes darting at the invaders of his regular spot at the counter.

Who are these kids? Where were you? What's going on? I interpret the questions correctly and roll my eyes in response, which he probably understands as a demand for patience.

I have a sour feeling in my stomach when I face the crowd, remembering Maya's stance on microaggression and racism, intended or otherwise. These kids weren't being mean, and they made the first step in fostering communication. But maybe I can contribute to a stronger connection.

"There he is," Mitch says. "You flew out of here like a bat out of hell. You good?"

I nod, grateful I didn't have to be the one to start the conversation. "Yeah, and hey," I reply, building up the courage to say something, "my name is Jay." I turn to Marcus. "This is my friend, Marcus."

The tall kid steps forward and clasps Marcus's hand the same way he greeted me earlier. "Yo, Marcus." Then he steps back and the rest of the group say hello. Marcus goes through this ceremony of masculine salutations mechanically, looking only slightly alarmed.

"I'm Mitch," the tall kid says and gestures at his friend, who has since retrieved his cap, "That's Tom"—and to the other two—"Richard and Harry. We go to school with Jay."

Encouraged by the friendliness, I brace myself and hope I don't alienate them. "And, yes, the Philippines, where both my parents are from, is located in Asia but that doesn't necessarily mean that we're like all the forty-seven other countries in that continent. And even though I *do* actually eat lots of rice, it's still stereotyping to assume that of someone you just met."

Marcus leans against the counter. "I'm not Filipino," he volunteers, "but I like rice."

The look of horror on Mitch's face confirms that he wasn't trying to be offensive earlier. "No, dude, I didn't mean that at all."

I raise a hand to interrupt. "Yeah, I know, that's why I didn't really say anything but my girlfriend"—*is she still my girlfriend?*—"told me I should. So it doesn't perpetuate some kind of racial profiling or something like that. I think." I sigh. "You guys are actually really great. I mean, I know y'all aren't trying to be jerks about it or anything."

"Mitch's just an idiot," Tom offers. The friends all laugh. "It's not a race thing. It's Mitch being bogus."

Mitch puts one hand behind his neck like he had earlier, which must be a habit when he's embarrassed. "I messed up," he admits. "But I'm really bad with names and faces to begin with. And I don't have any friends who are Asian, so I don't really know anything."

Harry leans back on the chair he's sitting in, the same way Marcus does. "But don't worry, Marcus," he says teasingly, "Mitch knows two other Black kids, so you're safe."

"Shut up!" Mitch says, really flushing red this time. He shoots his friends a sharp look before turning back to us. "I swear I'm not a jerk."

"I know you're not," I say. "I mean, you have good taste in food and all." I grin, letting him off the hook.

He drops his arm, looking relieved. "Thanks for being cool, man."

Big G interrupts, holding a tray with several orders for the customers and a stern expression meant for me. "Food's here," he announces to the room. He stares right at me.

I muster the most apologetic look I can, which isn't difficult because I'm feeling sincerely sorry for my behavior. Big G doesn't look sated but he doesn't call me out in front of everyone either, and I slip behind the counter to take over. With one more severe look to get his point across, he retires to the kitchen.

Richard grabs the closest chair and pulls it up to their table for Marcus to join them. "What do you say, Marcus?" he asks. "Feel like enriching Mitch with some culture?"

Mitch does not look amused at being the butt of the joke but also clearly wants Marcus to join them. He pushes his large order of fries to the center of the table, a silent peace offering.

Marcus grins. "I can be convinced," he says gamely, takes one of the offered fries, and sits down with them. The table erupts with good natured applause and cheering.

Mitch's group of friends stay all the way until closing, placing another order of fries and sharing easy conversation with both Marcus and me. We talk about families, traditions, and customs.

And as I watch this unsuspecting friendship develop right in front of me, I realize Maya was right.

I use my fear as a reason to hide from opportunity. It's a survival instinct to hide in the shadows to avoid being hurt. But when the time is right, it's worth the risk to take that step into the light and allow myself to be a little vulnerable. The reward could be a very good thing. Not just for me, but for every Filipino Mitch and his friends will meet from now on.

And the only difference between the two is a choice.

CHAPTER 48

BLOCKING OUT THE SUN

I have to stay longer after closing to clean up. Big G leaves a little earlier partially because his wife wants ice cream and partially because he's probably still irritated with me. He's been extra grouchy lately since Carmelita's demands have been getting more frequent. I picked a bad time to rub him the wrong way. I'm just grateful I haven't been fired.

Marcus happily leaves with Mitch and company. Any other time, I might have felt a little jealous at this new friendship but I already have too much going on to really care right now.

I go straight to Maya's house when I've finally locked up, hoping to repair the damage our argument caused. I know I crossed a line throwing being a manananggal in her face like that and I don't have a peace offering with me, but maybe admitting that she's right will be enough for now. And groveling. Lots of groveling.

Her father's car is in the driveway. I wonder if that is a good thing or if it will make things more difficult. I find out as soon as he, not Maya, answers the door.

"Maya doesn't want to see you," he says before I can greet him hello. I don't know what Maya might have told him but the very straight line his lips make hint that it wasn't favorable.

I open my mouth to argue but his eyes narrow in warning; I quickly change my mind. What can I really say to a father who thinks I broke his daughter's heart? He doesn't slam the door but it shuts with a very distinct click. It's the perfect punctuation to the finality I heard in his voice.

I stand there a little longer than I probably should, processing what just happened. I should turn around and leave but I lift my hand to ring the bell or maybe knock insistently. I stop myself before I do anything more I'll probably regret. I can't plead my case like this. Not while her father is her gatekeeper.

Back on the sidewalk, I mount my bike and take one last look at the house. I'm hoping to spot her in the windows but the windows are empty. I leave before her father shows up in one of them.

I have no destination. I don't want to go home. I made that mistake yesterday. There's no way I'm going to make it to my room without having to confront at least one person, and that just isn't going to end well.

The HotHouse has been my refuge this past week. But after annoying Big G like I did today, I don't want to give him another reason to be mad at me. And with the way my day is going, he'll find me loitering there and think I'm abusing employee privileges.

I don't know where Marcus and his new best friends went. And as pleasant as the afternoon turned out to be, I'm not in the mood to be the representative of all things Filipino American right now.

What kind of mood *am* I in?

I look up at the imposing metal frame proclaiming the entrance to the Lafayette Cemetery No. 1 and I realize that it's exactly the mood I'm in. How appropriate.

I walk my bike to the tree where Maya and I shared our first kiss. I hide under the shade of its wide branches, using the leaves as a shield against the direct burn of the sun. I sit on the dirt and feel a solidarity with the ground I've never felt before.

I'm dirt too. Kicked around and stepped on. I've never before had such a desire to dig a hole and hide. I've heard that absence makes the heart grow fonder. That sounds good. How long do I have to be gone for people to miss me?

But it's New Orleans, so how far can I even really dig before it's filled with water? Not far. Which just means it's another thing I can't do. Just another failure to add to the overflowing bucket of my trashed existence.

The summer started out so great and with so much promise. I was leaving my childhood at my peak and sliding into the next phase of my life with all sorts of advantages. In about the same time it takes to break in a pair of sneakers, I've managed to sabotage my life.

Epic job, Jay.

I lie on my back, really embracing being one with the filth. I lift my fists to my eyes, and while I don't quite scream, I also don't *not* scream. I'm trying to figure out what I'm supposed to do next. It doesn't take me long.

There's no move I can make. I don't have to dig an actual hole because I've metaphorically already dug a really deep one and I'm drowning in it.

I let my hands drop. I stare up, blinded by the light every time the wind blows through the leaves. Pretty soon, my eyes are filled with enough tears to block out the sun.

CHAPTER 49

SUCCESS

I'm beaten. Tired, hungry, and dehydrated, I finally make my way home. I'm not in any hurry to face the consequences of my recent behavior but I've lost my will to keep fighting. It looks like they always knew what was good for me to begin with anyway.

I see Mom at the kitchen window when I pull my bike in but she turns away when she sees me. Neither she nor Lola are in the kitchen when I open the door. It's Dad who is standing in front of the ladder to my room, blocking my favored exit strategy.

I'm too tired anyway. I have no intention of running anymore. "Hi, Dad." My voice isn't much louder than a sigh.

I think he sees the change in my demeanor because his shoulders relax and he even steps to the side when I walk by to get myself some water. My hand shakes when I reach for the handle of the refrigerator and I let it rest there a moment before pulling the door open. Just so I can get back a little control.

He doesn't say anything at first. He watches me take the pitcher, grab a glass, and pour myself some water. I'm aware he's staring at me even when I drain the glass. I lay it down gently on the counter when I'm done, but I don't let go. I stare at it because it's easier than facing my dad.

"What's wrong, Jay?" He sits down on one of the stools, away from the ladder, an intentional move to show that if I really want to run, he isn't going to stop me. Instead of the accusatory tone of a lecture, his words are surprisingly tender. It makes it harder to look at him.

"Everything," I mumble. It sounds dramatic, but maybe because it's accurate, Dad doesn't accuse me of being evasive. He waits for me to elaborate. "I can't do anything right."

When I don't expound further, he's a little more direct. "Did you really take all the garlic?"

I close my eyes because I can't lie and I'm afraid where it's going to go. "Yes," I admit, waiting for the hammer to drop. But it doesn't fall. I gingerly open my eyes again and see Dad waiting for an explanation. "I needed it. For work."

"Big G asked you to bring garlic?" It wasn't in his voice but I know how incredulous it must sound.

"Not exactly." I took a deep breath and let it out with words. "Big G said I was doing really well at the restaurant and he wanted to showcase what I can do by letting me make whatever I want as the special of the day so I created my own sauce blend that was really good but I needed a lot of garlic and wasn't sure he had enough so I took all the ones here at home just in case but I swear I planned on replacing it before coming home but forgot about it and didn't." I run out of breath just as I reach the end of the worst run-on sentence in history.

Dad takes a moment to process everything I blurted out before reacting. "You created your own sauce?"

In spite of myself, I smile. "Yes, and it was really good." I'm finally able to meet his eyes because I'm especially proud of myself. "We sold out before closing time."

Dad nods. "That's incredible." He hesitates, as if unsure of his next sentence. "Why didn't you tell us?"

I shrug and don't answer. I was afraid they wouldn't care. I was afraid they would trivialize something that I didn't want to admit meant so much to me. I was afraid. I'm back to studying my empty water glass.

"Maybe I wanted to see if I could do it alone," I mutter more to myself rather than in defense of myself.

"Just because you can," he says gently without rebuke, "it doesn't mean you should." When I don't respond, he continues in a lighter tone. "You know, if you had told your mom, she'd have had her friends over and you'd have sold out before lunchtime."

A different reality plays in my head. One where Mom would have been my first customer, already waiting in line with her friends in tow, insisting they try my concoction. They'd all compliment me loudly because they all would genuinely like it. After all, the flavor is heavily influenced by the Filipino palette. Their commotion, much like the commotion Mitch and his friends had made, would attract more customers and, as Dad predicted, we would have sold out before lunch was even over.

That reality didn't happen because I chose not to tell my parents. What other futures am I preventing by keeping more secrets from them?

I remember how proud I was to watch complete strangers enjoy something I made. I think of the peace I feel in the kitchen and the accomplishment of selling out. I bask in that glory and pure joy of doing what I love. That entire experience was a peek into a life I could live. Into a life I want for myself. It gave me courage to reach for it.

"Dad," I begin before I lose my nerve, "I don't want to be a doctor."

"Then don't."

I look up at him and he looks genuine. There is no anger in his voice or even disappointment. Just a matter-of-fact statement. I blink a couple of times, wondering if I am imagining this scenario but he remains as he is.

"I want to go to culinary school."

His bottom lip sticks out a bit, and he nods. His glasses slide down his nose. "That suits you well."

The tension is very much still between my shoulders, threatening to be a painful headache if I don't relax. I can't relax. This doesn't seem real. I've always anticipated this to be a more volatile conversation fueled by failed expectations and strong wills. Instead, Dad is receptive to my declarations without debate. Is it a trick?

"You're not mad?"

He tilts his head so slightly that if it weren't for the shift in his glasses, I might not have noticed. "Why would I be mad?"

"You and Mom have always pushed me toward medicine. Isn't it your dream to have me be a doctor like you?"

He surprises me by laughing out loud. "That was never our dream, Jay. That was yours."

What kind of Jedi mind trick is he trying to pull on me? That's not true. "I never wanted to be a doctor."

He leaned an elbow on the kitchen island and pointed at me. "Don't you remember? When you were five years old? You took my stethoscope and went around the room claiming you were a doctor?" He leaned back and snorted. "You wouldn't give it back to me! I was late for work!"

I vaguely remember the scene. Did I do that? Maybe I was just trying to get his attention.

"Then when you were seven, you wanted your birthday party to be in the hospital!" He removes his glasses when they threaten to fall off. "Your mother told you no and you cried!"

I forgot about that. I remember being so upset. "I had this idea that everyone would be wearing scrubs and roll my cake into the operating room on a gurney," I admit, suddenly remembering. "I wanted the room to be decorated with balloons and streamers."

"Of course we would encourage you. That's what you wanted!"

"I was seven!" My guard is up again and I'm defensive. "I didn't know what I really wanted then! I was just copying you!"

Dad holds up his hands, palm facing me in the universal manner one uses to try and calm a wild animal. "And now you're seventeen," he responds calmly. "You want something different."

I nod, not trusting myself to speak.

"Is this what's been bothering you?" When I nod again, his mouth tightens and his eyebrows wrinkle. "Hay, anak," he mumbles, more out of expressed frustration rather than just calling me his son.

He lowers his hands and considers me a moment before asking, "Do you know why I'm a doctor?"

"Because you went to medical school?" I'm sarcastic because I'm embarrassed for being so emotional while he's so calm. He raises an eyebrow and I relent. "I don't know," I admit. "Because your parents wanted it? Every Filipino parent wants their kid to be a doctor, right?"

"No, actually." It's my turn to be surprised. He smiles again. "Your lolo, my father, didn't want me to go to medical school. He said it was too many years of education and too expensive.

I wasn't earning while I went to school, which meant I wouldn't be able to help him provide for the family."

He reaches over and takes one of the ensaymadas still on the table. He unwraps it as he speaks. "We fought about it throughout my last year in school. I even took the entrance exam for the accelerated program in secret."

I can't imagine my father being a rule breaker. He goes along with whatever Mom decides, always a follower and never a leader. How is my dad the same young man that had the backbone to stand up to his own parents? Something I can't even do myself?

"When I was accepted into the University of Santo Tomas LEAPMed program, my mother was able to convince him to help me pay for school. And when I received my medical license, I began proving to them that it was worth their sacrifice." He looks as proud as he is humbled by his experience. "It was only when I was able to help send my younger sister to school that your lolo finally admitted it was a good idea for me to be a doctor." He chuckles as if sharing a secret with his former self.

"I'm a doctor," he finishes, "because I want to be."

This new understanding of my father leaves me in awe. He is so much stronger, so much more full of conviction than I could ever be. I suddenly realize how I've robbed him of an admiration so richly deserved.

"Do you know why your mom is a nurse?" It is an innocent enough question but there is an impish look in his eye.

"Not because she wanted to be?" I guess.

He grins, pleased I'm following along. "She's a nurse because she's very, very good at it." He finishes the last of the ensaymada he's eating with flourish. "Success in life is finding what you want to do or finding out what you're very good at."

He stands up, tosses the wrapper in the trash, and turns to face me. "You, son, are fortunate enough to have found both."

CHAPTER 50

THE FRIGHTENING TRUTH

Dad washes his hands in the kitchen sink, seemingly unaware of the shift in my universe. In one easy conversation, this unspoken heap of anxiety I refused to acknowledge is suddenly released, and it melts away in a stream of professed support and acceptance. The imbalance is enough to make me stagger.

I watch his back, feeling better about myself than I have in days and I'm suddenly compelled to hug him. I haven't expressed this kind of affection for either of my parents in years and I almost don't recognize the sentiment. I take one step toward him but before I'm close enough, he says over his shoulder, "You know, you should fix things with your mother."

The tightness in my stomach returns in full force and I'm frozen in place. He's right, of course. If this discussion should teach me anything, it should be that open communication can perform miracles. And I sure could use miracles.

"I know," I admit reluctantly.

He turns around completely and looks at me, leaning his hands on the sink behind him. He juts his chin in the direction of the door, a silent command for me to go find Mom. Now.

I want to defy him but my renewed respect for him makes me turn to the direction he indicated and walk to the living room, where I find Mom, alone, reading a book. She looks up, sees me, and tilts her head to the side, waiting.

She's not angry. She's not demanding anything. She's sitting there and watching me, trying to read my expression and the emotions behind them.

And I'm a mess. I'm just so tired. I know I can't keep adding to the facade. I've kept it up too long and it's heavier than I am strong. The longer we look at each other in silence, the quicker the invisible barriers between us crumble. I can't speak. Not because I'm afraid but because I don't know where to begin.

She closes her book, puts it on the coffee table in front of her and pats the empty space next to her. It's an invitation to sit. So I do. She speaks to me in Filipino without translating. Her words are slow and easy to follow.

"Talk to me, son," she says, her voice sounding more at home in her native tongue than it ever could in English. "What's bothering you?" When I don't answer right away, she puts one hand over mine and asks tentatively, "A girl?"

Not too long ago, Mom, Lola, and I were in the kitchen conspiring on ways I could woo Maya. They were my biggest cheerleaders. I miss that. I could really use a cheerleader now but I'm not sure that's possible anymore.

"Maya," I respond. "Her name is Maya. Maya Hebert."

Mom's eyes widen and the hand laying on mine so delicately grips me with urgency. "Mayaari?"

I brace myself for the reaction I know is coming, but for the second time this evening, I'm surprised. Because Mom smiles. Her eyes soften, and she puts one hand over her heart.

"You know her," I prompt, confused by her initial reaction.

She nods. "I knew her mother." She shifts into English easily but with a heavy accent. "We both worked at the hospital. We were friends." Her eyes lose focus, seeing the past and not the present in front of her.

I watch this play out, not willing to interrupt her memories just yet. I'm acutely aware of the minute changes in her expression: the twitch near her eye, the tug on her lips, the tightening by her jaw. She's reliving memories unshared.

"Did you know you and Mayaari used to play together when you were small?" It's strange hearing Mom call Maya by her full name but I suppose it makes sense if that's how she knows her. She gestures with her hands and I understand she must mean back when we were toddlers.

I've known Maya all my life? How do I not know this? It makes all the sense in the world. I can envision baby Maya and baby me easily getting along. We've always been friends, we just didn't remember we were.

"Tapos ngayon, magkasyota kayo! And now, look at the two of you—boyfriend and girlfriend!" Mom claps.

I'm baffled. What a complete deviation from Lola's backlash. Watching Mom react with delight feels like I'm being gaslighted. I shake my head again, trying to reconcile the two and failing.

"That's not how Lola reacted," I blurt.

Mom drops her hands. I watch her process what I said, understand what I mean, and finally make sense of my recent behavior. At the end of it, she looks tired and sad. "Your lola doesn't understand."

She knows but she isn't saying it. So I do. "She called her a mananananggal."

I watch Mom closely; no longer able to predict her reactions, I want to be able to interpret them. But she guards her expressions with an intentional look of neutrality. I've seen her do this when she's trying to manage an uncooperative patient at the hospital. So while it's unlikely I'd be able to guess what she's feeling with any accuracy, I can tell right away she isn't surprised.

"Alam mo ba kung ano'ng ibig sabihin nito? Do you know what that is?"

"A monster."

Mom searches my eyes but doesn't find what she's looking for. Instead, her expression must mirror mine, cautionary and suspicious. "And Mayaari?"

I don't know what she's asking. The question is loaded with unsaid information waiting to be unlocked. We're like two spies sizing each other up and trying to get the other to break first. What is the super secret code phrase Mom is waiting for me to utter?

"Maya says she doesn't want to be." I realize that by phrasing it this way, I admit I've spoken to Maya about this and she isn't denying it.

Mom picks up on that right away. Apparently, it is the right thing to say because she nods. "Her mother didn't want to be one either," she agrees. "That is why she tried so hard to find a cure for her condition, not just mask the symptoms."

My mom and Maya's mom seem to have a history more involved than I originally suspected. This goes beyond the standard Filipino network connection we joke about. There was a friendship there.

"I really think she might have figured it out if only—" She falters. "If only she had more time. She was an excellent nurse."

"You don't hate her?"

"Jay! We shouldn't hate anyone." She rebukes me as if I were five and just called someone stupid. "Hate is a bad word."

"Mom," I interrupt because it sounds like she's going to lecture me on the dangers of carelessly using powerful words. "She killed your baby!"

Her shocked reaction gives me pause. It looks like she wants to slap me but makes a hasty sign of the cross instead. "Jay! Don't say such things! Of course not! What a horrible thing to say!" Her litany of distress trails into Filipino I'm unfamiliar with.

"That's what Lola said." I'm no longer so sure of myself. Now I'm just trying to make sense of things.

She cuts me off with an impatient clicking of her tongue. I stop. When I'm quiet, she sits up straighter, closes her eyes, and folds her hands on her lap. She sighs heavily. I've also seen this before. This is how she centers herself before dealing with stressful situations. When she opens her eyes, she's not ruled by emotion but by calm reason. She speaks in English, each word measured.

"Jay, manananggals do not eat children. That is the superstitious belief of an older generation. Your lola is part of that generation."

"But that's how all the stories go, right? They split in half, grow wings, and suck children right out of their mothers' wombs?" I don't know why I'm suddenly defending Lola. It's not as if I want her to be right.

Mom frowns in the way she used to when I was younger and not listening to her most basic requests. It's the look she gives me when she expects better of me and I disappoint her. I'm disappointing her now.

"Manananggals change when their bodies are deprived of a specific protein. When that happens, their instinct is to seek it out." She leans forward without hesitation to explain this to me. "It's the same as when you're dehydrated, you will instinctively look for water."

I see what Dad means when he says she's really good at what she does. She doesn't struggle with medical terms the way she seems to struggle with everyday English and she's very comfortable in them.

"Manananggals aren't after the fetus," she continues. "They need a specific protein found in the amniotic fluid *surrounding* the fetus. Do you understand?"

I nod because there's more she wants to say but isn't going to continue unless I acknowledge her question.

"It's easy to assume the manananggal is after the fetus. The fetus depends on amniotic fluid to survive so if that's damaged, and without medical assistance, a miscarriage is unavoidable. But the fetus is not the main focus." The clinical terms make it easier for me to distance myself from the horrible circumstances. "Right at birth, a mother's amniotic sac often breaks. Sometimes it's still intact even after delivery. Once the baby is born, the sac is discarded but it can still contain the protein they need."

I knew this from health class. I mean, vaguely. The birth video they made us watch was so traumatizing, I barely remember anything else. But some of the terms she's using are familiar enough to make sense.

"Mayaari's mom worked on the birth floor with me at the hospital," she continues. "She was a very good nurse and took very good care of both the mother and child. And it also gave her access to what she needed *without* harming anyone."

She made a point to emphasize that, pausing and staring me down, daring me to argue. The narrative is so different from what I learned both from Lola and Maya. I can't help but ask. "Why did she change then? Why did Maya's dad have to kill her?"

I see tears in Mom's eyes but she doesn't blink so they don't run down her cheeks. This subject is difficult for her. She sets her jaw before responding, a visual indication of her determination.

"That's my fault."

"But," I protest, none of this is making any sense, "you're the victim."

"Mayaari's mother was my friend. When she told me what she was, I laughed in her face. Who would believe that?" She laughs without humor. "But then she needed my help, to try and find a cure for her condition."

"A cure?"

"She found ways to mitigate her symptoms but that wasn't the life she wanted for her daughter. We worked together to try and find a solution. And when I was pregnant with your brother …" She faltered. "We thought it was just what we needed."

"You were experimenting on yourself?"

"No, no, no, nothing like that!" She denies it immediately. I'm relieved to hear that. "It just meant we had the advantage. I would know when the time came, and she would have permission to collect a clean sample. The equipment in the hospital lab is much more advanced than what we have in the provinces. It would be the perfect opportunity to learn so much. It wasn't complicated at all. I had a cesarean delivery with you but the pregnancy was easy. We didn't think there would be any complications."

"What went wrong?"

She hesitates and I understand it's not because she wants to keep secrets but because it's painful to talk about. "We were walking home from the store together when my uterus ruptured." I don't know what that means and Mom must read that on my face because she continues to explain.

"It's very rare, Jay." Her voice is significantly softer. "And it's life-threatening. I lost a lot of blood very quickly and needed surgery immediately. She called the ambulance, did her best to slow the bleeding, and stayed with me when I lost consciousness. If it weren't for her, the ambulance would have not arrived in time, I would have lost too much blood. I lost the baby but she saved my life."

She closes her eyes now. The tears she'd been trying to hold back run down her cheeks. I should comfort her but I'm frozen in place, trying to make sense of this different reality.

"But the timing was terrible. Malas talaga. She hadn't changed in years, Jay. Years." She's as angry as she is tortured by this memory. "But the circumstances—the rupture, the blood, the stress, the blood moon, everything—triggered her change. And in a very big way." She takes a deep breath, interrupted by a sob she tries to control. "She didn't want to be a monster. She didn't want to hurt others anymore. And she made Jim promise to stop her. As a police officer, a father, and a husband, he was bound to. So he did. And it destroyed their family."

She covers her face with her hands, unable to stop her tears. "Kasalanan ko. It's all my fault."

I have never seen my mother look so vulnerable. She took on this guilt and responsibility, carrying it throughout her life without looking for absolution. I can't believe I never knew her pain. Without thinking about it, I wrap my arms around her in a fierce hug. She seems so small; I can't remember the last time I really hugged her.

It doesn't stop her from sobbing, and I instinctively tighten my hold, trying to protect her from all the hurt she's inflicted on herself by the fault in her memories. My mother does not deserve this.

"It's not your fault, Mom," I say softly in her ear. She shakes her head, refusing to let go of the guilt that's been haunting her. I don't let go. I refuse to. She needs to hear me.

"It's not your fault."

I say it over and over again.

Until she stops shaking.

Until she stops crying.

Until she believes me.

And only then do I let her go.

CHAPTER 51

SCIENCE AND MAGIC

Mom's crying alerts Dad and Lola. By the time I let her go, the whole family is in the living room.

Lola looks at me with suspicion, but it seems seeing my relationship with Mom mended softens her opinion of me. She doesn't say anything but sits on my other side and lays a gentle hand on my back. Dad kneels next to Mom and kisses her hand. It's his way of letting her know he's there for her if she needs him.

We huddle together, a family like we haven't been for a while, and I'm rejuvenated. I didn't realize until this moment, how big of a foundation they are to me. I believed independence meant I needed to do things alone. I thought I had to distance myself so I could prove I'm capable of being by myself. But that's not necessarily true.

With my family, I'm capable of so much more.

"Naku! Anong oras na?" Mom suddenly exclaims, looking at the large decorative clock hanging over the fireplace. "What time is it? It's already dinnertime and I haven't even started cooking yet!"

You would think, from her state of alarm, she's the head caterer for a wedding reception rather than a mother cooking for three other adults, who are all more than capable of feeding themselves. I look at Dad, hoping he hears my silent plea. Mom and I aren't done yet.

He gets up while simultaneously keeping a firm hand over hers to let her know not to stand. "We'll handle dinner," he declares, looking pointedly at Lola. "The two of you look like you still have things to talk about."

I don't know who is more grateful, Mom or me. She doesn't argue. Lola follows Dad back to the kitchen, giving us privacy. We don't say anything as we watch them leave.

"Mom?" I'm still off balance from the twists in this corkscrew of revelations. "If Maya's mom figured out how to deal with her"—I struggle with the word—"um … symptoms, does that mean Maya can too? She doesn't have to turn?"

Mom reaches for the tissue box on the table and dabs at the residual tears, a way to gain back control. "Maria, her mother, was able to prevent the change from happening for years. We didn't have a cure, but she found ways to live with her condition. She adjusted her lifestyle. It's like being a vegetarian. Or living with diabetes."

"Except you turn into a flying baby-eating monster when you miss that insulin shot," I mumble, angry at the situation Maya is in and not because I'm being judgmental. Mom swats me on the arm anyway.

"Stop that! I already told you. That's inaccurate." She frowns at me; I recognize the displeasure.

"I'm sorry," I apologize immediately. She's right. I'm being stupid. "Maybe it's the medical professional in you that's able to look at it like a disease and not a curse."

"Everything is magic until it can be explained by science."

"How are you just a nurse and not, like, a scientist or something?"

"What do you mean *just* a nurse?" I meant for it to be a compliment but she takes it as a full affront. "There's nothing easy about being a nurse, anak."

"I didn't mean it like that."

"But you said it like that," she points out. "Akala mo, porke lang babae ako, hindi ko kaya? You think just because I'm a woman, I can't do it? Of course I can!"

She's clearly insulted. I shrink as she sits tall and proud. "There is no ranking system in science, just a difference in specialization. Yes, I could have been a scientist or a doctor like your father."

Properly chastised, I ask, "Why didn't you?"

"I like people," she responds quickly, an indication that this question is something she'd considered before. "I took up medicine because I want to help people. If I were a scientist, yes, I could be helping, but I would be just in a lab and not see anyone. Ayoko naman na ganoon. I didn't want it to be like that."

She juts her chin out toward the kitchen where Dad is. "Doctors see patients but parang hindi rin. It's like they aren't treating patients, they're treating the problem. Nurses treat patients."

I'd never thought of it that way before.

"Nurses aren't failed doctors." She's scolding me, and I deserve it. "Remember that. We all work together in different ways to help others. That is what this field is all about."

"I want to help Maya," I say, redirecting the conversation away from my mistake.

"It's a lifestyle change," she repeats, back to being the capable health professional she is. "There are things she needs to do to keep it under control."

"She eats balut every day," I offer.

"Her mother did that too. We suspect the soup in the egg has the kind of protein her body requires. We don't understand why it's not enough."

We lapse into a moment of silence. There has to be more. More to work with. More to understand. What had first been introduced as little more than a fairy tale has evolved into a medical mystery. Maybe what we're looking for isn't a magical solution but a practical one?

"What if," I blurt, fueled by sudden inspiration, "what if she needs to eat it raw?"

Mom makes a face, demonstrating how she feels about the idea of consuming a raw partially formed duck egg. But her expression turns thoughtful as she considers my idea.

"It would be the difference between eating raw vegetables and cooking them, right?" I prod. "A lot of the vitamins leach out and are destroyed by the heat. What if the same things happen to protein?"

Mom isn't looking at me. Her gaze is beyond what she's looking at as she processes this new hypothesis presented to her. "You may be right, Jay. Protein functions are dependent on their shape. Heat weakens the bonds allowing them to keep that shape." She finally looks at me, her eyes filled with a mix of pride and joy. "Naku, anak! I think you're right!"

I grin, feeling good about this conclusion. "Gastronomic science to the rescue!"

"You need to make sure she knows that!" She makes a move to stand, as if to indicate I need to spur into action immediately. My grin is short-lived.

"She's not talking to me right now," I admit sullenly.

"Hay naku, Jay." She slumps back down. "Ano nanaman ang ginawa mo? What did you do?"

"Why would you assume it's *my* fault?" I exclaim, feeling more defensive than I had any right to be. She just looks at me—a mother who sees right through her child's theatrics. I drop my gaze to the floor. "I called her a monster." I cringe. I can sense Mom's dismay without even looking at her.

"Jay," she says, laying a hand on mine. I reflexively look up and meet her eyes. They are free of judgment or resentment and instead are filled with insistent determination. She makes sure I'm not just looking but also that I really *see* her before she continues.

"I failed her mother. You must not fail Mayaari."

CHAPTER 52
CHAPTER 52
INDEPENDENCE DAY

I tried calling Maya repeatedly. At first, her phone rings and rings without anyone picking it up. After a few tries, all I got was a busy signal. Her phone must be off the hook.

I went to her house after work, without any luck. Her father's car wasn't there but no one was answering the door. I thought I saw movement in the upstairs window but it could also have been a trick of the light or my own wishful thinking.

The only things I saw through the fence are her ducks. She wasn't with them. I banged on the door a few times, calling her name. I only left when the neighbors looked at me like they were about to call the police.

I don't know what else to do. It's been three days. She's successfully locked me out of her life.

"Send her flowers," Marcus suggests when I complain to him. "They like flowers."

"That's not cliché at all," I reply sarcastically while I count the money in the register at the end of the day. We weren't supposed to be open today. The HotHouse used to always be closed on the Fourth of July, but that was before he hired me. And of all days, we stayed open longer than usual. "Not *all* girls like flowers. I thought you were better than that."

He scoffs. "I know better than to screw up as bad as you did."

He's not wrong, but I respond with a scowl. He doesn't know exactly what I did. All he knows is I insulted her family, which is a vague description of what I actually did anyway so it's not like I lied.

Big G walks in, wiping his hands on a dish towel. "Women are complicated," he grumbles. I share an amused look with Marcus. Big G would normally be the last person to pile on the gender divide but he's been having a difficult time navigating the unpredictable territory of catering to a pregnant wife.

"Ice cream or burgers this time?" I ask. It seems his biggest challenges deal with providing the desired food for consumption. Extra frustrating when you're a chef.

"She's well past cravings." He wipes his brow with the dish towel. "I understand the discomfort and backaches. I mean, I *don't* understand but it makes sense." He rolls his eyes upward.

My guess is he's fresh from an argument in which Carmelita accused him of patronizing her. We've witnessed it firsthand before, and because it wasn't directed at us, Marcus and I found it rather funny.

"You don't understand anything," she had said to him, impatience lacing her voice. "You're not pregnant." He made the mistake of saying he didn't have to be pregnant to understand. She did not take that well.

"What I don't get," he continues, "is how it's eighty degrees inside the house and she complains it's too cold? Then ten minutes later, it's too hot? Even when the temperature hasn't even changed!" He looks utterly confused. He throws the towel up. "I can't do anything right."

We can tell he's at the end of his rope because there's no way he'd have talked about his wife like this with a couple of teenagers. Big G prides himself on being a role model and fancies himself as a mentor of sorts. Today, he's acting like we're a couple of married men who can relate.

"My mom says that's normal," I offer, trying to act older than I am. I've never actually had this conversation with Mom but it sounds like something he needs to hear. He grunts, probably because he's looking for solutions, not explanations.

"Maybe give her flowers?" Marcus suggests, grinning at me.

"With my luck, it'll make her sneeze," he mutters. "Jay's right. I just have to accept that there's no arguing. She's growing a human being inside her, I can handle always being wrong for a few more weeks." He thinks about what he just said then points at Marcus. "Maybe not flowers but a present isn't a bad idea."

"Presents are always a good idea." Marcus grins.

"Finding the right present is the tricky part," Big G agrees.

"Speaking of presents," Marcus says, turning attention back to me. "It's Maya's birthday. Today is the perfect time for a present. You can apologize and celebrate her birthday in one go."

"I regret telling you things," I complain.

"Get her a bouquet of fireworks," Marcus suggests. "Except you run the risk of her aiming them at you if she's still mad." He laughs at his own joke.

"Not helping, Marcus," I growl. I'd throw something at him but I didn't have anything that would make a good projectile close to me, and Big G would probably yell.

"A mixtape." Marcus shrugs. "I mean, it's classically romantic but still personal." I've never made a mixtape before. Marcus has a bunch. He compiles music from different artists into one cassette tape for different occasions. Making one for the person you're dating is just as cliché as the flowers he suggested.

"You need something bigger and more memorable," Big G counters. "Pull out all the stops. Not just because it's her birthday but because it's the first time she'll be celebrating it with you."

"Or you can wait until *after* the holiday to apologize so you don't have all that pressure."

"No, no"—Big G waves his hands in protest—"that will only make it harder to apologize. Believe me." He taps a finger to his lips. "What you need to do is find the perfect present for Maya."

I stare at him, feeling dread instead of hope. Because the perfect present for a freshly turned manananggal would probably be his pregnant wife. And Maya knows it. It's her worst fear coming to pass. It's her eighteenth birthday. The change happens tonight, with or without a blood moon. I need to reach Maya before she turns or else she may not be able to resist and she'll never forgive herself.

"Sure." I swallow the realization, hoping to hide emotions too difficult to have to explain. "Yeah, the perfect present. I'll do that. Thanks." I don't want to brainstorm ideas anymore. I have to put an end to the conversation before the pressure makes me throw up.

Big G and Marcus share a triumphant look, as if they've solved my problems together. Meanwhile, my sense of urgency is hitting new heights. I look out the window.

Maya is quickly running out of time.

CHAPTER 53

OUT OF TIME

The sun is setting.

The sidewalks are filled with backyard BBQs spilling out into the streets. Smoke from the grills rises in the air, and the smell is enough to make you hungry even after you've eaten. Temperatures are high again but it doesn't seem like anyone cares. Kids are running around with sparklers lit before it's dark. It's red, white, and blue everywhere you look. American flags are on all the poles, and bunting is strung between houses. People are wearing themed attire, complete with red, white, and blue beads. Because if there are no beads for the occasion, are you even in New Orleans?

It takes longer than usual to get to Maya's house. I'm hitting every possible obstacle, from a child dropping an ice cream cone in front of me to an unscheduled, impromptu parade of tourists already drunk on red, white, and blue drinks. It's a testament to my self-control that I don't just run them over with my bike.

When I get to her house, the front porch hurricane lamp is lit. I see her father's car in the driveway but I'm fueled with purpose enough to distract from any irrational angst. I jump off my bike before I reach a complete stop, leap over the low fence, and bound up the steps.

I alternate banging on the door and ringing the bell repeatedly. The neighborhood is celebrating and will neither notice my suspicious activity nor care. Though at this point, it wouldn't matter if they did call the police. One of them is already inside.

"Maya!" I yell, my voice cracking. "Maya! Open the door!" I crane my neck, trying to see anything I can through the windows. There's movement. I brace myself, knowing it's probably going to be her father. Maybe if I move fast enough, I can get past him and into the house.

But when he opens the door, it's not the same stern face that stonewalled me a few days ago that greets me. Instead, it's the panicked expression of a helpless father. His uniform, sans the tie, isn't tucked into his pants. The top buttons of his shirt are open. He's out of breath, and wild eyes with dilated pupils look frantically past me.

This is all wrong. A cold dread takes hold of my throat. I lose my ability to speak.

"Where is she?" His voice is strangled, like he can barely get it out. He has one hand on the handle of the door and the other gripping the frame, his knuckles turning white. "Where is she?" he asks again, his voice louder.

I shake my head.

He lets go of the door and runs his hand through his hair, further adding to his bedraggled appearance. Without warning, he slams his fist against the wall next to him. The drywall gives way to a crater the size of his hand. It snaps me out of my mute state.

"She's missing?" When he doesn't answer my obvious question, I add, "Since when?"

His fist drops to his side. The impact caused damage to his knuckles as well. There's no blood but it's scratched with red marks almost as angry as him. "Since I got home this afternoon," he says. "She didn't leave a note."

He looks at me. His desperation is woven into his every fiber. He suspects exactly what I do. Maya has already turned and we're too late.

"We need to find her." I'm stating the obvious but her father seems to understand I'm demanding it of myself and not of him. He doesn't respond with sarcasm like Marcus or I would. He nods, far more concerned about finding her than he is about putting me in my place.

"She's not in the house. She's not in the garden." He's sharing what he knows. It's methodological and efficient. Years of being in law enforcement have trained him this way. "My next guess would have been that she was with you."

I'm even more of a failure under his accusing gaze. I shake my head, ashamed. "I haven't seen her since—" I falter. "Since our fight." *Since I called her a monster. Since I broke her heart.*

He swears with a vehemence I've not experienced before. He turns his back to me and storms into the house. I follow, sparing a glance at the damaged wall. I leave the door open in case a quick escape later becomes necessary.

"Do you have any idea where else to look?" he demands when I catch up to him. He has one hand on his radio, ready to relay information. Everything is moving too quickly for me to keep up, and my mind blanks. I can't think.

He swears again, but instead of rattling me, it shakes me out of my confusion.

"Her mom," I say. It gets his attention, but not in a good way. His lips twist into a growl. "Where did you find her mom?" I prod.

He stops, understanding what I'm asking. He slowly lowers the radio to the table and lets go. It's a non-threatening action but it looks so deliberate it feels like a threat.

He doesn't answer right away; instead, he narrows his eyes and looks me up and down, taking a measured step toward me. I fight the urge to take a step back. I need to stand my ground. And try not to flinch.

He must know Maya has told me everything but he's also not just going to unburden his deepest secret just like that. He stops an arm's length away from me, tilts his chin down so he can see me better, and I know he's judging me. Weighing what he knows against me with what he can learn. I wonder what he sees past this sweaty teenager before him. Does he see how much I care about Maya? Can he tell what I'm willing to do for her?

If he can, he's a better detective than I can ever give him credit for because I don't even know myself.

"How did you know where to look?" I ask.

"She told me," he admits in a voice filled with warning, raising his chin like a dare.

I should be intimidated. I'm not just facing Maya's father. Standing taller than his six-foot-plus frame, he's also the entire police department personified. A man who puts the safety of the public ahead of his own happiness. Ahead of his wife's life. He is a force that cannot be messed with.

But I'm not intimidated. I'm not afraid because what he said sparked a glimmer of light against the darkness. And the hope I feel is enough to conquer all my fears because now I know.

"I know where she is."

CHAPTER 54

THE END IS NEAR

We take his car; it's faster than weaving through the crowd on a bike. He puts the siren on, an amplified scream of our own silent desperation. The crowd responds by getting out of our way. If they could see the look in his eyes, they would move even faster. I sit in the passenger seat, safely buckled, watching his tight grip on the steering wheel. He wants to bear down on the gas pedal. I can see it in the way he twitches. And because it's also what I want him to do.

The sky is a brilliant display of deep orange and blue, bordering on black. Like a rip in the heavens is bleeding. I can make out the faint shape of the moon, looking full, preparing for its grand appearance. I plead for the sun to slow its descent but celestial bodies don't listen to me.

When we pull up at Lafayette Cemetery No.1, the bleeding of the sky is gone, replaced by a dark purple, a brightening moon, and a sinking feeling in my stomach. Maya's dad blocks the entrance with the car and pulls out the key, leaving the lights on. We open our doors at the same time, but his movements are so much more practiced than mine. By the time I make it out of the car, he's far ahead of me. But because I didn't tell him exactly where in the cemetery to look, it's not the direction I go.

He heads to his wife's grave without a second look at me. I don't bother calling out to him. He's too far gone. I turn the other direction and run toward the tree where we had our first kiss. No one knows that tree like we do. It's our safe space.

I'm running as fast as I can. I don't notice the rocks from the uneven terrain displaced by my steps. I don't notice the sweat building up from the combination of stress and effort. I don't hear the distant squeals of delight or the pop of roman candles.

I'm desperate to see but also afraid of what I may see. The cemetery isn't well lit at night, and the shadows made by errant fireworks shot by impatient families play on my nerves. I try not to let what I see in my peripheral vision distract me from my focus.

It's difficult to make sense of the shapes in the near darkness. I think there's someone hiding in the nook and my spirits rise ever so slightly. Maya.

Except I don't find Maya.

I find *part* of her.

I knew the possibility was there. I knew what I *might* find but I'm not prepared for what I *see*.

I stagger backward, hitting the back of my head on a cracked tomb behind me. I don't feel the pain. My knees are weak, and I sink to the ground, my back scraping against the rough concrete. My eyes adjust to the darkness, and when colors explode in the sky, it's just enough for me to see better in bursts. I can't reconcile this vision with reality. Sporadically painted in shades of pyrotechnic red and blue, the scene becomes even more surreal. I'm in a twisted, horrible nightmare.

It is Maya, but only from her waist down. Standing impossibly straight. She's clad in clean bright sneakers and loose shorts. Then everything just ends, like someone erased her upper half. Just … gone.

She told me what was going to happen but my limited imagination didn't envision this. An impossible scene like an incomplete drawing. Almost peaceful. Nothing to indicate that half a person is missing from this picture.

I'm lost in the torment. I don't notice that Maya's dad has caught up with me. I don't notice the flashlight beam facing me. I don't hear him calling my name. But when the beam of light is trained on Maya's half form, that's when I know he's here.

I follow the light back to its source, the heavy standard-issue flashlight in his hand. He sees what I see, and his reaction is similar but also different. It goes beyond shock. Because he's seen this before, and he knows what it means.

We're too late.

He takes a step back before falling to his knees with a sob that will haunt me for years. It's the worst possible scenario. Everything he's sacrificed before must be sacrificed again. And this time, he loses everything.

The hourglass has bled out. He's lost his wife and now he's lost his daughter too.

He crumples on the ground, a shattered man. The light shakes with every broken breath he makes. I walk past him toward her form. The smell of wet flesh mixes with the moist foliage. It's stronger as I find the courage to come closer. Is it morbid curiosity that propels me forward?

With his light still trained on Maya's incomplete figure, I see things a little clearer. Her waist isn't as neatly severed as I first thought. Ripped, bloodless flesh hangs in shreds around the edges of her waistband. I avert my eyes. I'm not ready to see more.

There's something next to her feet. It's not the mini backpack she always carries with her but it's roughly the same size. A simple sack tied closed by a familiar cord. I get down on one knee to inspect it.

On the cord hangs her mother's agimat. And in the sack, enough salt to kill her.

CHAPTER 55

THE DARKNESS AND THE LIGHT

What do we do?" I have to repeat myself because her father isn't hearing me. The light is in my eyes, so I can't see his face, which may be a good thing because I don't want that haunting me too.

Finally, he hears me, pulling him away from the agony in his head to the hell in front of us. He gets to his feet and joins me, shining the light away from Maya's unbelievable form to the bundle in my hands. I open the sack and show him the salt inside. The agimat is in my hand.

"This can't be happening," he mumbles in a voice so low I can barely hear him. "Not again. Not Maya." He steps back and I'm concerned he's going to run and leave me.

"We have to stop this," I insist. "What do we do?"

He turns and faces me and I see a crazed look I had never seen before. "You don't understand," he spits out. "You can't understand! *This is my little girl!* I can't lose her!"

It's enough to make me take half a step back, as if I'm trying to get away from his blast radius. He's right. I don't understand what he's going through. I can't possibly. He's gone through this with his wife and now has to do it all over again. How many more hits can his soul take before it's shattered?

But then I think about Maya.

"Maya doesn't want this either," I remind him, my voice so much steadier than I feel. "She doesn't want to hurt anyone." I hold up the sack of salt, evidence of her unspoken wishes. "She wants us to stop her."

He squeezes his eyes shut, shaking his head, unwilling to hear what I have to say. He doesn't want the truth. The truth means losing his daughter.

"Maya is the strongest person I know." The tears I didn't know have been pooling in my eyes run down when I blink. As terrified as I am, as hurt as I am, this is so much worse for him. I take a step toward him. "She gets that from you. And she needs that from you more than ever."

He doesn't open his eyes but I see his breath is steadier. He's struggling to accept the situation but he's making progress.

"You raised her well," I continue, hoping I'll stumble on the right words he needs to hear. "She's kind. She's compassionate. She knows what's right and what's wrong. You need to trust you did your job. You need to trust her."

He opens his eyes and they are tortured and pleading. As if I hold the fate of his daughter in my hands. As if I had the ability to manipulate the reality of the world we both live in. We see in each other the hopelessness of this situation. We're the only two who do.

"What do we do?" I ask again.

He swallows. His voice shakes when he answers me. "We need to sprinkle some on the exposed center." I'm glad he said *we* and not *you*. Because even though I know I'll have to be the one to actually do it, I don't want to be alone in the decision. "She'll sense it and return here."

This is what Maya wants. Just like her mother, she left us with the tools we need to stop her. Just like her mother, she'd rather die than be the monster hurting people.

I hear, rather than see, him unclip the gun from his holster. "She'll come after us," he warns. The sweat on my skin cools, and I shiver in the hot night. He moves away from me until he stands where I did, with his back leaning against the tomb. Then he tells me to do it.

He shines the light back on Maya's half body. There's no avoiding it. I'm standing over it now, and the smell of wet flesh and fresh blood is overwhelming. Not the smell of a hospital but the smell of a butcher shop. The exposed entrails are covered in a translucent film of white, and the areas that are the red of inner organs. Despite the smell, there's no actual blood dripping anywhere.

With shaking hands, I scoop some of the salt Maya left behind and pour a little on one side of her torso. As soon as the salt hits the raw organs, there's a violent reaction. A sudden bubbling and unnatural smoke erupt from the combination. The wet flesh smells like it's burning. I recoil, spilling most of the salt I had in my hand uselessly on the floor. I almost drop the entire bag.

It's as if the bottom half of her is its own being, flinching at the introduction of an invasive element, and reacting as if in pain. I can almost hear the voiceless screams. I look back at her father for guidance but can't see him with the light trained on me. I lift the hand holding the agimat to my eyes, trying to block the light so I see him better. He angles the light away, and I drop my hand.

That's when he fires.

I instinctively crouch, getting down as low as I can to the ground without falling forward. And when I look up, I see he didn't angle the light away to help me see better but because there's something more important to look at.

Above me is a manananggal. It's not Maya. It's a full-fledged nightmare of a monster.

Illuminated by the beam of his flashlight, it hovers by beating its large bat-like wings in the air, as wide as a full-grown person. Time slows, and I watch this first encounter play out in front of me like it's broken down frame by frame. The yelling behind me is garbled and intelligible. Even the fireworks that burst behind the manananggal seem to languish unhurriedly. The explosions cause a backlight, helping to define all the horrid lines that make up this demonic illusion.

Entrails dangle loosely from its severed half, bloodless but exposed. Unlike Maya's well-groomed silky hair, the growth from its head is tacky and matted, looking like it has never been washed. So long that it hangs completely over its torso and almost covers its entrails. The specter would not be complete without the sharp teeth and impossibly long tongue.

This can't be Maya.

When I blink, time speeds up again, the world moves faster than I can follow. The manananggal rises higher in the air, disappearing from the spotlight. The light jerks to follow, not fast enough. It's like chasing a shadow.

I scramble to join Maya's father, hoping to get under the safety of his firearm. He hadn't hit his target. Had he meant to? Or was it just a warning?

The beating of its wings should be drowned out by the random fireworks at the distance but my hearing is tuned to the wind moving and the hissing that is out of place in this world. We wanted its attention, and we got it. Is this really better?

I think of Big G and Carmelita. I think of the family they're excited to build together. I think of the baby that will bring them joy. And I think of how Maya does not want to take that away from them. Or anyone.

Yes, this is better.

But when light catches the manananggal right before it attacks, I wonder. There are two possibilities, and neither of them are favorable. We're going to die. How will Maya feel when she discovers us dead? And if, somehow, we survive this, how will I feel when we kill her?

Maya's father is holding his gun steady in his hand, braced by the other holding the light. He has her dead to rights, there is no way to miss. He knows what he's doing. He's done this before.

He doesn't pull the trigger. I see his tears and the anguish reflected on his face. He doesn't see a monster. He sees Maya. And he'd rather die than hurt his child.

I have no weapons to defend myself. The only things I have in my hands are half a bag of salt and Maya's necklace, an abandoned trinket. I don't think about what I'm doing. I throw the open bag at the attacking form like it's a grenade. I knock her father off balance as I throw myself on him. He never fires.

The manananggal rears back with a horrible scream. It doesn't like salt.

I sit up and scramble backward until my back hits something hard and unmoving. The flashlight, knocked out of her father's hand, rolls uselessly away from reach. There's still the faint glow of the streetlights, the random fireworks, and the fullness of the moon, but it feels like we are plunged into complete darkness.

My breath comes in waves, it's all I hear. I don't hear the distant popping. I don't hear the cries of a broken man. I don't hear anything but my breath and the pounding of my heart. It's amplified in my ears, composing a cursed soundtrack for this grisly scene.

My fingers dig into the dirt and grass. Bits of rock wedge themselves under my nails. I push back on the crypt behind me. There's nowhere left to go. Nowhere to hide. Nowhere to run. My eyes hurt from not blinking. I can't. I'm too scared.

A dark form blocks out the moon. It's not difficult to guess. I close my empty hand around loose dirt. I'm out of salt. The only thing I have is the agimat she left behind. Not a weapon, perhaps a shield?

I hold it above me like the talisman it's supposed to be and I yell Maya's name.

The winged form screams again but stops its advance. It hangs in the air, suspended by unworldly rules. It writhes in place like it's struggling with invisible bonds but it stays, and, unbelievably, it listens.

"Maya!" I yell again. "You don't have to do this! There's another way."

The writhing stops. It beats its wings but slows its movements, waiting for me to continue. I see her dad from the corner of my eye. He's reaching for his light.

Inspired by this development, I move slowly, trying to get my feet under me as I speak. I'm not yelling anymore. I'm also not quiet. The conviction in my voice is loud enough. "You said you needed clarity of spirit. You told me I had that. Remember?" I dangle the agimat between us, hoping the physical item will tie to an intangible memory. "You're right. I do have clarity of spirit. You gave me that."

I put the cord around my neck and let the agimat fall on my chest. In the faint light, the manananggal's eyes are shark-like and predatory; I fixate on them. "I know there's another way," I insist. "I know you're capable of it. You helped me know myself. I know myself because of you." Suddenly, I'm brave enough to step forward. "You did that. For me." The manananggal does not react.

"Maya." The more I say her name, the more courage I find in myself. I stop seeing the manananggal with monstrous wings and dangling innards and start seeing Maya, the extraordinary girl I fell in love with. It's not self-preservation that drives me. Not anymore. I'm going to save her. I'm certain of it. Or die trying.

"I'm sorry I called you a monster." I swallow the shame of that memory. "You're not a monster. I was wrong. I made you feel like one. I made you think there's no other way. But *that's not true.*" One step forward. "You're just like me. We're both products of two worlds. You don't have to be one or the other. You're both. Like me. And we can find our way together." Another step. "It's not what you are that matters. It's what you do. And you don't have to do this."

I pinch the agimat between my fingers and lift it up. "This is your moment, Maya. And you don't have to do it alone. We're here with you." I gesture to her father, who trains his light on her. I see her clearer now. The manananggal, yes, but also Maya. One more step. "*I'm* here with you."

I'm standing so close to her now; there will be no getting away if she decides to stop listening. "Remember me," I implore her. "Remember *us.* Remember how it feels to be together. Remember standing here with me and choosing the light." I stare into this creature's eyes; they look nothing like Maya's. But there's something undefined swimming in that pool of darkness. A little light. I see it. I see her.

"Choose the light, Maya." The talisman warms in my hand like it had when we performed the ceremony together. Is there actual magic in this? She said the strength imbued in it can be called upon when needed. I need all the strength I can harness. For her.

"*Be* the light, Maya," I insist, speaking to the pure soul I know is buried under the curse. "You can do this. I believe in you."

The manananggal screams. Louder than before because I'm also standing closer. I stagger backward, lose my balance, and fall ungracefully to the ground.

I failed. I'm going to die.

The figure spirals up and disappears from the spotlight with unnatural speed. Maya's dad frantically tries to follow with the light, tracking the movements with jerky inaccuracy. Until finally, the light lands back to where Maya's other half is standing. Because what had been separated has begun to rejoin.

CHAPTER 56

THE SACRIFICE

"Maya!"

It's difficult to see. Not because we don't have enough light but because there is suddenly so much wind. The winged half of her spirals above, creating a semi-tornado as it closes the distance. I see the fabric of her shorts ruffle when loose rock and dirt spin in the air. I can't see much else through the dust, but I can tell that though the artificial twister seems powerful, her legs do not move.

I have to close my eyes against the wind. I don't see what happens and the sounds are far more disturbing without vision. If I thought the scream of the manananggal was enough to curl my skin back, the gurgling and unidentifiable screeches are what hauntings are made of.

When the air stills, I dare open my eyes. Just in time to see Maya, now whole, collapse to the ground.

I scramble forward, clawing the grass for balance, but her father gets to her before I do. He checks for signs of life, expertly, intuitively. Meanwhile, I fixate on the ugly open gash in her side.

Blood drips out of the wound. The skin around it is charred and blackened, blistering around the edges. At first I think it is the result of the warning shot her father fired but then I realize. *I did this to her. This is because of the salt I poured.*

"Put pressure on the wound." The voice sounds far away but when I look up, I see Maya's dad by her head, only a few feet away from me. "Jay," he calls, snapping me back to the present. "You need to put pressure on the wound. To control the bleeding. She has a pulse but it's weak."

I gingerly put my hands on her, afraid I'm causing her more pain, but she doesn't react. I press harder. Her blood seeps through my fingers. I scan around me as if I'll find what I need just lying on the ground. There's nothing, of course. I look down at my shirt, covered in dirt. It's not ideal but it's what I have. I hastily remove it, fold the fabric inside out into a messy wad, and use that to cover the gash, putting firm, steady pressure on it.

I look back up at her father and he nods once, a sign I am doing what I'm supposed to be doing. If I look close enough, I can see Maya's chest rise and fall. But her breathing is weak and irregular. My vision blurs. I think it's a trick of the dim light but it's because I'm crying.

Her father stands. "The ambulance is on its way," he tells me. He must have called it in. I didn't even hear him do it. "I need to meet it at the entrance and let the paramedics know where to go. Keep pressure on that wound," he instructs again. Then he's gone, leaving me responsible for his daughter's life.

I shift positions so I can be closer to her face without losing the leverage. There's no sign of the wings, the fangs, or the long tongue that had been there just a moment ago. It's just Maya, as I've always known her. But she's not smiling or laughing or being anything she should be. The light I've always seen in her is dimming.

I should've been with her. I could have prevented all this from happening. If only we didn't get into that stupid fight. If only

I didn't call her a monster. If only I wasn't so late. I could have saved her.

I wish I could stroke her hair or cradle her face. I wish I could caress her so she knows I'm here. But I don't dare ease the pressure I'm keeping on the damage I caused. Sirens wail in the distance, a promise that help is on its way.

"Maya?" I say her name, hoping it's enough to bring her back. Hoping she'll hear me and wake up like they always do in the movies. Hoping she'll sleepily open her eyes and smile at me.

But she doesn't.

"Maya? Can you hear me?" There's no change. *Where are the paramedics?* I blink to try to get the tears out of my eyes. I'm not very successful. "Please hear me. Maya, please stay with me."

Flashlights turn in my direction, dancing like I'm in a club. But it's not because it's a party; the paramedics have arrived, and they're running to us as fast as humanly possible. It's not fast enough. I look down at the shirt I'm holding, and it's already soaked in blood. Did I even slow down the bleeding? Did I do anything but hurt her?

"I'm sorry," I whisper. "Don't die. Please don't die."

I beg her. I beg God. I beg the universe. I beg anyone or anything willing to listen.

But no one hears me.

CHAPTER 57

THE UNCERTAIN FUTURE

Are you nervous?" asks Mom.

"Shouldn't I be?" The collar of my freshly ironed shirt feels tight around my neck. I tug at it.

"Don't worry. You're ready for this."

"Am I?" I don't feel ready for anything. Much less this.

"Jay." Mom's sitting next to me in the car. She knows I'm distracted, and she wants my full attention. I sigh and reluctantly twist in my seat to face her. She smiles, her expression so much softer than the tone of her voice. "Kaya mo 'to. You can do this."

My stomach twists at the memory of me saying similar words to Maya a few weeks ago. It feels like it just happened, but at the same time, it feels like it happened a lifetime ago. To someone else.

The light turns green, so Mom shifts her attention back to the road. I watch the world go by outside the window. The sun is so bright it's enough to make you believe the night never happened.

I close my eyes. I'm in the past, seeing Maya collapse to the ground. I see the blood through my fingers. Memories happen in flashes, like the explosions of fireworks above us. Black-and-white images washed in red, white, and blue.

I open my eyes again when the engine dies. I look out the window to see we've arrived. Mom doesn't unbuckle her seatbelt but she's not done talking to me. I unbuckle and wait patiently for the advice I'm sure is coming.

"Jay, I know you've been through a lot," she begins, and the knot in my stomach tightens. I don't want to talk about anything. It's just making everything worse. "It doesn't seem like it now but things will get easier. You're stronger now, a better version of yourself."

I nod because that's what she's waiting for. And because that will make this conversation end faster. She pats my knee. Strangely, I'm comforted.

Ever since Mom and I talked, before everything blew up at the cemetery, we've had a much better relationship. She isn't on my case as much, and it's so much easier to talk to her. And she's one of the few people who understands, on a very raw level, what I went through with Maya.

I rode with Maya's father to the hospital that night. That's where Mom found me, inconsolable, my shirt covered in Maya's blood. I was in a daze. No one else could get through to me but her. She gathered me in her arms like I was a little child, rocked me when I broke down and cried. She found me a clean shirt, got me something to eat, and even got me to sleep when I couldn't stay up any longer. Then she took me home.

I put one hand over hers. "Thanks, Mom," I say. "And not just for the ride."

Her smile is so understanding, and I'm reminded of how much I've underestimated her. This woman who left a homeland she loved to start a life of better opportunities for her family; this devoted daughter who makes sure her own mother is taken care of; this loyal wife who always looks out for her husband; this caring human being who gave up a better paycheck so she could help people and be a friend to others; this incredible mother who continues to give without demands even when I was too selfish to notice.

I see her now, and I'll never underestimate her again. "I love you," I say. The look on her face tells me it's something I have not said frequently enough.

"Mahal din kita, anak," she says. "I love you too. And I'm very, very proud of you."

I kiss her on the cheek and get out of the car. She starts the car again and drives away. I watch her go, waving my goodbye.

Marcus is waiting by the door. He's not dressed in his usual attire, and he looks just as uncomfortable as I do. He greets me with the—now standard—Mitch & Co. greeting we've adopted since the pivotal day at the HotHouse that made us all friends: clasping hands and bumping shoulders.

Marcus came to the house the day after the whole incident. He sat with me and kept me company even when I didn't want to talk. Sometimes he'd prattle on about his day and the recent dumb things Mitch did for a laugh. And sometimes, I did laugh. Eventually, I emerged on my own.

I never told him what really happened. The official report is that it was all caused by malfunctioning fireworks. There are always several reports of burns and injuries due to fireworks on the fourth of July, so it was easy enough to stick with the story. Especially when it came from a police officer. You don't really ask more questions.

Marcus may never know, but that's OK; he doesn't have to. All that mattered to him then was that I was hurting, and he was there to help me heal. Because that's what best friends do.

"Are you ready for this?" he asks.

I'm better after Mom's affirmations and having Marcus here helps too. I nod. "Let's do this."

I take my key and open the door. It's dark when the door closes behind us but I know where the light switch is and feel for the toggle. The long fluorescent bulbs mounted on the ceiling of the tight kitchen flicker on. Even the problematic one. I don't need the broom this time.

Marcus reaches for an apron. He has his own now. I was finally able to convince him to take on the responsibility and commit to steady employment. He's already here most of the time anyway, he may as well get paid. And after that first surprise envelope he received from Big G for his assistance, he was much easier to persuade.

It was good timing, too, because shortly after he was hired, Carmelita gave birth, and Big G needed more help. The more time Big G spent with his family, the less time he had for the HotHouse.

So he promoted me. I'm a manager. I even have a new uniform. With a collar. And now that Marcus works here, he's the one I'm officially managing. Big G still comes around several times during the week, but only when it suits him; often, he just wants to show his new baby to his customers. I run most of the restaurant's day-to-day operations. It's something I didn't realize I already knew how to do until he left me to do it.

At least until school starts again. Then I have to focus on other things. Like graduation and college. Grown-up adult stuff. Things I don't believe I'm ready for at all. But since when did that stop me?

"Is the cop coming?" Marcus asks as he starts his morning prep. He's already so efficient in the kitchen. He's one of those people who can accomplish anything he puts his mind to.

"He said he'll swing by around lunch if it's not too swamped at the station."

Maya's dad is a recent regular at the HotHouse. And not just for his Monday fish fry that Maya used to pick up for him. He drives by a couple of times during the week and stops in for conversation. We don't talk about that night but having shared the experience together, having someone else know what you know makes a difference. That's what I am to him. Someone who knows.

I must've stopped what I was doing and just stared into nothing because I twitch when something hits me on the back of my head. It snaps me out of my self-inflicted daze. It's a plastic spoon, and it was Marcus who threw it at me.

"I asked if you were good," he repeats. Apparently, I hadn't heard him the first time.

I put the spoon on the counter. "Yeah," I reply. "Just distracted, I guess. The last time we did this, I wasn't the one in charge. What if no one shows up? What if everyone shows up and we can't handle it? It's a Saturday. We're going to be packed."

"Listen," he says, pointing the spatula he's using for prep at me, "the last Feature Dish of the Day was a smashing success. Yes, it was so busy you needed my unemployed butt to help you out but we've got this. And if it's too much, we'll call reinforcements."

I nod. "I know. I know." I've already gone over all the possibilities with Big G, and we have contingencies for every scenario. Including calling him to come in.

Marcus returns to his mixing but says over his shoulder, "I know why you're distracted." I don't challenge him because I don't want him to be right. But he continues his guessing anyway. "You miss Maya."

Of course I miss Maya, I want to say, but I don't. I've snapped at him many times before, and the only one who's annoyed at the end is me, so I've learned how to control myself. It's better this way.

The doctors were baffled by her injuries. She stayed unconscious because she had lost too much blood. Her blood pressure had dropped so low they were afraid there wasn't enough blood getting to her brain. The burns on the side of her torso were so extensive they were classified beyond a third-degree burn, but the wound was strangely localized, and there was no smoke inhalation detected at all. And they just couldn't wake her up.

What they didn't know was that her body was likely lacking that important protein she hadn't been able to get when she changed. It's something science hasn't yet been able to explain. And that, not the transfusions, skin grafts, fluid transfers, medication, or surgeries was what was killing her.

It took a week for the hospital to stabilize her but Maya still did not regain consciousness. They theorized her body had gone into shock and had to put itself into a coma to recover. But there was no improvement. Her breathing remained labored, and even with numerous plasma transfusions, her skin looked pale and thin. Her cheeks were sunken, and she'd lost so much weight in such a short time. It was only a matter of time.

I was a mess, a husk of who I used to be, dissolving inside. I didn't go to work for almost two weeks and stayed at the hospital whenever they would allow me. Thanks to Mom, I was able to stay past the regular visiting hours.

"Well, stop it," Marcus demands. But before I could frown at him, he gestures to the front of the shop with his chin. "She's outside."

I follow his gaze and see Maya standing at the locked doors of the HotHouse, her hands cupped over her face, trying to see inside. I grin at Marcus, abandon my station, and try to act nonchalant as I make my way to the door.

It was also thanks to Mom that Maya survived. Whenever she could, she would sneak the raw balut soup into Maya's feeding tube. It wasn't the exact protein she would've had from the amniotic fluid she really needed but it kept her alive.

The biggest bump in her recovery happened when Carmelita gave birth.

Mom was there to deliver the baby. Carmelita's water never broke, and the baby was delivered completely encased in the unruptured sac. It's a rare occurrence but it was exactly what Maya needed. Mom was able to collect a pure sample of untouched amniotic fluid and feed it to Maya.

I wasn't there when it happened but she almost immediately regained consciousness. Her vitals improved, and she began to respond to treatment. Mom saved her life. "I owe it to Maria," Mom said, then she cried.

Maya had to be flown to Boston for further burn treatment. I hadn't seen her in a week. I didn't know she'd arrived.

Maya waves at me through the glass when she sees me coming. She steps back when I unlock the front door. But the moment I swing it open, she leaps into my arms.

"Whoa!" I say, trying not to hold her around the waist. "You don't want to rip your stitches or anything!"

She leans back but doesn't let go of me. "I missed you!" she declares, ignoring my concern.

"I missed you too," I say. "So let's make sure you don't get sent back to the hospital for not taking care of yourself." I let her inside the restaurant and lock up behind her. We aren't open for another hour. "When did you get back?"

"Late last night." She looks past me and waves. "Hi, Marcus!"

"For the record, your homeboy here didn't even see you at the door!" he yells back at her. "I'm the one who spotted you!"

"Yeah, yeah." I dismiss him with a wave. "Thank you, Marcus." I'm too happy to care anyway.

"Thank you, Marcus!" Maya adds, her voice melodic. He holds his spatula up in acknowledgment. That's all he wanted.

"Why didn't you call?"

"It was super late by the time we got home, and I thought it would be fun just to surprise you on your big day." The dimple in her cheek is a sight I have missed for so long. She's gained back most of her weight; she looks healthier. Happier. "Look at you, Mr. Manager on Feature Dish Day!" She hugs me again. "I'm so proud of you."

Her eyes sparkle, and I can't help but smile. It's been such a rough month. Some days felt like they overlapped with each other and formed one long day. I haven't felt like I've been able to take a good breath. But seeing her, standing stronger than she'd been all month, is the breath I need.

"How do you feel?" I ask, gently running my hands up her bare arms. I'm afraid to touch her. I'm afraid to break her.

She tilts her head to the side, her hair, tied up in a high ponytail, swings along with it. She lifts her tank top a little to show me her scar. The wound is not nearly as angry anymore. Multiple skin grafts have smoothened the area but we both know it's her steady diet of raw balut eggs that progresses any treatment she has. "The doctors are all congratulating themselves for their good work." She laughs. "But your mom knows what's up."

"Does she know you're back?"

She laughs, a confession of sorts. "I don't know if Dad told her," she admits, passing on the blame. "I haven't spoken to her yet. But I'm following instructions." She takes a small container out of her mini backpack. In it is a single balut egg.

She and Mom have been in contact. Not just for health reasons. Maya learns more about her mom this way. Beyond the journals and beyond the rumors. And it's healed Maya's soul more than any potion could.

Suddenly, she has a future again. She's made it through her eighteenth birthday. Barely, it's true, but she did it. And now, with the proper diet, she can conquer the world. Not destroy it.

When the summer started, we were a couple of kids who had an uncertain future, dark secrets, and limited options. We didn't know where we belonged and we didn't know what we were capable of.

Now, just two weeks before the start of our final year in high school, we're a couple with an uncertain future, a shared knowledge, and infinite possibilities. We belong here and we know what we're capable of.

Anything we want.

What a difference that makes.

THANK YOU

John Lacson
My safe space anywhere in the world.

Cale Lacson
Second generation. Laughs at my jokes, whether or not it's deserved.

Caden Lacson
Second generation. Always finds light in the darkness.

Holly Rogalski
Diverted my attention away from a different project in order to obsess over this one.

H. M. Lawson
The first person to read Twice Removed before it was ready for the rest of the world.

Chhabria James
Introduced me to my own, very relevant, cultural history.

Dawn Abron
Safeguarded the dignity of color.

Jessica Bayuga
Gave Jay a home and secured correct representation for all things NOLA.

Lynette Thornburgh
Kept me on track in spite of an alarming number of ducks.

Stefanie Anastasia
Beta read Twice Removed in its entirety over the span of two days.

Martin & Aya Tinio
Lent me the perfect name.

Cara Tinio
Demonstrated such faith in me by blindly volunteering tribute without knowing how it will be used.

The Grayslake Arts Alliance Writers Group

The rising tide to raise all our ships.

The Grayslake Arts Alliance Beta Book Club

Supports the efforts and successes of local authors with valuable and encouraging feedback.

The Village of Grayslake

Giving a family of immigrants a place in American history.

27 Houses

Shared a space and all the positivity that went with it.

Something's Brewing

Supplies fuel and hype.

Carolyn Sideco

Adopted us into the Bayou Barkada.

The Bayou Barkada

The bridge for today's Filipino American and their heritage.

Kathy Waghorn

Identifying Jay's strength and guiding me through this discovery.

Credit:

Aaron Amar : *Quiapo font used for title.*

EDELPONA : *Bagwis Baybayin font.*

Kuya Bai : *Baybayin Translator.*

ABOUT THE AUTHOR

ZEE LACSON

Zee Lacson, a first generation immigrant, has lived half her life in one country and the other half in another. Born and raised in Manila, Philippines with her grandparents, father, and twin brothers, she now enjoys the small town life in Illinois with her husband and twin sons.

She has had practice in many professions. Engineer. Educator. Photographer. Artist. Storyteller.

Reverie was her first published story in 2020. Revenant, its sequel, was released the following year. The Woolgathering Trilogy was completed in 2023 with the final book, Réveil.

She's never been a big believer of monsters hiding in the dark but she eats lots of garlic and will sleep with a little light on.
Just in case.

Reviews help nourish authors.

Feed me.

Leave a review for

Twice Removed

Follow Zee Lacson: